THE SECRET IN THE RUBBLE

BY

DENISE DAISY

ISBN: 13:978-1466422148ISBN: 10:1466422149

ACKNOWLEDGMENTS

Here I go again, my chance to put into print the names of the people who impact my life. It's funny how life plays out like a story. And in every great story there are those characters you never forget. Anyone who truly knows me, knows my favorite character of all time would be Sam Wise Gamgee. I think you're blessed if you have at least one Sam in your life that leaves their signature across your heart. I'm happy to list a few.

To my pumpkin pie, Journey Grace, I love you. You are the dearest little girl in the world. I love the way you think and the way you sit patiently and wait while I write. I cherish our life together; you are growing up so fast. I told you one day when you were bigger that you could read mommy's stories, when you do, and you read this, know that my heart has always burst with love for you. You are indeed my wonderful Journey of Grace. Mommy loves you.

To Awa, Binney and Kendall, I miss living with you three, but you are adults now and have turned into beautiful women. I am proud of all three of you and enjoy every visit and every phone conversation and every hilarious facebook status. You keep me laughing. I love you so.

To my mother, Mary Frank, thank you for not giving up, thank you for trying, thank you for your love. I love you.

To Fiona Joy Hawkins, we've never met, but thank you for your beautiful music and especially "Contemplating" it inspired many touching scenes in this story.

To my Sam Wise, Carleene Parra, again, what can I say? You are the best. Always there, always encouraging, always proof reading and always excited about the future. I adore you.

To Paul, again, thanks for everything, I wish you the best in this new chapter of your life story.

DEDICATION

This book is lovingly dedicated to Nick Redick, a true Falcon.

THE SECRET IN THE RUBBLE

Those who see you stare at you,
they ponder your fate:
"Is this the man who shook the earth
and made kingdoms tremble,
The man who made the world a desert,
Who overthrew its cities
and would not let his captives go home?"
Isaiah 14:16

PROLOGUE

It was once said that dead men tell no tales. Nothing could be further from the truth. For the corpse spoke and the tale it told thundered across the expanse, shaking the mountains, awakening them from years of dormancy and sending boulders plummeting to the valleys below. Birds took flight, screeching across the sky, relaying the blood stained message, written on the dead men's forehead. It was a single word that shook the earth's foundations, for it had not been spoken for over six hundred years. No one dared utter it for it was forbidden. Yet there were some who dared whisper it in secrecy, as a source of hope, for all who still believed in deliverance.

CHAPTER ONE

Elam paled. The last thing he wanted to do was to repeat the word. He looked to the men gathered around the table. All dropped their gaze, none wishing to relay the message. No matter how courageous they appeared, each one held an enormous fear where Abaddon was concerned. The man they once held in high esteem, following his directives without question, had turned into someone they hardly recognized. They watched in horror as he spilled blood with no remorse and boldly wore the white stone that once belonged to his dear friend Ariston. The pendant hung around his neck along with a vial of the murdered Prince's blood. Since his men could not look into his eyes without permission, their gaze always landed on the barbaric jewelry, a constant reminder to them of the lengths to which he would go and to the depths he'd fallen.

It was often rumored as to where he received his incredible power. His outward appearance remained the same but it was the spirit that gazed from his eyes that immobilized them in fear. It was dark, evil, yet luring, consuming everyone who entertained it with a deep lust for power and admiration. It was that spirit that spawned the notion that Abaddon died some time ago and that the impious one now occupied his body. Whatever reason, his approval was intoxicating, addictive.

Each man at the table would do the unthinkable to receive the honor of being asked into his elite. None of them would ruin that chance by uttering the message the dead man brought.

Makram had the most to fear. He was supposed to have disposed of Haytham and for six hundred years it was believed he had. No one knew why he didn't. Perhaps it was because he couldn't, yet Elam knew that wasn't the case. He supposed the real reason was because Makram was a noble man in the midst of corruption; and although he chose to side with Abaddon, he did not entirely agree with his directives. Whatever the reason, Makram's secret was soon to be disclosed, and as much as it grieved him, Elam knew he was the one to reveal it.

Elam swallowed hard, his throat constricting in fear. Delaying was no longer an option. It was time to relay the message.

"They're all dead; every one of them. Their slayer left a message inscribed on their foreheads." He stopped there and lowered his gaze from the vial of blood to the surface of the table. His heart seized, pounding against his chest. The silence in the room unnerved him; and, for a brief moment he tried to remember what peace felt like.

Abaddon spun the ceremonial dagger lying on the table. It was the same weapon that started the bloodthirsty coup almost seven hundred years ago; the knife that tore into the heart of Ariston, killing the first Prince of Eden.

The blade became invisible as it whirled and then took form again as it slowed and stopped. Abaddon caressed the knife running his fingers reverently across the blade and then back down the handle.

"And how is it that I send ten men over to kill the prophesied scribe and nine of them end up as corpses and you return unscathed?"

Elam swallowed, trying to moisten his dry mouth. His allegiance was in question and if Abaddon thought him a spy, aiding the other side, his execution would be imminent. His stomach grew sick and he feared he might vomit. When would this end? Could the world ever go back to the way it used to be? Could the name the corpse brought back really deliver them from this pervading darkness?

"Your thoughts betray me."

Abaddon's accusation hissed, igniting a terror. How

could he be privy to his thoughts? He had not allowed him access. Had the darkness reached so far? Or were the rumors true and the impious one taken residence in his body?

Elam felt the color rush up his neck and into his face, revealing his guilt. His mind searched for an explanation, a quick excuse to give reason for his demeanor.

"No, my Lord. It is not my thoughts that betray you, but the one named in the message. There is a betrayer in our midst and now I must find a way to reveal it to you and my heart grieves in the task."

Abaddon sneered in disgust, "Please spare me your sympathies. Do you not think I am aware that there are some who would switch their allegiance if given the chance? I fear no one. There is not a man alive who can thwart my plan. Name the apostate and I will kill him."

Elam dare not raise his eyes yet he could no longer take the image of the repugnant vial; so he closed them while uttering the forbidden word.

"Haytham."

The silence was deafening save for the sound of Elam's pounding heart. A low rumble erupted as the floor around Abaddon's chair began to shake. Elam opened his eyes and immediately wished he hadn't; for the sight of Abaddon's pupils turning milky white and rolling back in his head burned an image into his memory that he would surely take to the grave. A gust of foul smelling sulfur swept across the room extinguishing the flame of each candle; casting the room in utter darkness. A hideous shriek ripped into the blackness, the sound of it bringing each man to the brink of insanity. Makram gurgling, gasping for his final breath of air was the last thing Elam heard before icy fingers wrapped around his neck, forcing him against the cold stone wall. The grasp so tight he could barely swallow. If it lasted much longer he was sure to lose consciousness and join Makram in the afterlife. A frigid vapor wafted into his face, no doubt the call of death. His heart seized within him while he waited for the inevitable. In a way he welcomed the escape, yet he feared his life choices would only transport him from one torture to another. Then to his surprise Abaddon's grip lessened and then he summoned him with his mind so the others in the room would not be privy to their conversation.

Elam drank in the cold air, filling his lungs to capacity, then immediately gave Abaddon permission to enter into his consciousness, "I am listening; my Lord."

"And how is it you survived when the others lost their lives?"

Elam knew he must choose his thoughts carefully. He had one chance to survive, he would take it and hopefully it would be enough.

"I survived, my Lord because I set a plan in motion some time ago. I have kept connections, friends who believe me to be sympathetic to their cause. I have chosen these contacts carefully preying on those who are plagued with doubt. It's a weakness I can easily penetrate. Haytham has an elite circle as well; I have infiltrated it, gaining the trust of one. While the other nine attacked, I spent my time collecting information. I left immediately, knowing the report I carry must make it back. I have with me the names of ten who could possibly be the scribe. One however, is a writer; she goes by the name Bronwyn Sterling."

The room remained dark and still; not even the men gathered around the table made noise. Had it not been for the feel of Abaddon's fingers curled around his throat, Elam would've thought he'd been sent to the abyss.

"I have a mission for you." Abaddon's thoughts entered his head after an extended silence. "If you complete it with success, I will elevate your status among these men. You will lead my inner circle and no one will surpass your authority. You will have your choice of the royal manors where you and your family will live in luxury and privilege. You will walk in significance and everyone will envy your station in my kingdom."

The thoughts of Abaddon poured into the chalice of Elam's mind like an intoxicating drink and he swooned at the notion not once considering the price of the prize. And in an instant, his allegiance to the darkness was established.

"I humbly accept the task you require of me."

"Do not accept it in humility, Abaddon's thoughts hissed. "For a humble man will not succeed. Accept it proudly; let arrogance drive your ambition to complete it. I have no use for meek men in my service."

Elam swallowed hard fearing the icy grip once again, "I understand my Lord."

"Listen carefully to your directives. It is up to you to discover the best way to carry them out. It is why I chose you. You possess a scheming spirit that has caught my attention. You have full authority and access to whatever you require to launch your operation. Once you have carried out my directives, you will receive your reward; then and only then we can all celebrate after finally fulfilling the quest we have waited years to complete. Am I clear on this?"

He nodded, savoring the favor of his leader.

Abaddon removed his hand from Elam's throat and then lit a nearby candle bringing light back into the secret chamber. The men seated around the table were shocked to see Elam alive and standing, unharmed.

"Dismiss the men," Abaddon gave the order through his mind.

Pride engulfed Elam, corrupting his wisdom. Dismissing the men meant only one thing. He was now part of the elite inner circle. He could only imagine what they would be thinking. They would be jealous and talk among themselves of how they should have been the one selected instead of him. The thought of their gall in the matter incited bitter feelings. He deserved the promotion.

After all he was the one who took the risk in relaying the blood stained message.

"Leave us."

The dumbfounded expressions on their faces pleased him and once the room was cleared Abaddon continued laying out the devious plot.

"The Scribe opened the book; it is just a matter of time until the second prophecy is located. Whoever is the first to possess it controls the portal and will receive the first clue to the treasure. We cannot lose that power. You must prevent them from finding it first. Use your contact on the other side to gain information. Then put together a small army, you will need one to overtake Haytham. Kill the Scribe, destroy the book and then bring Asa and Haytham to me."

CHAPTER TWO

Black Hickory trees circled the two-story home, sitting several yards off the road, like an oasis in the middle of the desert. Storm clouds boiled on the horizon as they did almost every scorching summer evening; causing the breeze to pick up, bending the trees and blowing open the screen door. Madison Sterling took advantage of the chivalrous wind and darted outside; balancing the laundry basket on her hip, she pulled the clothes from the line; rescuing them from a certain soaking.

Bronwyn remained hidden, watching from a distance. Her parents would welcome her surprise visit and the look on their faces would be priceless. Madison sent numerous facebook messages to Bronwyn, all seeped in guilt suggesting her daughter visit more often; each letter insinuating her dad might not make it another year. That was absurd. Martin Sterling was only sixty five and in great health. Bronwyn knew it was her mother's way of manipulating a visit. She loved her parents and welcomed every time they dropped in but for some reason she found it difficult to return home.

The wind picked up, pushing harder, shoving against the thick boughs of a massive Hickory growing close to the house. The tree seemed to summon her, trying to gain her attention by scratching its gnarled branches across the top of the house. Its skeletal fingers pointed to the small attic window. Bronwyn inched closer squinting her eyes. Something was materializing just behind the clouded pane.

A gust of wind swept across the property; shrieking as the sky continued to darken. It snatched a bed sheet from her mother's grasp, carrying it across the yard and toppling lawn chairs along the way. The sound of its lament chilled her. The old Hickory slapped against the house, harder this time, drawing her attention back to the small oval window. She pushed against the powerful wind making her way toward the house all the while her eyes fixed on the dark porthole. The branches of the black hickory blew aside revealing red glowing eyes watching her from inside the attic.

Bronwyn gasped and sat up. Her room in Sandalwood Inn was dark, quiet. The only thing that caught her eye was the red glowing numbers 4:35 on the alarm clock. Letting out a long sigh, she ran her hands through her ebony hair. The chilling nightmares of her youth were returning and she hated it. It had been years since the face with glowing eyes appeared in her dreams.

Shivering she turned on the bedside lamp and looked around. The gentle billowing of the drapes from the open window was the only movement in the room. She climbed from her bed, pushed back the curtains and peered outside. The sun had not risen, yet the sky was changing from a dark blue to deep violet as an early morning fog blew across the ground. Travis's truck was sitting outside, gassed and ready for her departure just as he told her it would be. She looked at the time. 4:37 AM. Her alarm was set for five. If she lay back down, she could grab ten more minutes of rest, but she knew that would be impossible. She was much too motivated about her trip. It had been quite a while since she experienced the bliss of solitude. Months of traveling on the crowded touring bus was beginning to take its toll. A cross country road trip alone would be therapeutic. She would have hours to think and decipher through all the events of the past week and maybe some repressed memories of her childhood and the old manuscript would surface.

Dressing quickly she hurried downstairs with her cumbersome suitcase in tow. The aroma of fresh brewed coffee and muffins greeted her nose. Mavis woke early just to prepare food for her departure. Bronwyn smiled at her kindness. Veering away from the kitchen she decided to load her suitcase in the truck first before stopping for a bite to eat. She rolled her heavy bag onto the front porch and stopped abruptly at the sight of Falcon leaning against the front of the truck; a cigarette hanging from his lips despite the early hour. Ascending the porch steps, he grabbed her suitcase.

"Morning Scribe. Glad to see you're up and ready, I was hoping we'd get an early start."

Her heart dropped into her stomach. Did he say we?

Following Falcon off the porch, she watched as he tossed her suitcase in the storage area behind the seat. It fell alongside another piece of luggage that didn't belong to her. Her heart sank further. No way! This was not part of her plan! She eyed him suspiciously, "I'm going on this trip alone."

He smirked, "Like hell you are."

"Yes I am," Her mind was resolute as she placed her hands on both hips. "I am capable of making this trip on my own."

Falcon took a draw off his cigarette and blew a long line of smoke, never removing his eyes from hers, "No you're not."

She shifted her feet; uncomfortable at his gaze, "You don't think I can do this by myself?"

He gripped the cigarette between his teeth, "It don't matter if you can or can't, which you can't. You're not going alone and that's it."

The two engaged in a brief stare before Bronwyn ended it by stomping back into the inn.

"Where's Travis?" She demanded of Mavis as she barged into the kitchen.

Looking up from her paper, Mavis gave Bronwyn a sympathetic smile. She took a sip of her coffee and then nodded her head toward the screen door. Travis had just left the sheds and was heading to the inn. Bronwyn stepped outside on the porch and placed her hands back on her hips, "Falcon is here and he says he's coming with me."

Travis mounted the steps, "He is. I asked him to accompany you."

"Well I don't want him to. I want to take this trip alone."

He walked past her heading for the door, "You can't go alone."

Frustration boiled inside of her. Travis wasn't going to fix her problem. He and Falcon were in cahoots and she suddenly realized she had no say in the matter; however, it was not in her nature to give in so quickly. She whirled around blocking the entrance with her body, "Why can't I go alone?"

Travis's eyes smiled at her antics even though his mouth didn't, "Bronwyn, I know you do not completely comprehend the magnitude of the quest. So I will remain patient. To sum it up, you opened the book yesterday and now the enemy has been unleashed and will be looking for you as well as the second prophesy. You're not ready for a confrontation with them. Falcon is. He can protect you. That's why you're not going alone. In fact you're not to go anywhere alone anymore. Falcon is your bodyguard. He will be with you all the time."

"And I have no say in this at all?"

Travis did not respond and by his silence she knew his answer. His mind was set; his words suffocating, so intrusive of her personal space. Closing her eyes, she sighed; disappointment manifesting itself. Her two blissful weeks of solitude were now invaded by the rogue Falcon. Her heart plummeted at the thought. Falcon still frightened her. If it was so important for her to have protection why couldn't Travis do it himself?

"He scares me," She whispered her thoughts.

"He is a bit unorthodox…"

"A bit?" Her eyes flew open.

Travis gave way to his smile, "He's eccentric and a

revolutionary to the core, but, he is extremely trustworthy. And, since I am not at liberty to accompany you, I believe Falcon to be the best there is." His words seemed to be the final say on the matter. Proceeding to move her aside, he made his way into the kitchen.

Mavis exchanged places with Travis joining Bronwyn on the back porch. She handed her a thermos of hot coffee and a paper bag full of warm muffins. Bronwyn gratefully accepted the thoughtful breakfast, despite the fact that her appetite escaped her the moment she realized Falcon was accompanying her all the way to California and back. She gave Mavis a quick hug goodbye.

"He scares me too," Mavis whispered, "But Travis is right, Falcon is good at what he does. You'll be safe with him, and Travis knows that. He wouldn't trust your care to anyone else."

Bronwyn sighed defeated, "Let's see if I can squeeze this two weeks into one. The sooner this is over the better." Mavis grinned and gave her a loving hug. "You take care. I'll see you soon." Bronwyn nodded and headed for the truck only to find Falcon leaning against it gloating as he gave her one of his impish grins, "Let's go scribe. You're wasting time."

Walking past him she yanked the cigarette from his mouth tossing it to the ground, crushing it beneath her sandal. "You want to protect me? Then don't kill me with second hand smoke. Besides it's too early in the day for this."

"I knew she was going to be trouble" Falcon directed his words to Travis as he climbed into the cab of the truck.

A smile pulled at the corner of Travis's lips and danced across his eyes.

"You haven't seen trouble yet," Bronwyn threatened as she slammed her door.

"Seatbelt," Falcon said, instantly meeting her

challenge.

“I don’t like wearing them.”

“I am not moving this truck until you put it on.”

“Oh get real. Don’t begin to try and convince me you care about safety. I rode on the back of your motorcycle remember?”

Falcon shot her another impish grin yet still refrained from starting the truck.

“Yep, it’s going to be a long interesting two weeks.”

Realizing that her stubbornness was only delaying the inevitable she jerked the seatbelt with a force that could pull it from its encasing and reluctantly fastened it around her.

“Now that’s my girl,” Falcon mocked, then started the engine and pulled away from the inn.

“Let‘s just pray those two don’t kill each other,” Mavis said as she headed back inside.

Travis watched until the truck disappeared down the highway and then made his way into the inn to sound the alarm.

CHAPTER THREE

The morning sun remained low in the sky, offering little light to the winding road. A white misty fog hung in the trees blanketing most of the mountain range. Falcon offered no conversation. Staring out of the windshield, he sped down the narrow highway, taking each curve at an alarming speed. Despite the poor visibility he never let up on the gas. Instead, he tore thru the patches of fog like a madman, the tires protesting on every curve. Had it not been for the seatbelt, he insisted she wear, Bronwyn was sure she would end up in the driver's seat right alongside him.

"Slow down!"

At her demand Falcon pressed on the gas increasing their speed just as the truck rounded another curve. Again the tires squealed. Bronwyn peered out of her window and gasped as the truck hugged the edge of the highway. The drop off on her side was at least a mile deep.

"This is your way of keeping me safe?"

He accelerated again not affected by her protest and she figured one more demand from her would only result in Falcon increasing their speed again. She leaned her head against the back of the seat and closed her eyes. If she were going to plummet to her death, she'd rather not watch. She clutched the door handle bracing for the next curve. Closing her eyes proved to be the wrong decision. It only took a few more turns for nausea to set in. Taking in a deep breath, she placed her head against the window hoping the coolness of the glass would relieve some of the queasiness. The smell of the blue berry muffins began to overwhelm her. Pushing the metal lever, she lowered her window, welcoming the rush of cool air blowing into the cab of the truck.

Falcon took his eyes off the road and for the first time

since they left the inn he looked at her. Pleased with her discomfort, he jerked the truck over to the side of the road, tossing pebbles and stirring up a cloud of dirt. She jumped from the truck as it skidded to a stop. The sound of her retching brought a smile to his face. He took advantage of the opportunity and lit up another cigarette.

Bronwyn wiped her mouth with the back of her hand and sat in the dirt. She wanted to cry. She was angry. Travis would have never treated her this way. Why hadn't he come on the trip instead of Falcon? As she looked into the deep ravine that lay before her, she was almost inclined to jump, just to rid herself of the two torturous weeks that lie ahead. Better yet, she wondered if she had enough strength to push Falcon over the edge. She didn't want to kill him, just harm him enough to get her revenge. She was sure he would be alright. After all, he said he could fly. Her thoughts pleased her giving some relief to her misfortune.

"Take a swallow."

Falcon stood beside her, a water bottle in one hand and a cigarette clutched between the fingers of the other. She had no desire to take anything from him but she did have a bitter taste in her mouth. Reluctantly, she accepted the bottle; drinking the cool water, sloshing it around in her mouth. She didn't swallow; instead she spit the water out directly on Falcon's bare feet.

"If that's the way you want to play Scribe."

He walked closer to the ravine and took in a long draw while starring out over the hazy canyon and exhaled a cloud of smoke. Bronwyn watched his eyes follow a hawk gliding across the vast sky beneath them. The bird let out a lonesome cry as it flew past and in some way it seemed to communicate with him. She felt a tinge of shame for her anger.

Taking a final draw, he tossed the cigarette; crushing the butt with his bare heel. He said nothing as he climbed into the cab and started the engine. Grudgingly, Bronwyn

pulled herself up from the ground and took in a deep breath of the morning air. She filled her lungs with the scent of spruce and pine knowing they would be at the base of the mountains soon and it would be some time before she would be able to smell the pleasing aroma again.
Before her door was completely closed Falcon took off down the road. This time he took the curves at a much slower speed.

The sky was in full light by the time they reached the base of the mountain. The road no longer wound in twists and turns but stretched out before them in a straight line, widening to a broad, populated four lane highway. Bronwyn glanced in the mirror. She could see the massive mountain range growing smaller as they left it behind. Her heart stung, yearning for Travis. The mere thought of him, far away, hidden in the immenseness of the mountains caused her spirit to ache.

Falcon hadn't spoken a word and neither had she. Both drew back into their corners waiting for the next round of conflict to present itself. If Falcon stayed on schedule they would make Texas by early evening. Her stomach churned at the thought of how she would explain Falcon to her parents; not to mention how she would explain leaving her job with the troupe and her impulsive move to Moonshine. Her mother was sure to ask a multitude of questions and pry until she wore the truth out of her.

Her cell phone suddenly came alive with notification signals interrupting her thoughts. She startled at the sound. It had been over a week since she used her phone, and now, she was paying the price for her absence. Pulling it from her travel bag she viewed the screen.

"My God!"

Over fifty-three missed calls, forty-seven voice messages and seventeen texts. She scrolled down the call list. Twenty-eight of them were from Ryan's attorneys. She sighed; now that she had closure with Ryan, and offered him the use of the script, the harassing phone calls were sure to stop. Several of the missed calls were from her mother; all of them recent. She hoped her parents were well and there was no emergency that would entail so many calls. A couple of calls were from her California neighbor Jamia, and two missed calls from Bethany. Bronwyn noticed those had been placed in the past hour and thought that was a bit strange. The ringing of her cell startled her once again, the screen lit up interrupting her review. The ID on the screen said Mother. She sighed, got to face it eventually.

"Hello."

"Well I guess I can call off the search party!"

"I'm sorry mother. I've been out of range."

"No kidding. Your dad and I have been worried. We called your last engagement and they said you all never made it there."

"We had some engine problems and were stranded for a while. It's a long story. I'll fill you in tonight."

"Tonight?"

"Yes, is it alright? I'll be home tonight."

"Alright!" Madison responded so loudly that Falcon could hear her. "Honey it's more than alright. Your dad will be so happy. What time will you be here?"

"Around seven-ish."

"Dinner will be waiting, so don't eat before."

"Don't go to a lot of trouble momma."

"Are you kidding? I'll kill the fatted calf for this one!"

Bronwyn laughed.

"I love you hon, you be careful."

"I will. Bye."

She hung up the phone, now more nervous than before. She'd told her mother she would fill her in, now she had several hours to come up with a story. She should be able to think up with something; after all she was a writer. She glanced over at Falcon and again wondered how he would fit into her deception.

Another call. This time it was her neighbor, Jamia. She lived in the beach house closest to Bronwyn's and Ryan's, keeping a close watch on the properties and all the comings and goings of the occupants; eagerly catching Bronwyn up on the gossip every chance she could.

"Hello Jamia."

"Boy are you a hard one to get a hold of," her cheery voice rang out, "I could call the white house and talk to the president easier than I can get a hold of you."

"Sorry, I haven't had use of my phone in a while."

"I wondered what became of you. I was beginning to worry."

"No need. I'm fine."

"Listen. A couple of men have been snooping around your place asking a lot of questions. They tried to smooth talk me into giving them my spare key and letting them inside. I didn't of course."

"Did they say what they wanted?"

"Said something about the condo coming up for sale but I know that's a lie. It's a rental. Anyways, I called the owner and he said he has not listed it nor is he planning to. I saw one of them again today. Should I call the police?"

"No. It's more than likely some of Ryan's attorneys, although they shouldn't be coming around now."

"They don't look like attorneys hon. Believe me I've seen my share of attorneys and these two don't fit the bill. They look like a couple of thugs."

Bronwyn's stomach churned again. It could be paparazzi or reporters from some scandalous grocery store magazine. She desperately hoped the news of her pregnancy with Ryan hadn't leaked out. Wilbur had called Ryan, what was to stop him from calling the press? She wouldn't put it past him, especially if he thought he could benefit financially in some way.

"It's probably just reporters. Don't give them the time of day and don't give them any information."

"I get you honey. I won't say a word. So when are you coming home again?"

"Actually I am headed home now. I should be there in a couple of days."

"Great! I miss hearing your stories. You better have some good ones. You don't worry hon; I'll keep the reporters away. See you soon."

Bronwyn hung up the phone.

Falcon spoke for the first time since they left the side of the road, "Someone's snooping around your place?"

"Yeah, probably just reporters or the paparazzi. The condo is actually in Ryan's name. They're looking for him not me. They come around from time to time trying to get pictures of him. They just snoop around looking for anything they can find for a good story. They have no shame." She sighed. "I just hope Wilbur hasn't talked to the press."

"Wilbur's the fat man in your group?"

She nodded, "Yeah he's the one who called Ryan and told him I was in Moonshine and that I was pregnant. He'd sell his own mother for a dollar."

"Where is he now?"

"With the troupe. According to their schedule they should be performing in Texas tonight."

"Where exactly? I'll send someone to shut him up."

Bronwyn chuckled at the thought.

"Wilbur's harmless."

Falcon wasn't amused, "You laugh?"

"He's a greedy annoying bastard but hardly a threat."

This time it was Falcon who let out a mocking laugh.

"When are you going to get it Scribe? What's it going to take for it to sink in that head of yours that you are involved in a war and our adversary wants you dead? You haven't heeded any of our warnings. You continually wander off after Travis asked you not to. You planned on making this trip alone...." He shook his head in disbelief.

She immediately took offense with his insinuation of her ignorance to the severity of the situation. Maybe Falcon in his revolutionary ways was looking for a fight and over sensationalizing the whole thing. She had yet to encounter any adversary as he called it. The only person she ever saw stalking her was him. Besides, how could anyone know who or where she was?

"I just think you're being a little over cautious. After all no one knows my identity, or where I am. I would have probably done better alone, you being with me is a dead giveaway, no pun intended." She felt a surge of confidence in her declaration and grinned at her candor.

He sighed, "I see the need to educate you scribe or we're going to be in some serious trouble."

Her exasperation shot out. "Oh by all means, please do. I have been begging for some answers."

He glanced in his rearview and switched lanes, passing a slow moving Kia before he spoke.

"The second prophesy is vital. Whoever has possession can access the portal. They work as a type of key. Abaddon has possession of the first one, which is why he can use the portal at will. He fears us having access and infiltrating Eden to reclaim the kingdom. He fears even more the story you will write because it's sure to end his reign. You can bet he has sent his best through the abyss. His men are crafty and devious. They will stop at nothing to find you because they know you will lead them to the prophecy. Believe me when I say, everyone wants their hands on it."

Bronwyn looked out her window at the miles of empty space; nothing but undeveloped land for as far as they eye could see. Only a dilapidated old barn dotted the horizon every now and then... emptiness. It was how she felt about her situation. Empty and void of any inspiration or knowledge of the world in which she was commissioned to write about. All this talk about prophesies. It all seemed like a chapter out of the latest fantasy novel, and suddenly she felt a seed of doubt beginning to take root.

"They'll be gravely disappointed." She muttered. "I haven't a clue where the prophecy is."

"It doesn't matter if you know or not. You will inadvertently find it. All they care about is locating you. The only advantage we have right now is that they were expecting the Scribe to be a male, but if Wilbur mouths off about you to the media or anyone else that's snooping around, he will lead the enemy straight to you. Have you forgotten Wilbur was the one who gave you away the night before the festival? That's why I want to send someone to him to shut him up. Now where is he?"

"Shut him up how?" She remembered witnessing Falcon easily slit a man's throat in the garden nearly a week ago. Although she disliked Wilbur and his self-fulfilling ways, she did not think him deserving of sudden death.

"Don't worry Scribe, my men will just scare him, threaten him a bit, and hurt him where he is most vulnerable, his wallet."

Bronwyn smiled at the thought. "They're playing in Ft Worth this weekend at the Starlight Amphitheater; they have a new script so I'm sure they are there rehearsing."

"It's done then." Falcon said.

Bronwyn finished going through her voice messages and texts. Bethany hadn't left any voice messages when she called this morning. Ryan left a text telling her he had never seen her more beautiful than she was at the cabin. He told her he had been a fool to leave her in the first place, and hoped that maybe one day their paths would cross and he would be the man she deserved. He gave his apologies for not being there for her when she lost their child, stating that if he had known, he would have immediately been by her side. She rolled her eyes and deleted the text, hoping he would not attempt to contact her again. What was done was done. She had not fallen out of love with Ryan; rather she realized she had never truly loved him in the first place. Travis made her aware of that the night in the garden when he told her the true definition of love. True love was a selfless act. A day had not passed without her reliving that evening in her head. And now, sitting in the cab of the truck miles away from him, she had no desire to torture herself with such thoughts. She needed a distraction. She leaned forward and turned on the radio, scanning the channels. All of them offered the same mixture of country music and static; nothing worth listening to. Reaching over, Falcon pressed the button on the CD player. Within seconds peaceful instrumental music filled the cab of the truck. Bronwyn smiled and leaned her head against the back of the seat. So this must be what Travis listens to. The melody was calming, relaxing her, even inspiring her as she thought of Eden and the book she was soon to write. She dozed off and on throughout the day, listening, thinking and composing a story in her head. Falcon drove in silence allowing her solitude.

CHAPTER FOUR

Bethany dug through her travel bag looking for the letter. It was in there somewhere. She hadn't thrown it away although the thought to rip it to shreds had entered her mind. Instead, she decided to save it as some sort of evidence, just in case the circumstance demanded it. And she had been right. Call it premonition or whatever, but somehow she knew she would need it.

Frustrated, she dumped the entire contents of the bag on the floor, rummaging through them until the crinkled envelope caught her eye. Snatching it from its hiding place she headed back down the hallway to the front entrance where the cagey detective was waiting. She was glad to help him in his investigation, and felt some sort of vindication in the matter. Her concern over Bronwyn was now justified. She wasn't being a nosey intrusive friend, but rather a true friend, looking out for Bronwyn's best interest whether she realized it or not.

"Here it is," she said handing him the letter. "Hope you're an expert on languages 'cause I have no idea what tongue she wrote this in. I didn't even know she could speak another language but then I'm finding out there's a lot of things about her I don't know."

Elam took the envelope and pulled out the letter, his eyes scanning over the written words. Raising his eyes from the paper he narrowed them in on Bethany, "The rest of you are free to leave however, I'd like you to remain behind if you don't mind."

Bethany glanced over at Marcus, "Looks like you rehearsing without me for a while if that's okay?"

"Take all the time you need," Marcus was generous. "If our Bronwyn is any kind of trouble, we're glad to help. I had a bad feeling about leaving her behind but she'd made up her mind. She's a stubborn one, that girl."

As soon as the others left, Elam placed the envelope in his pocket, pointed to a settee in the lobby, and escorted Bethany to it. "So you've known Miss Sterling for quite a long time?"

"We met in the sixth grade and have been best friends ever since. She's like a sister to me. We are both only children, my parents weren't the best; hers were, so I spent a lot of time at her house."

Elam smiled at her, and it lasted longer than she thought it should, so she shifted in her seat and continued talking. "I know her better than anyone, so you can imagine how concerned I've been. And that letter was just weird. I don't know what to think."

Pulling a couple of photographs from his coat pocket, he handed one to Bethany. "Was she ever in the company of this man?"

Bethany nodded, "Once that I know of, she'd been out all night and when she came back to the inn she was with him. That was the crazy day when Ryan Reese showed up; oh did I mention she was engaged to him?"

Bethany's mouth suddenly felt dirty as if she'd spoken out of turn. She had no intention of betraying Bronwyn even though she was upset with her. Now she feared she'd said too much. But to her surprise the detective didn't seem shocked at her disclosure. Perhaps he already knew, after all he was an investigator. She took comfort in the fact that he was a professional and would never allow anything she said to leak out to the press. She handed the picture back. "Except the guy has a scar underneath his left eye."

Elam nodded as if he already knew and handed her the next picture. “How about him?”

Bethany smirked, “Oh yeah, Travis. She did spend an awful lot of time with him. He’s married though, so she was kind of disappointed about that. I think he’s the reason she stayed up there.” Again, her mouth felt dirty. She handed the picture back as to remove all guilt.

“Would you happen to have a picture of Bronwyn?” Elam asked. “It would help tremendously for us to have a visual of their latest victim.”

“Victim?” Bethany’s heart faltered. “Is she in trouble?”

Tucking the picture back into his coat, his face turned grim.

“She could be. Our objective right now is to get her away from these two men, if in fact she is still with them.”

Bethany agreed. Bronwyn needed to come back home and get her mind clear. She picked up a copy of their latest program, turning to the author bio page.

“This is her, you can take it with you; we have plenty.”

If Elam’s expression, when he gazed at the photograph, didn’t bother Bethany enough, what he mumbled did. Pulling his eyes away from the picture, he focused once again on Bethany, asking her for the Sterling’s address before giving her his card, promising to be in touch.

“Would you happen to know where she is?” he asked the question as an afterthought while leaving.

"She's staying at the Sandalwood Inn in Moonshine." Bethany offered still puzzled over his words. "Travis owns the inn. You can find them both there."

"Already looked," He said, "The entire town is deserted. We didn't find anyone."

CHAPTER FIVE

At seven fifteen, just as Bronwyn predicted, Falcon pulled into the long gravel driveway of her childhood home. The wheels of the truck scattered the small pebbles, announcing their arrival. Bronwyn shivered when she saw the house; purposely refraining from looking up toward the attic window. Her nightmare continued to haunt her; already she could feel the discomfort and anxiety rising as she stepped from the cab of the truck. Yawning, she stretched her cramped legs and stiff back. The front door of the house flew open. An attractive woman in her early sixties bolted outside, her arms outstretched in front of her as she headed toward Bronwyn, a joyous scream escaped her lips.

"Baby!" Madison embraced her daughter. Bronwyn returned the hug holding on tightly. Falcon watched the display from the cab of the truck. It was no surprise to him that Bronwyn's mother was a beauty. Her body was fit and slender; her shoulder length hair adorned a stylish fashion. Her brown eyes sparkled while her mouth laughed. Following close behind Madison was Bronwyn's father, Martin. He sported a full head of wavy hair despite his age; and only in the past year had it began fading from a rich brown to shimmering silver. His blue eyes smiled behind a pair of bifocals that he quickly removed and placed in his shirt pocket.

"You got one of those for me?" He asked. Bronwyn pulled away from her mother and wrapped her arms around her father's neck. She took in a deep breath inhaling his aftershave. It was an aroma she cherished.

The sound of the truck door closing brought all attention to Falcon.

"Oh," Madison's shock revealed itself in her face. "You brought someone with you."

Bronwyn forced a smile attempting to disguise her nerves. In the fourteen hour trip she neglected to come up with a simple story to explain Falcon. Talk about writers block. And, she was expected to write an epic?

"Yes I did… This is…"

"The names Dakota," Falcon approached her parents with an outstretched arm. "I'm Bronwyn's boyfriend. Nice to meet you both."

Bronwyn stood speechless as Martin grabbed Falcons extended hand and shook. "Martin Sterling. Nice to meet you, this is my wife Madison."

Falcon nodded "Please to meet you ma'am."

Madison graciously escorted her guest to the front door. However, Bronwyn was an expert at reading her mother's body language, and from her posture, she could tell her mother was not at all thrilled with Falcon's presence.

The delicious aroma of dinner greeted the tired travelers as soon as they entered the door. Bronwyn smiled knowing exactly what meal was waiting for them on the dining room table. She took in another deep breath inhaling the ambiance of the room. There was a comforting familiarity; and yet, there was also a disturbing spirit camouflaged somewhere inside the walls. It was that spirit that kept her visits at bay for some time now. She took a quick inventory of the room. Everything was as it always had been. Only a few subtle changes, such as a flat screen TV to keep up with the latest technology, new wooden blinds on the windows and different place settings on the table. Madison scrambled to set another place and soon they were enjoying a meal of cedar plank salmon that Martin grilled to perfection.

Falcon gallantly pulled Bronwyn's chair catching her off guard. He winked and flashed his impish grin before taking his seat next to her.

Martin reached for Madison's hand, "Let's pray." It

had always been custom in the Sterling home to pray before each meal. This ritual was made complete by taking the hand of the person sitting beside you as the blessing was offered. Bronwyn lovingly took hold of her mother's hand; giving it a tight squeeze. Madison returned the affection, thankful that her daughter was home safe. The feeling of warmth was interrupted as the rough calloused fingers of Falcon clasp around Bronwyn's free hand. Looking his way, she found his head reverently bowed and his eyes closed. Martin prayed a long drawn out supplication, thanking God for the surprise visit from his daughter. He politely offered thanks for the nice man who delivered her safely to them, then gave thanks for the wonderful woman who sat by his side, and eventually got around to thanking God for the food. As the prayer ended, Falcon surprised Bronwyn by kissing her hand, displaying affection for the benefit of her parents, but she didn't care to impress. Instead, she quickly pulled her hand away and placed it in her lap.

The silverware clinked against the china as everyone dug into the delicious meal. Madison passed a basket of warm rolls down the table; starting the conversation, "How long will you be staying dear?"

Bronwyn took a keen interest in buttering her roll to keep from meeting her mother's inquisitive gaze. "Unfortunately only tonight. It's one of those in and out trips. We're on a bit of a tight schedule."

Madison continued to pry, "Aren't you rehearsing a new show?"

She could tell by her mother's tone and forced smile that she already knew the answer to her question. Suddenly, she felt fourteen instead of thirty four, and had a peculiar feeling her mother was aware of more of her personal affairs than she was letting on.

"We are so sorry we didn't get a chance to see your last show," Martin apologized picking up on the charade.

Bronwyn sipped her iced tea, "I'm glad you didn't. It

definitely wasn't one of our best."

"So you're doing a new one then?" Madison took a bite of her salad; continuing her strategic questioning.

Bronwyn thought a minute as how to answer her mother without causing an uncomfortable interrogation at the table.

"They are, but I'm not in it. I left the troupe."

"So I heard," Madison smile was patronizing; igniting a flame of anger inside Bronwyn. If she already knew, why was she beating around the bush asking questions? Her mother had an agenda and Bronwyn knew it.

"Really? Who told you?"

Madison took another bite of her salad pleased to have the upper hand.

"I called Bethany when I couldn't get a hold of you. She told me you turned in your resignation and quit. She said it came as quite a shock to everyone."

Bethany! She should have known. Bronwyn could only imagine the conversation Bethany and her mother must have engaged in. Bethany was upset with her the day the troupe left and obviously took her revenge by confiding to Madison of all the strange goings on and Bronwyn's questionable behavior. Her stomach dropped. She sincerely hoped Bethany had not mentioned the pregnancy and miscarriage. Yet by the troubled look growing in her mother's eyes Bronwyn was certain she had.

"She said she's been pretty worried about you. Said you haven't been yourself lately."

Bronwyn's heart fell while her mind desperately searched for a sane way to explain the situation.

"She left the troupe because she is writing a documentary," Falcon came to her rescue. "I have her on contract. We're doing a film on the Legends and People of the Appalachian Mountains. I'd say it was providence that led her to us. One look at her and I knew she was who we wanted to write our story. Her friend Bethany was not privy to this information therefore does not understand Bronwyn's decision to leave the troupe and remain in the mountains. She is simply taking the chance as it presents itself to fulfill a lifelong dream. We are headed to California to retrieve some of her belongings. She will be relocating to the mountains to do her research."

Falcon's improvisation left Bronwyn speechless. She watched in wonder as he effortlessly led her parents in a brilliant discussion of Appalachian history and culture. As much as she hated to admit it, Travis was right. He was good at what he did. A secret agent able to take on any role needed; and as his charade played out, she caught a glimpse of him that was quite fascinating. He hadn't embarrassed her in front of her parents as she feared he would. Instead, he performed a good of role as any actor she'd ever known, instantaneously transforming into an intelligent film maker, the most appropriate character he could have ever improvised. Bronwyn decided to watch and remain silent; allowing him to continue his great fabrication, putting her parents troubled minds at rest.

With dinner and the conversation coming to an end, Martin invited Falcon poolside to smoke cigars. Standing from his chair, Falcon triumphantly kissed Bronwyn on the top of her head, "Need anything dear?"

"I'm good, thank you." she continued the charade but refused to call him by anything affectionate.

Giving her a sly wink, he headed outside with Martin but not before taking their plates into the kitchen. Madison waited until the screen door shut behind them before she spoke, "Well he seems very nice."

"Uh huh," Bronwyn agreed half-heartedly. The last thing she wanted was to get into a discussion about her love life, and she could tell this was exactly where the conversation was headed.

"I have to admit I'm a bit surprised," Madison continued much to Bronwyn's disliking. "Bethany mentioned Ryan came to see you recently. She hoped you two might get back together; but she said you turned him down. What was that all about?"

Bronwyn's annoyance with Bethany was rising. It was pretty bold of her to speak out of turn. Besides, how could she possibly know what transpired during her conversation with Ryan, unless she was snooping around asking more intrusive questions. Bethany was only doing this out of retaliation. She would call her the first chance she got and set her straight.

"It was nothing really. He still wants to produce the screenplay we wrote. I finally gave him permission."

Madison wiped down the counter and then hung the cloth over the sink. She dried her hands on a towel and turned to face Bronwyn.

"Are you sure you're okay dear? Bethany is very concerned."

Bronwyn sighed, "I'm fine mother, really I am. Bethany is nosey, not concerned. She's just upset that I don't tell her every thought I'm thinking. I needed a break from the troupe and Bethany. She's a dear friend but she's beginning to invade my personal space. I needed a change. You understand that don't you?"

Madison eyed her daughter and Bronwyn knew the interrogation was far from over.

"How long have you known Dakota?"

Bronwyn thought quickly. She dare not mention a time frame just in case her father was outside asking Falcon the same question. It would be detrimental to their façade if they gave conflicting answers.

"Long enough," Was the only information she offered.

Madison wasn't satisfied. "Bethany mentioned a married man by the name of Travis. She said you fell in love with him. She never mentioned anyone named

Dakota."

Bronwyn's fury rose. How dare her. She was definitely going to have words with Bethany. "She didn't mention him because she doesn't know him. Mother, please, do us both a favor and don't engage in anymore conversations with Bethany. I'm really ticked off at her right now. As usual she's jumping to conclusions and talking about things she doesn't know anything about."

Bronwyn could tell her mother was not completely convinced but knew better than to press the matter. Madison desired peace more than anything and would do nothing to hinder the happy unexpected visit. Bronwyn took advantage of the pause in the conversation.

"Momma, do you still have all my writings from years back?"

Madison inspected Bronwyn a minute before answering. "Yes honey I do. I have kept everything you have ever written. It's all boxed up in the attic."

"Mind if I snoop and take a few things with me? Being asked to write this documentary has boosted my confidence a bit. I want to go through some of my old work and possibly resurrect an idea."

"Honey you can have whatever's up there. It all belongs to you."

Bronwyn poured two cups of coffee and briefly told her mother of the mountains and the beauty of where she had spent the past several days. Madison listened intently and for once asked no questions. Bronwyn neglected to mention the name of the town; for some strange reason she felt the need to protect it. They chatted for some time discussing Madison's friends, her garden club activities and the house for an underprivileged family her father was helping build. Bronwyn mostly listened hoping the conversation would not veer back toward her personal life. Taking their empty mugs to the sink Bronwyn glanced out of the kitchen window checking on Falcon. He seemed content puffing on cigars with her dad.

The cuckoo clock on the wall struck ten. A little bird burst through to miniscule wooden doors and tweeted ten cuckoos then disappeared back inside with the cranks and dials. Bronwyn wished to go exploring in the attic and hunt for the old manuscript; but she feared if she mentioned it her mother would volunteer to help. Instead she feigned exhaustion yawning loudly.

"It's been a long day. Road trips can be so exhausting. I think I'll turn in since we're getting another early start in the morning." She noticed her mother's disappointment and wasn't sure if it stemmed from the briefness of their visit or the fact she didn't retrieve more personal information.

Bronwyn gave Madison a kiss on the cheek. "I'll spend more time here on our return trip back. Maybe two or three days if we can spare them."

Madison smiled, "I'd like that." Giving Bronwyn's hand a loving squeeze she slipped out back to join the men. Bronwyn took her opportunity and in spite of a dark premonition and incredible fear manifesting inside her, she stole upstairs to the attic in search for her writings.

CHAPTER SIX

A solitary bulb swayed hauntingly back and forth casting eerie shadows across the walls; offering a scarce amount of light for the unwanted trespasser. Bronwyn paused before entering. The peculiar heat sensation she experienced in Moonshine spread through her at an alarming rate; and for once she thought maybe it was her bodies warning system, letting her know when she was in extreme danger. There was something about the attic that didn't sit right with her. True, it was dark, musty, and housed every old and antique thing her mother owned. Almost every child was fearful of the attic or basement yet there was something more. Something drew her there, and yet frightened her to the point where she couldn't bear to look at the door as she passed in the hallway. During many of her childhood nightmares she would wake on the steps leading up to the eerie room. Once she remembered waking in the attic, on a chair looking out the small oval window and screaming for someone to come and find her. That was the dream that unnerved her parents to the point of seeking counsel for her. She hadn't thought of that moment until now, and with that revelation, other suppressed memories began to surface. Shaking the thoughts from her mind, she took a deep breath and stepped inside convincing herself she was older now and she could do this. No problem.

A cool draft crawled quietly across the floor, accompanied by a shiver racing up her spine. Taking a quick survey, she strolled past years of discarded memories and abandoned dreams. Most every item in the attic was reminiscent of her childhood. All the pieces of her life, now covered in layers of dust, tucked away and hidden in the black room. She browsed past shelves of trophies, plaques and ribbons. Some awarded for her writing skills, others for piano competitions, swim meets and children's theater. She eyed several large rubber bins stacked in the back corner. The light from the small bulb barely reached this part of the room; nevertheless, she made her way to the bins. Written on the first, in Madison's expert penmanship, was the words *Bronwyn's Work*. She breathed a sigh of relief. Thanks to her mother's obsessive organizational skills this would be easier than she anticipated. Now she could locate the manuscript and leave the spooky room.

She blew the dust from the lid and pried it open. Stacks of notebooks lay inside; all school projects. Bronwyn read through each title, disappointed when she reached the bottom. Nothing resembled an old manuscript written by a ten year old. Replacing the lid, she shoved the heavy bin aside. The label on the one beneath it read: *Bronwyn's stories.* She eagerly dug through the manuscripts lifting them from the bins one at a time. Again, she reached the bottom without finding anything. She continued her search until all the bins had been opened. Disappointed she paused to think. Barak mentioned her parents taking the book away and forbidding her to continue. If he was right, and her parents *had* taken the book, perhaps her mother destroyed it. The thought burdened her and she hoped that wasn't the case. If she couldn't find it, she would be forced to ask her mother what had become of the book, and that would be a catastrophe. Defeated, she replaced the last bin and turned to leave. At that moment she noticed a small metal container, resembling a safe deposit box, sitting alone in the opposite corner. Her heart seized. This has to be it! As she stooped down to lift it from its dismal hiding place, a small key fell from underneath it, disappearing as it slid across the dark floor. By now she was on all fours, feeling along the ground, until her fingers touched cold brass. Grabbing the key she carefully placed it in the lock and turned. A deafening click echoed across the still room. As she lifted the lid, a sudden gust of wind swept through the attic swinging the lone bulb. She startled and looked toward the door thinking someone must have entered and caused the sudden rush of air. However, the door was closed. Terror cozied up against her sending a chill through her body. A peculiar sorrow dug at her heart, tears stung her eyes and her attention was unwillingly drawn to the dark porthole. She gazed out into the black sky a vague memory trying to claw its way to the surface. Again, she saw the waterfall and Travis standing in the rushing stream. The vision lasted much longer than before but this time she saw another figure in the distance, approaching fast. Urgency tore into Travis's expression and the critical nature of it caused her heart to pound even now. A sudden flash of lightning right outside the window brought her attention back to the box cradled in her lap. Lying in its metal hiding place was a beautifully bound notebook. Holes had been carefully punched into an antique looking parchment. Blue silk ribbons were woven through the holes binding the papers to the soft leather cover. The word Moonshine was etched in silver calligraphy.

Her hands trembled as she lifted the manuscript from its bed. The heat sensation wrapped around her neck as dozens of memories flashed spontaneously across the screen of her mind. Her stomach knotted at the vivid pictures of once forgotten events. Despite the intensity of the heat, an icy chill forced a path up her spine while intimidating shadows came alive, emerging from the corners and closing in on her weakened state. The air grew thin as a sinister spirit sucked the oxygen from the room. She gasped for breath yet inhaled scalding wet air. Her head felt light; the room began to spin. Another gust of wind blew causing an abandoned floor lamp to topple over with a crash. She spun around and screamed when she saw Falcon standing directly behind her. Frightened, she nearly gave him a beating with the coveted book.

"What are you doing in here? Why did you sneak up on me like that?"

"I'm not to let you out of my sight, Travis's orders."

She hugged the soft book against her body in an attempt to control her shaking.

His impish grin melted into a reverent spirit as his eyes fell upon the manuscript; and his face grew more solemn than she had ever seen it. His eyes went from the book and back on her.

"You found it?"

She nodded. He smiled but this time there was nothing impish in his grin. "It's been here all this time."

"Twenty four years," she whispered, and then, as if she'd just discovered buried treasure, "Want to see if the prophecy is hidden inside?"

His face grew grave. "If it's in there and we open it, the enemy will know you have it."

She shrugged. "I don't care. Let them know."

Falcon narrowed his eyes; his examination made her uneasy. After a brief stare down he escorted her over to the dangling bulb. Pulling over one of the rubber bins, he offered her a place to sit. Placing the book in her lap, she carefully began to unlace the ribbon that held the pages shut. Falcon remained standing, guarding her as she opened the soft leather cover. With trembling fingers, she glided her hands over the papyrus. A smile formed on the corner of her lips as she read the handwritten words, inscribed twenty four years ago, in her best penmanship.

"Once Upon a Time, the world was beautiful, perfect, and good. On the earth there existed the amazing city of Eden. All royalty lived in Eden, because it was their home. Everyone lived in beautiful castles with exquisite gardens. There was no need for gates or moats or drawbridges, because, no one was afraid. Fear did not exist because everyone loved each other more than they

loved themselves. When all you have is love, then there is no reason to fear.
The royalty were beautiful people, strong and wise. They were chosen to rule the earth. There were three princes who were also brothers; they ruled the whole earth as well as all of Eden. Their names were, Ariston, Brennun, and Asa. Ariston was the oldest, Brennun was the middle brother and Asa was the youngest. Ariston and Brennan found wives and married. Asa hadn't found his lady until one day..."

The heat continued to rise; her heart racing wildly as she read. There wasn't a doubt, the story Barak and the council told her at the Citadel, now presented itself in her own handwriting, and told in the innocence and purity of a child. She read over the names of the three princes again. Ariston, Brennun and Asa and swallowed hard.

"One day a beautiful young woman came to the city of Eden. She was a story teller. Her name was Kenalycia. She was a good and kind maiden, traveling the earth, entertaining everyone with her stories. The people loved when she came because her stories were the best.
Prince Asa heard that the story teller was coming so he went out to meet her. As he listened to her story, and watched her emerald eyes dance as she told it, he knew he could love no one else from that day forward. When she finished and the people dispersed, Asa called her to himself and asked if she could tell him a story. Kenalycia was honored at his request. They walked for a spell and stopped at a beautiful waterfall. They found a secluded spot behind the falling water and it was there Kenalycia began to tell Asa a story. Now Kenalycia was clever, and knew if her story ended Asa would go home and she might never see him again. So she made her story to carry on, informing Asa he would have to come back the next day to hear the rest. Asa was pleased the story was

on going, for he wanted another chance to be with her. The next night they met at the falls, and again they sat behind the water and Kenalycia continued her story. Again, she made her story longer and told Asa it would be continued on the next night. He was happy. He loved hearing her story but more than that, he loved hearing her tell it and how her voice would change at exciting or sad parts. He loved watching her mouth form the words and he loved the way her green eyes smiled and danced. Kenalycia's story continued for a long time."

Bronwyn's heart ached as she read her own words. She had read the name Kenalycia before. It was carved into the back of the white stone pendant she found in the small wooden box near Travis' bed. It was no doubt his love's necklace; the one possession he had of hers. Tears flooded her eyes. She didn't want to cry in front of Falcon; she could feel his gaze upon her and knew he was watching her. Yet despite what she wanted, a tear found its way from her eye, escaping down her cheek and splashing upon the stiff parchment. The single tear landed right on the word waterfall, smearing the ink. Panicked, she wiped her cheek to prevent more from falling onto the book. A loud clap of thunder erupted outside shaking the room. She looked at Falcon, his eyes locked with hers and for a moment neither of them spoke. And then, it happened, another flash, another vision. This time it was Falcon's face plastered across the screen of her mind. The image evoked a terror, chilling her as the seed of distrust began to take root. Was this a premonition? He watched her intently, and she had a dreadful suspicion he might be privy to her thoughts. She removed her eyes from his stare, placing her attention back on the book. She would read the rest of the story later. Right now, she would flip through the pages and search for the prophecy.

Carefully turning the pieces of paper, her eyes skimmed over the words. There was only story, nothing resembling an ancient prophecy. She flipped through to the last few pages, nothing. Disappointed she decided to start at the beginning scanning each page carefully in case she missed it. As she closed the book, her eyes fell upon a small slit in the leather of the back cover. The corner had been turned down just a bit as if to make a hidden pouch. She reached for the soft suede and pulled. It tore away easily revealing a yellowed parchment. Her heart leaped in her throat as she removed a beautifully scripted letter. The handwriting was hers but the script was in a language unknown to her. Running her slender fingers across the page, she turned her attention to Falcon.

"I found it."

By the look on his face, he was more than aware of what she held in her hand. Reverently, he knelt beside her; all the while keeping his eyes fixed on the paper. With quivering hands, she offered him the coveted treasure.

"You will have to read it. I'm afraid I have penned it in a language I do not know."

Removing his eyes from the parchment, he gave his full attention to her. His face was somber.

"This is an honor I am not worthy of." His words seemed strange and out of place for the roguish guy she knew him to be, and for some reason, his declaration made the quest seem all the more vital. If he couldn't read it then who would?

"Well, the way I see it is, you are here, and no one else is. I can't read the language and you can, so in my book that makes you worthy." His eyes smiled although his mouth didn't. Her rationalization of the situation must have been convincing. He took the parchment from her and read it silently. When he finished he closed his eyes and sat in silence. She waited patiently as he allowed the words to soak in.

Another clap of thunder shook the house in fury while

the lighting continued to dance outside of the small octagon window. Falcon remained unnerved, his eyes closed as if he were praying, and it was then she remembered Falcon had no need of a cell phone because his people were able to communicate with their minds. She figured that might be what he was doing so she continued to wait while the wind began to howl outside. After a few minutes he opened his eyes and looked at her.

"You ready?"

She swallowed hard and nodded but before he could begin reading, a bolt of lightning hit near the house followed by an intense crackle. The small bulb lost its light, casting the attic in bitter darkness. An earsplitting thunder clash rocked the room, drowning out her scream. In the blackness Falcon took hold of her; lifting her to her feet.

"Hold on to me I'll help you downstairs". Without difficulty he led her from the attic and down the steps. His hand clutched tightly around her arm steadying her so she wouldn't lose her footing on the staircase. The strike knocked out all the power; casting the rest of the house in darkness as well. Still, Falcon led her through the rooms with ease stopping in the kitchen. Her suspicion grew and she wondered if he had the ability to see in the dark. It would explain why he could wear his sunglasses even at night. When they reached the kitchen Bronwyn stuck her hand in a drawer; rummaging around for a flashlight, a candle, or whatever would give them a bit of light. Falcon gently removed her hand and withdrew a tall slender candle. Grabbing a holder off of a nearby shelf, he removed the lighter from his pocket, and lit the wick bringing light into the room.

"You can see in the dark can't you?"

The flame lit his infamous grin confirming her suspicion. He picked up the candle, lighting her way to the bedroom.

The rain pounded against the roof, and the wind

rattled the glass in the windows like an angry intruder demanding entrance. Falcon closed the door to the bedroom and placed the candle on the nightstand. Kicking off her shoes, Bronwyn crawled up on the bed and grabbed the soft blanket draped across the antique footboard.

Falcon removed a gun from the back of his jeans; laying it on the night stand. Before she could protest, he removed a knife and placed it underneath the pillow.

"What if my parents see those?"

He smirked, "The door's locked, besides, they're in bed."

Peeling her eyes of the weapons, she returned her attention to the prophecy he held in his hands. "Okay, let's hear it."

He gave her a final glance before reading.

"Listen inhabitants of Eden and all people of the earth, you who have been misled and mistreated, whose lives were stolen by the one you called friend. Traces of deliverance have come! The spirits are whispering. They whisper words of remembrance, words of resurgence, and words of rebirth. The scribe has returned home to the land of protection and has opened the first two books.

Draw you battle lines and prepare for war! The doorway is open and all dominions are released. Be diligent to know truth and do not be swayed from what you know to be right. For some among you will be influenced by the darkness and join forces with the enemy, threatening your redemption. The betrayers have crept in unaware and are living among you. Wolves in sheep clothing they are, eating at your tables, and then spying upon you when your backs are turned. Be careful that you are not deceived. Their words will be convincing, they will offer pleasing and beautiful promises of knowledge and power, yet in the end, the only thing you will get for your allegiance with them is death.

To the Scribe, pen your story. The beginning is yours. Follow your heart and you will preserve life. All depends on your ability to make the right choice. In time you will be led to the secret place. Enter without fear, it is there you will find the third book, and the third prophesy.

He who holds these words in his hands and heart has the only key to the second portal. The Scribe alone knows the location of the second portal.

Falcon rolled the parchment back into a scroll, flicked on the lighter; holding the flame to the end.

Bronwyn's eyes widened, "You're burning it?"

"I've committed it to memory and I read it to Travis. If I burn it, then it can't fall into the wrong hands."

A small red flame began crawling across the scroll. Falcon made his way over to the fireplace, and tossed the burning parchment inside. The tiny flame consumed the entire scroll, and within seconds the long awaited prophecy was gone.

Thunder protested in anger, rattling the windows and shaking the house. The wind howled a lament, sweeping through the trees in search of something it would never find.

Feeling the need to protect the book, Bronwyn held it close fearing that Falcon may burn it as well; or, that the wind would crash through the window and rip it right out of her hands. Strange as it may seem, her book felt like an old friend. Despite the terror, it brought a great deal of comfort along with a strange connection to something or someone, but she didn't know exactly what. The mysterious bond created a desire to read more; consuming every word just in case the book was taken from her again. However, the scarce bit of light emanating from the dancing flame was hardly enough to make out the aging words, so she closed the book, holding it close like a child hugging a teddy bear.

The branches of the black hickory scratched against the window pane bringing back the nightmare of early this morning. She shuddered and shook her head trying to erase the mental image. Noticing her anguish, Falcon came back over to the bed. Sitting on the corner he lifted her chin so she eyed him directly.

"Don't lose confidence. Remember what I told you before. I will give my life to save yours. You have nothing to fear as long as I am with you. But if anything should ever happen to me…"

She shook her head in protest. She never was a plan "B" type of girl and didn't want to discuss that turn of events; but, Falcon was all business at this point and continued on in spite of her protest.

"Scribe," His words were firm. "We just read a prophecy stating that all dominions had been released and you can bet they are roaming earth looking everywhere for you. If anything should happen to me, make your way back to Travis. And, should the worst happen and you end up in Abaddon's keep. Do what's necessary to stay alive, for if anything happens to you, all hope will be lost."

She cradled her head in her hands pouring out her objections.

"I'm not sure I can do this."

Falcon nodded in frustration and lifted her face to his again.

"Well if you can't then I guess we're all damned aren't we? There's no room for doubt. You're the scribe now get your act together."

His unsympathetic remark appalled her. She wasn't asking him to coddle her; only to understand the overwhelming burden placed on her shoulders.

"The prophecy said all depended on my ability to make the right choice. I'm sorry if I disappoint you, but that is a huge burden to bear. I'm not afraid as much as overwhelmed at a task I don't think I am good enough to accomplish. I mean….it's embarrassing to admit but I've never had anything published, all my efforts have been rejected….." her voice trailed off in shame. "Maybe I'm not that great of a writer."

The thunder applauded her confession while the wind howled in delight. Falcon shook a cigarette from the carton and lit up. Taking a draw, he looked toward the window and the dancing lightning outside.

"It's who you are that matters Bronwyn." His tone was soft, the sarcasm gone. "True there are many scribes who are masters at prose, who studied their craft at great universities. However there are some things that cannot be learned no matter the brilliance of the mind or the prestige of the school attended. Those things are a part of the soul and are the very essence of the person's identity. You are someone special Bronwyn; believe that. The private ponderings of your heart have cried out and captivated their attention. You were chosen because they saw the most hidden parts of you, parts you don't know exist as of yet….and they were pleased." He took another draw and brought his eyes to hers and then with a crooked smile, he continued, "You have forgotten who you are."

Something in his announcement stole the breath from her lungs and for a brief moment she sat frozen her eyes locked on his. A feeling of familiarity swept through her.

"Who am I?"

The thunder resounded outside as the tiny flame on the candle flickered and then diminished all together, and from the darkness he answered.

"You're a storyteller."

CHAPTER SEVEN

The rain continued through the night and on into the next morning. The fierceness of the storm had long subsided, leaving a drizzle falling over the city. Bronwyn woke to the sound of the steady rain tapping against the window. Keeping her head on the pillow, she glanced around the room. Her mind re-engaging as she gradually began to recall the events of last night. Her heart sank when she remembered she was sharing a bed with Falcon. Rolling over she found him sitting beside her, reading the coveted book.

"Morning, Scribe."

Brushing the hair from her eyes, she sat up and glanced at the flashing twelve o'clock on the alarm.

"What time is it?"

"Around seven."

She climbed from the bed and dressed in the privacy of the bathroom; then met her parents in the kitchen for a quick breakfast while Falcon showered. Her father commented on the unexpectedness of last night's storm and her mother lambasted the weather man, accusing him of not forecasting correctly the entire summer.

Before Bronwyn could pour a cup of coffee, Madison asked if she would take a quick ride with her to the pharmacy, to pick up a prescription. Bronwyn's stomach fell. The last thing she desired was a one on one with her mother. She knew from experience that a barrage of questions and opinionated advice was what the quick trip to the pharmacy was really about. Despite the inner urge to deny the request, she found herself in her mother's Buick, heading down the driveway. Just as she had expected, her mother immediately voiced her concerns over Falcon and the impulsive decision of leaving the troupe and relocating in Moonshine. Without warning, Madison turned to her and asked the question Bronwyn had hoped she never would.

"Honey, did you lose a baby?"

Bronwyn's heart fell, this had to be Bethany's doing. She wondered if Falcon could send someone to shut her up as well. Turning her head, she watched the misty rain blow against the widow.

"I did."

Madison was quiet but only for a moment, "Just for the record, Bethany and I are both hurt that you didn't trust us with this information. We would have loved to help you through it."

Bronwyn pursed her lips. "Bethany had no right to tell you."

"Don't blame her honey," Madison jumped to Bethany's defense. "She assumed I already knew. One would think a mother would know about things like this." Her words were biting.

"Mother, there are some things I would rather deal with on my own. I can manage my disappointments. I'm doing fine."

"Are you really?" Madison's tone turned to sarcasm.

"That's not what I've heard. Bethany is really worried about you, and to tell you the truth, so am I. Honey, she said you have been staying out all hours of the night with a married man. Is Dakota married honey? I sincerely hope he is not!"

"Who's Dakota?" Bronwyn asked before remembering it was the name Falcon used when he introduced himself to her parents. It was too late to retract the question. Madison's eyes were locked on her.

"Dakota is the man you arrived here with yesterday. I believe that is what he called himself, although Bethany has never heard of him either."

Bronwyn's anger rose. "You talked to Bethany again

last night?"

"Honey I'm concerned!"

Bronwyn sighed there was no way of defending herself. Any truth she could tell her mother would sound even more bizarre and would confirm in her mother's mind that her daughter was definitely losing her grip on reality.

Madison pulled her car into a spot near the front of the small pharmacy.

"Well… Is he married?"

"No! He's not married mother. As usual Bethany doesn't know what she is talking about."

Covering her head with her purse, Madison made a quick dash in the pharmacy leaving Bronwyn fuming in the car. She stared out of her window, wishing she and Falcon were in the truck, heading far away. Despite their distrust of one another, they shared camaraderie.

In no time at all Madison climbed back in the car and offered Bronwyn the small paper bag in her hand.

"I had my doctor call these in for you. They will take some of the stress off of you, help you relax, put things back in perspective."

Bronwyn folded her arms in front of her, refusing the package.

"Send it to Bethany. She can use it more than me."

Madison sighed and drove back to the house without saying a word. As they pulled into the long driveway Bronwyn noticed the truck was gone. She sighed; Falcon must have left to gas it up. She hoped he would hurry back; right now she wanted to leave more than ever. She'd grab a quick cup of coffee and her travel bag so they could get on the road as soon as he returned. Now that she had recovered her book, there wasn't any need to stay and hang around. She hated to leave with a rift, but knew no amount of persuading would convince her mother of what she had already believed to be true.

Martin sat at the table drinking his coffee; his

expression alerted Bronwyn that something was wrong.

"Where's Falcon?"

"Who the hell is Falcon?"

Damn it! Why couldn't she remember the script? She really needed to pay attention.

"I mean Dakota. Where is Dakota?"

Martin sat his mug on the table.

"He left, to go look for you. He's pretty upset. He didn't like the idea of you going somewhere without telling him."

Bronwyn's face flushed in embarrassment. This looked bad, and she was sure she wouldn't be able to explain.

"What? Are you kidding me?" Madison voiced her concern. "Is this the kind of relationship you're in? You can't take a quick trip with your mother to the store? Oh this is scary! I have heard about men like this, over possessive and controlling. They always end up as abusers. Honey we're concerned. How well do you really know him? Bethany said it's only been a week."

Falcon entered the kitchen on the tail of her last words. With his jaw clenched, he lowered his sunglasses, looking only at Bronwyn.

"Say your goodbyes we're leaving."

Aghast, Madison looked over at her husband, wanting him to intervene.

"Martin?"

Her father peered over his bifocals. "Are you ready to leave hon?"

Although she would have liked nothing more than to defy Falcon for embarrassing her as he did, she wasn't up to the challenge. All she cared about was removing herself from her mother's suspicion and the awkwardness of the moment.

"Yes. I'm ready to leave." Giving her parents a quick kiss goodbye; she left them standing on the porch, more concerned than ever.

"Don't ever do that to me again," Bronwyn gave her reprimand as Falcon backed out of the narrow drive. "As if I didn't have enough explaining to do. What you did looked really bad."

Falcon jerked the truck onto the road and then checked the rearview.

"Scribe, I am only going to say this once more so listen well. You are to never leave my side. Not for a minute, not ever. You do something like that again and you'll be sorry."

All her anger toward Bethany and her mother was nothing compared to the fury she felt for this smart-aleck she had known less than a week. And then, a feeling of empowerment engulfed her, readying her for the challenge. She wasn't going to take anything else.

"Are you threatening me?"

"Yes."

She bit back, "I don't like being threatened."

"I don't care what you like. Do what I tell you and I won't have any reason to threaten you."

She sat back hard against the seat crossing her arms in front of her. "Why make such a big deal about running a quick errand with my mother? You're being ridiculous. Nothing happened. I refuse to live in fear...."

His sarcastic chuckle interrupted her tirade.

"What's so funny?"

He checked the rearview again, "Scribe, you don't know fear."

Again, she met the challenge, "Oh really? I'm beginning to believe you use scare tactics as a means of control. Funny, I've yet to see the enemy. Everything up till now has been all talk. Maybe you give your adversary more credit than he deserves."

Even though Falcon said nothing, she could see her words annoyed him and she was happy. Feeling pleased with herself for not backing down, she turned away to watch the falling rain. She wasn't going to waste her time worrying if he was mad at her or not. She didn't care. The person causing her the most trouble right now was Bethany. She would give her a call and tell her what she thought of her meddling, but figured it best to wait until she was calm.

The rain continued all morning with no sign of letting up. They drove along in silence; the only noise being the repetitious song of the wipers slapping against the misty windshield.

Falcon hadn't spoken since his reprimand. She sighed; must every day of this trip start out at odds with each other? If this was the way it was going to be, then it would be a long day.

Bronwyn spent most of the morning looking out her window at miles of emptiness. Bored, she tried the radio, and as before, the only song playing was either static or blue grass. She pushed the CD into the player and leaned her head against the seat.

Without saying a word, Falcon opened the glove box, removed the old book, and handed it to her. She took it; opening it with reverence, to where she last read.

She read the first few lines in silence before Falcon asked her to read aloud. Taking a deep breath she began:

"*After many weeks of meeting behind the water fall Kenalycia decided to tell Asa the truth about her story. When he arrived she lowered her eyes in shame and spilled out her confession. She admitted purposely making the story with no ending, so she could be with him night after night. She promised to end her story and he would be free to do whatever he desired with his evenings. Asa smiled and told her that he also had a confession to make. However, he did not lower his eyes. He looked right at Kenalycia and admitted, that as much as he enjoyed her stories, they were not the reason he came night after night. The reason he came was to be near her. He asked her to never end her story. From that night on Asa and Kenalycia were inseparable.*

The familiar ache of her broken heart flared up again. She wished Falcon hadn't asked her to read it out loud. She feared her voice might quiver at any minute and then he would know of her desire for Travis. Besides, it was difficult to read about this woman that intrigued him. She pictured her to be a flawless beauty, hidden away somewhere in Eden, waiting for Travis to come and rescue her. Her heart hung heavy in her chest so she took in a deep breath before turning to the next page. Before she could read, the truck jolted, spinning violently across the rain slick highway, sending the manuscript flying out of her hands. Everything was a blur as the truck skidded sideways off the road; sliding backwards down a shallow embankment. Despite her seatbelt, she banged her forehead against the window as the truck came to an abrupt stop. They sat in silence as the wipers swiped furiously at the pounding rain.

Falcon killed the engine.

"You alright Scribe?"

"What happened?"

"Tire blew."

She picked the beloved manuscript from the floorboard.

"Need help?"

He smirked. "You stay put. I can do it myself." Opening his door, he ventured outside, disappearing into the blinding rain.

Realizing now would be a great time to try and sooth some ruffled feathers, Bronwyn took advantage of her privacy and placed a call. She'd calmed down quite a bit and hoped her mother had as well. Since she hated leaving things the way she did, she decided to call and give an impromptu performance convincing them that everything was okay. Punching in the number she waited. A surprised Madison answered.

"Everything alright honey?"

The concern was evident in her voice.

"Everything's fine mother." She forced a cheery voice. "I hated the way we left things. I wanted to call and let you know I'm fine and that I love you. It was really good seeing you and daddy."

Madison's voice softened.

"I love you too honey. That's why I worry about you so much. You'll always be my baby."

"I know mother. We'll have a better visit on the trip back. I promise."

"Will Dakota be coming with you?"

"Yes."

There was a noticeable silence before Madison spoke again.

"Honey, please don't get upset, just hear me out on this. I just spoke with Bethany; and she said detectives came to the theater very late last night and asked a lot of questions about you and Dakota."

Bronwyn's sigh was loud enough for Madison to hear on the other end.

"Momma, please. I am sure the detectives were hired by Ryan to find me so he could ask for the rights to the screen play. Maybe he forgot to call off his guard dogs. I'll check into it but don't worry, Falcon's not a criminal."

"So Falcon's his name huh? Why is he using a pseudo name then?"

Damn it! She did it again.

"Honey we're concerned. These detectives weren't hired by Ryan. They are conducting a serious investigation about illegal activity taking place back there in the mountains. Your dad and I would feel so much better if you didn't travel with Dakota. Seriously honey, you just met him. How well do you know him?"

Bronwyn closed her eyes and massaged her temples with her free hand; all the while wishing she'd never placed the call.

"Momma, there are things I can't tell you, and if I could, you'd never believe me. You just gotta trust me on this one."

This time it was Madison who sighed.

"Well whatever it is you can't tell me, you're gonna have to tell the detectives. It's just a matter of time until they catch up with you. Your dad and I told them where you were headed and what vehicle you are in."

"Mother! Why?"

"You can't expect us to lie to the authorities. I answered them truthfully and you'd be best to do the same."

"Okay mother," Bronwyn cut her off before the conversation turned sour again. "I'll tell them whatever they want to know. I have nothing to hide." Even as the words slid from her mouth she felt guilt for her lying. She had everything to hide. Her only comfort in the matter was they were doing nothing illegal. Saying a quick goodbye she hung up the phone; wishing she'd never made the call.

The driver's door opened blowing in the misty rain. Soaked, Falcon climbed in, his tee shirt clinging to his skin and water dripping off his face. His breathing was labored and his hands bloodied. He hit the power locks securing both doors before starting the engine. The back tires spun in the wet grass trying to find their traction. He pressed down hard on the gas. The truck swerved a couple of times before it shot out of the ditch roaring back onto the highway.

Agitated, Falcon drove with intensity, focusing on the road ahead. Within a few minutes they entered the city limits of a small town. Taking the first exit ramp, Falcon turned the truck into the parking lot of a nearby truck stop. The highway oasis provided every comfort for the cross country travelers, allowing them to pull their rigs in for any needed maintenance, while they enjoyed a nice home cooked meal in the small diner. Afterward, they could shoot a game of pool in the dimly lit arcade, shower in the locker rooms and replenished any needed supplies at the market before hitting the road again.

Dozens of semis sat parked in rows in the back of the lot; some were at the pumps refueling, along with other smaller vehicles traveling the long stretch of highway. Falcon parked the truck directly in front of the mechanics garage. The sound of idling engines filled the cab as he opened his door. Stepping into the falling rain, he left her with a warning before slamming the door.

"Stay put and keep the doors locked."

She watched him enter the garage and approach one of the mechanics on duty. *Stay put?* Rebellion began rising inside. She was tired of everyone dictating their demands; her mother, Bethany, and worse of all, Falcon. She hadn't forgotten his little charade this morning, or his idle threat. She would meet his challenge. If she obeyed his every command, then she was allowing him to set the precedent of how things would be.

Feeling the effects of driving for five hours without stopping, she decided to do as she pleased, stretch her legs and make a quick trip to the restroom. She locked the doors as he instructed. She'd give him that much, besides, she wanted to make sure the book was safe. Dodging the rain, she took retreat inside of the small diner. The cashier pointed the way to the restrooms located past the arcade in the back with the showers and lockers. The smell of country cooking reminded her how hungry she was. She didn't eat breakfast because of the quick trip to the pharmacy and their hasty departure afterwards. She hoped the tire would take a while to repair so they could sit at a table and dine instead of getting a meal to go and eating in the cramped cab.

Entering the restroom, she noticed a woman sitting in

the floor, leaning against the wall. No matter the cleanliness of the place, she shuddered at the thought of someone taking refuge on the floor. She skirted past, making her way to a stall when the woman reached out to her. Her voice so feeble, Bronwyn barely heard her call for help.

"Are you okay?"

The woman took time in shaking her head, and when she looked towards Bronwyn; her eyes seemed glassy and unfocused.

"I need my insulin."

Bronwyn looked around the floor for a bag.

"Where is it?"

"In my truck." The woman slurred her words

Bronwyn's heart fell. There were hundreds of semi's outside how could she find this woman's rig not to mention retrieving her medication?

"Maybe I should call for help?"

The woman shook her head, rolling it against the wall.

"No, I just need help getting to my truck. I'll be okay once I get my insulin."

With no other choice available, Bronwyn helped the woman to her feet and slipped outside into the blinding mist.

CHAPTER EIGHT

Although the mechanic was accustomed to dealing with intimidating truckers, there was something menacing in Falcons demeanor that persuaded him to put all other work aside. Falcon hadn't responded favorable to the fact that it would be a couple of hours before someone could get to the job. He pulled the dark glasses away from his eyes and insisted the work be done immediately. The mechanic felt a strange sense of dread when he looked into Falcons eyes and decided it would be best to get the work done and send this delinquent on his way.

Satisfied, Falcon went back to get Bronwyn. They could grab a quick bite to eat. Nearing the truck his eyes fell on the empty seat.

"Damn it!" He banged his fist against the window, whirling around, scanning the parking lot. He bolted into the small diner, figuring she would be easy to spot in the sea of overweight bearded faces. He scanned the room his eyes inspecting every table.

"Hi Handsome!" a gaudy waitress greeted him while balancing a tray of food on her shoulder. "Have a seat in my section honey and I'll bring you whatever you need."

He pushed past her, heading into the convenience store. Not finding Bronwyn in there, he bolted down the narrow passageway into the dimly lit arcade. Nothing but a couple of men shooting a game of pool, and another fellow placing quarters in an old pin ball machine, illuminating flashing lights and sounding off bells. The men glanced briefly at Falcon and then returned to their games. Leaving the room he continued on down the narrow hallway pushing open the door to the women's locker room. A hefty woman wrapped in a towel stretched to capacity startled at his abrupt entrance.

"Scribe!" He called out ignoring the woman while walking through the room kicking open the doors to every stall and pulling back the plastic curtains hanging in front of the showers.

"There aint no one in here but me." The plump woman bellowed while holding one hand on her towel and another on her hip. "And unless you want an eye full you better get the hell out of here."

Falcon left the room disgusted at the thought. He entered the men's room. Nothing!

Dread grew inside of him as he retraced his steps; again scanning every room he passed through, all the while knowing every second was monumental. If the enemy had grabbed Bronwyn from the truck they could be miles down the road by now. He bit down hard on his lower jaw at the thought. He exited the diner pushing past the cheap looking waitress who called after him offering a later rendezvous. Back in the falling rain, he scanned the gas pumps and rows of parked rigs in the back lot. Suddenly, he caught sight of a beautiful brunette, drenched from the rain and walking alone amongst the semis. His eyes narrowed in fury. It was time to make good on his threat and show her just what their adversary was capable of. After today, she would never doubt again. He slipped quietly into the alleyway near rows of trash dumpsters and waited patiently.

CHAPTER NINE

Dodging the rain, Bronwyn made her way back to the diner. She hadn't meant to be gone this long, and for that matter, she never intended on taking a walk in the blowing mist. Now her clothes were soaked and clinging to her. Realizing it would be a miserable ride in the frigid cab, wearing wet clothes, she decided to grab some dry ones from her suitcase; hoping the truck wasn't on the jack just yet.

A bolt of lightning zigzagged across the sky giving a warning to veer to the side of the building instead of walking out in the open. When would the rain end? She'd had her fill of it.

Picking up her pace, she made her way toward the diner, staying close to a long row of dumpsters lining the way to a back alley. Just as she was wondering about the wisdom of walking near metal dumpsters during an electrical storm, someone reached from the shadows, yanking her inside. Terrified, she tried screaming but before a sound could escape her lips, a forceful punch to her stomach, knocked the breath from her, stealing her cry for help. Strong hands hurled her against the metal side of a trash dumpster. The cold dirty steel slapped against her face; had she not turned her head, the impact might have broken her nose. She swung her leg out behind her, attempting to kick her abductor. He was fast, anticipating her next move. He pulled her off the dumpster with such speed, not allowing her to get her bearings, and slammed her into a neighboring trash bin. He repeated this move several more times, all the while pulling her deeper into the alleyway. Every slam against the hard metal dulled her senses, which along with the blowing rain blurred her vision, so she could not focus on her abductor or a way of escape. Panic rose at the thought of being raped by some roadside serial killer and she wished she had heeded

Falcon's repeated warnings not to venture out alone. Then, a thought what if her captor was one of Abaddon's men? It would explain the crushing strength. If that was the case, maybe Falcon noticed she was missing and was looking for her, after all he'd left her parent's house this morning in search of her.

Realizing the air had returned to her lungs, she decided to try yelling again; hoping that amidst the pouring train and diesel engines he would hear her. Unfortunately, her attacker was one step ahead, quickly covering her mouth, smothering the call for help. He drug her a few feet further before pinning her to the dumpster. Moving in close, he pushed against her so tightly she found it difficult to take in a breath. The lack of air, combined with the sheer terror, depleting her energy, caused her to grow faint, making it almost impossible to hold herself up. She'd have fallen, had the man not leaned in with his hip pinning her to the dirty metal wall. Keeping his hand firmly over her mouth, he pressed his lips against her neck and whispered.

"Where were you scribe?"

Her heart dropped. *Falcon?* The sound of his voice frightened her.

"I told you to never leave me didn't I?"

Remembering his threat, that if she went off on her own again she would be sorry, filled her with anger, vanquishing any fear that may have manifest during the attack. With renewed strength she hoisted her leg, kneeing him violently in his groin. He pulled her off the trash bin and threw her to the wet ground, but before she could get away he pounced on top of her, yelling over the rain.

"What business did you have over there among the semis?"

Her eyes flared in anger while she stared at him in defiance, never intending to answer his demanding question. He raised his arm, striking her across the cheek with the back of his hand. Her jaw rung in pain as the copper taste of blood entered her mouth. Her heart faltered, not believing what was happening. The seed of distrust growing inside of her was now in full bloom. Grabbing a fistful of mud she slung it in his face, fighting back, knocking the dark glasses from his eyes. He grabbed hold of both her arms, pinning her to the ground; and leaned in close to her face.

"How long do you want to do this Scribe? Let me warn you, you are no match for me. I'm going to win. The question is; how much pain are you willing to endure? Now tell me, what were you doing over there?"

Lying on the ground, with water pooling around her, she curled her hands into fists, struggling to pull up against him. Her efforts were futile. He raised his hand to strike again, but her words stopped him.

"I was helping someone."

"Who?" he asked not letting up on the force in which he held her to the ground.

"I don't know, some woman who was sick, she asked me to help her to her truck."

Falcons hand fell across her face again splitting open her lip.

"I told you to trust no one but me."

She spit the blood in his face. "You expect me to trust you after this? You're crazy!"

Falcon leaned over practically lying on top of her. Placing his mouth directly on her ear, he whispered angrily. "Better I rough you up a little, than they kill you. Just so you know, that wasn't a simple blow out we had back there. Our tire was shot out. I left two men on the side of the highway dead. One got away and he is looking for you. If he finds you, he will do much worse than this."

She turned her face away from him; wanting to cry, but wouldn't dare give him the satisfaction. Not that he would notice, with all the rain spilling onto her face.

Deep inside she wasn't sure she believed him. All the talk about the enemy and still she had yet to see them. Right now the only person who posed a threat was straddling her. She wondered how Travis would have handled the situation, and if he would agree with Falcon's aggressive little lesson. He had referred to him as a little unorthodox but this behavior was far more than just eccentric; and even though Travis trusted Falcon she wasn't sure she did. There was something about him that just didn't seem right. For right now she would give into him only because she had no other choice. She would watch and wait; time would tell, and if she wanted to take off on her own, she would plan it in a way where he would never find her.

She let her body go limp, no longer resisting him. He pulled himself off and sat on the ground beside her, then offered his hand. She refused it, stubbornly sitting up on her own. She wiped the blood from her lip; it stung and felt twice its normal size. They sat in silence while the rain pooled around them like two junior high boys who had just fought it out. He gave her a slight smile.

"You're filthy Scribe. I'll get your things; you can shower up before we leave."

Falcon's presence in the locker room accompanied by a very muddy and blood stained Bronwyn sent the hefty woman along with a couple other ladies flying out the door. Falcon sat on the vanity waiting outside the stall while Bronwyn showered. His menacing appearance caused anyone who entered the restroom to change their plans. Once she was done he took his turn cleaning up, then they decided on a quick lunch while the mechanic finished up on their tire.

Bronwyn decided on a bowl of soup and a cornbread muffin since her lip was beginning to swell. Even though she was in dry clothes she continued to shiver, and hoped the warmth of the meal would remove the chill.

The adrenaline rush of the attack left her weak; that combined with her extreme distrust over Falcon cast a greater pall over an already gloomy day. To add insult to injury, they ate in silence, forced to listen to a talk show host interview Ryan about his latest movie, from a television in the corner of the diner. Falcon shook his head in disbelief as Ryan prattled on about refusing to use a body double, insisting in doing all his own stunts. And just when she thought her day couldn't get any worse, the local programming was interrupted by a breaking news report. A grave looking reporter stood under an umbrella; speaking into his microphone.

"A grisly discovery on Interstate 40. Two white males, stabbed to death, were discovered in a small ravine seven miles off of the Briarwood exit…"

Murmurs from the diners sounded throughout the cafe as they realized the closeness of the gruesome sight. Grabbing a remote control, the gaudy waitress, turned up the sound, so all could hear the ghastly report.

"No vehicle was found at the site, however fresh tire tracks were discovered in the grass. Authorities are speculating the victims may have been killed elsewhere, and dumped at the scene. Local police are combing the area, beginning with several truck stops and rest areas nearby. Anyone with information should contact the local authorities immediately."

Bronwyn pushed her bowl of soup aside. Falcon had told her the truth, which also meant he was the killer the authorities were searching for.

"Should we leave?"

Keeping his head low, he glanced around the diner and then cut his eyes over to hers.

"Not yet. Getting up now will make us look suspicious. We need to leave pretty quick though. This place will be crawling with the police soon."

Bronwyn's stomach dropped. Fiddling with the salt shaker, in an attempt to calm her nerves, she leaned across the table, lowering her voice.

"Why didn't you tell me what happened back there? We could have bypassed all this if you'd just told me."

Falcon scanned the diner again before locking eyes with her.

"In order for you to survive this quest Scribe, you need to trust. Your ability to choose wisely will be our salvation. Believe me, you will meet up with the enemy, it's just a matter of time, and he will not be anything you're expecting. He will appear, kind and good. If you trust in only what you see, you will die." He leaned across the table before delivering the next few words; "I know you don't trust me and I'm warning you now, there will come a time when you will trust me even less. If at that time, you react by what you see, all could be lost. So get over demanding answers, and start trusting."

There was no time to decipher his ambiguous words, for Falcon was looking past her, into the large parking lot, at the two police cruisers pulling in.

"Time to move."

CHAPTER TEN

The cheap looking waitress squinted at the photograph before grabbing the reading glasses dangling from a chain around her neck. Lifting them to her eyes, she examined the picture more carefully. “Yep he was here, handsome fellow, looks just like him, ‘cept he had a scar under his left eye.”

Elam smiled as he replaced the photograph in his jacket pocket. “Was he traveling with someone?”

“A woman, ‘bout the same age as him, thin, pale, but pretty.”

Elam retrieved another picture, “This her?”

The waitress replaced her glasses once again.

“Sure is. ‘'Cept she wasn’t smilin’ much. Didn’t look too happy to be with him though. I think they were fighting. I noticed she had a swollen lip. She ordered soup but barely ate any. I don’t care how hot the guy is, in my opinion, if he’s beatin’ on you… leave, ya know?”

“Definitely,” Elam agreed. “I wish all women thought the way you do.”

The waitress reveled in the handsome detective’s approval, not knowing he thought her capable of taking down any man that looked at her crossways.

“How long ago did they leave?”

She pulled a pile of receipts from her pocket, fumbling through a few before stopping at one.

“By the time on their receipt, I’d say ‘bout an hour and a half ago.” She grinned revealing a gold tooth. “He left me a big tip.”

Elam thanked the waitress, leaving her to tend to the hungry diners and headed for his car. Next stop, California.

CHAPTER ELEVEN

Needing a breath of fresh air, Bronwyn lowered her window, inviting the night breeze inside. She loved the outdoors at nightfall. The scents of the earth always seemed stronger in the evening. Manmade sounds diminished, giving way to nature's orchestra, it was always peaceful, and she certainly needed peace. The events of the day had her on edge; starting with her mother's quick trip to the pharmacy, and ending with Falcon's surprise attack. All the thoughts rambling through her head were tormenting, doing nothing to calm her troubled spirit. She had tried sleeping, hoping to escape the onslaught of questions and conspiracy theories crowding her mind. Despite Falcon's instructions in the diner to quit demanding answers, she found herself looking for a logical explanation of it all. Her mother's call telling her of detectives looking for Falcon haunted her thoughts. What if she were part of some elaborate illegal scam? What if she'd let her guard down because of her infatuation with Travis and was actually being duped. The farther she traveled from Moonshine, the easier it was to second guess it all. But, there was the fact of her old manuscript, and the cabin in the mountains, and the book with her name and handwriting. It had to be real. She leaned her head toward the open window and inhaled. The rush of air stirred through the cab and must have stimulated conversation from Falcon.

"So tell me about your pretty boy."

His topic choice surprised her. She wondered if he noticed her troubling thoughts and was trying to distract her, trading one turmoil for another.

"He's not my pretty boy anymore."

Falcon smirked, "You seem to be an intelligent woman, what was the attraction to a guy like Ryan

Reese?"

She laughed not believing she was actually having this conversation with Falcon.

"First, it was his looks. I happened to find him quite handsome as does most of the female population in this country. After all, he is considered the sexiest man alive according to all the magazines."

Falcon laughed, "That's what made you love him?"

"It wasn't only that. We had a lot of fun together too."

Falcon nodded in disbelief, "I have a lot of fun with my friends but it doesn't mean I want to marry them."

She felt foolish. Her past engagement suddenly resembled a junior high crush.

"Well I am not with him anymore so I guess it doesn't matter." She hoped her declaration would be the final say in the matter ending and unwanted discussion. Falcon had different intentions.

"And why is that? Didn't he come to Moonshine and beg you to take him back?"

"Yes he did," She answered smugly feeling a bit vindicated in the matter.

"And why didn't you?"

"Because Travis made me realize that I never really loved Ryan."

"Oh so you're in love with Travis now are you? Good luck with that."

She felt her face turn as crimson as the setting sun before her.

"That's not what I said. I meant Travis allowed me to realize that I was only in love with my created version of Ryan."

"And how did he make you see that?"

"He accused me of not really knowing what love is. Then, he explained true love to me."

"He did, did he?" Falcon seemed amused. "Please, tell me what he said."

She could quote word for word what Travis said that night. A day had not passed since, that she had not replayed that scene inside her head. As the sun disappeared on the horizon, she took a deep breath and recited Travis' words:

"If I say I love you, do I love you in the same way I love the mountains, or the smell of the earth after a good rain, or the way I love music? Do I love you because the way you look ignites a passion inside of me? Is my love for you only contingent on the way it affects me, how it makes me feel? If this is so, I only truly love myself, and I only love and want you for how it affects me. Or, do I love you, the person who looks at me from those emerald green eyes? Do I love you, despite the times you are angry, and bitter, and unlovely? Do I continue to love you, although your heart belongs to another? Can I send you away, knowing I will never experience you, but you, will experience all you've ever dreamed of? I can if my love is for you and not myself."

She felt awkward in the long silence that followed. Then, almost inaudibly she broke it, "I hope I can love someone like that one day, but I am afraid I'm too selfish." For the first time since they left the truck stop, Falcon took his eyes off of the road and smiled. There was nothing impish or wicked in his grin.

They drove all night. Falcon thought it best not to stop, saying that the further away they got from the crime scene the better their chances of not being detained. Bronwyn volunteered to drive but as usual he refused. He did volunteer to allow her to stretch her legs, so around eight-thirty he pulled off the main highway. They traveled a few miles down a secondary road before stopping at an overgrown field; in the middle, an old abandoned house sat in solitude. Of all the places, Bronwyn wondered why he would stop here. It looked haunted and spooky; she had experienced enough fear lately. She didn't need to add to it.

Falcon climbed from the cab, immediately lighting up a cigarette. It had been hours since his last smoke and she figured he was desperate. Following him out of the cab, she stretched her legs, but quickly recoiled in pain. The little bout at the truck stop was setting in, leaving her sore.

Falcon blew a line of smoke into the evening breeze, "Sorry about that."

She rolled her eyes, "I'm sure you are."

He took in another draw, narrowing his eyes in on her.

"You don't trust me do you?"

In light of their surroundings, his question seemed threatening. Had he asked it at the truck stop, or while they were eating in the café, it wouldn't have frightened her as much. But here, in the black of night, in the middle of nowhere, standing helpless in the overgrown yard of an abandoned house, it sent a chill.

"Not entirely."

Clenching the cigarette in his teeth, he stepped toward her. Not wanting to appear fearful, she remained her ground, determined not to move away. He pressed in close, still she didn't move. He was taller, so she found herself starring into his throat, wondering what his intentions were.

Placing his hands on her shoulders, he turned her to face the dilapidated house. They'd left the rain and storm the further west they drove. Now standing in the open field the moon showed bright in the sky overhead, spotlighting the ram shackled home.

"What do you see?" he asked her.

She shrugged, confused and somewhat apprehensive about the moment.

"Just a run-down old house."

"Is that all?" he asked keeping the cigarette clenched between his teeth.

She looked around, "Well, there is some dried out decaying trees, and a broken down fence, some busted windows but that's pretty much it."

He sighed and when he did a gust of smoke enveloped her face. She pulled away from his grasp coughing.

"It's a pathetic shame." He said crushing his cigarette with the tips of his fingers and tossing it into the tall grass.

Anger began to boil inside, at his condescending attitude. She still hadn't forgiven him for what he did at the truck stop. She refused to take any more.

"Really?" She bit back. "You're referring to me?"

"That I am. At least you got that one right."

She wanted to punch him, to give him the thrashing he inflicted on her; however she knew it would only result in him laughing at her lame attempt.

"How am I a pathetic shame?" her voice quivered with the words. She wasn't sure if the quiver was born out of anger or the haunting truth inside her that her life was pretty pitiful.

"You are not the pathetic shame," He corrected her and she was glad he did. At least she felt a tinge better. The shame is in the fact that you are our redemption and you are not ready to be. Not now, anyway."

"Well I could have told you that," She said; and when she did, she began to laugh at the thought of it. She, Bronwyn Sterling, the savior of a world she knew nothing about. The thought was preposterous. Maybe it was the extreme exhaustion she was experiencing or perhaps the anxiety she felt in being with the cad Falcon; whatever the reason, she couldn't stop laughing. She took in a deep breath but the laughter continued. Falcon shook his head in disbelief and lit up another, starring at her while he smoked.

"You know what I could use right now?" She asked him in between breaths. "I could use a drink. I just realized I haven't had alcohol in almost two weeks. I was trapped in Moonshine and never even had a swig." She threw her head back, hysterical at her own words.

Falcon flicked the ashes from his cigarette. "Strong drink isn't for the noble, who hold the lives of others in their hands. It's for the common, so they can drink and for a while forget their misery."

"Then fill 'er up!" She laughed again but allowed it to trail off when she noticed he wasn't smiling. This time she stared at him narrowing her eyes in deep inspection. She had to admit his words were stimulating, and it surprised her that such insightful words could come from a man like him. Since he was being philosophical she decided to ask him the question but couldn't resist a bit of sarcasm.

"What do you see then? Is that night vision of yours illuminating something I can't?"

He let out a thin line of smoke and looked towards the house.

"I see what once was. I see a man coming home from work and his children running to meet him. I see his wife standing in the doorway smiling, thankful he's home and that their children love him. I see a fireplace with a welcoming fire and a dinner table with a family gathered around it. I see beds where the children dream. I see a tree with a swing, and a dog wagging his tail and barking while the kids play. I see a woman hanging clothes out to dry and stopping for a moment to chase her kids through the trees." He took another draw, and expelled the smoke slowly as if he were lost in a memory.

"I see time marching through; an enemy they couldn't stop no matter how hard they tried. I see what once was, and not the shell of what is. I see what can be again, if a renovator would come and see the potential. I see something that, if given the proper care, could bring happiness to a family again." He took one last draw before he finished. "You don't need night vision to see these things Scribe, just a heart."

She felt ashamed. She should have seen all of that. After all she was the writer; she if anyone should have seen the story in the rubble. Falcon was right, it was a pathetic shame. When did she lose her wonder? When did she start existing, and quit living? She gazed at the house, bathed in the glow of the moon, and tried to imagine what it was like in its prime and then her eyes fell on Falcon, and suddenly she knew why he had stopped here, and what he was really trying to show her. He was the house. He wished her to see who he once was, to look past the rough chain smoking façade to who he really is. She felt the same about herself, hoping he and Travis could see past the bitter, heartbroken woman she'd become. She wanted a do over, a remote control where she could rewind life to the place where she began messing up and start fresh. And then it hit her. Tonight was her do over; a fresh start. And as she stood in the overgrown field, under the sky filled with stars, she knew someone, somewhere, in the great expanse of it all was renovating her life; because they saw potential, they knew who she really was and who she was destined to be.

CHAPTER TWELVE

Bronwyn took a sip of the strong coffee, thankful for the morning brew. She'd intended on sleeping much later than she actually did. She and Falcon drove nonstop, after their visit at the ram shackled house, arriving at Bronwyn's condo sometime around seven. After Falcon staked out the place, making sure no one was hiding in the shadows, awaiting their arrival, he and Bronwyn collapsed in bed for a well-deserved rest. But their peaceful slumber was interrupted two hours later by Jamia's persistent rapping on the patio door. She'd waken to take her three Bichon's for their walk when she noticed a strange truck parked outside Bronwyn's place. Being the one person who constantly kept an eye on the beachside condo, running off Ryan's attorneys and nosey paparazzi, she banged on the door determined to have it out with whoever was trespassing.

Falcon reached the door first, shirtless, and with his hair in a wild mess. He was in no mood to be interrogated by the neighborhood watch. Bronwyn heard his verbal assault on Jamia and bolted down the stairs just in time to hear Jamia threaten to call the police unless she saw Bronwyn. The two looked as if they were ready to have an all-out brawl when Bronwyn appeared at the door diffusing the situation. After answering an onslaught of questions from Jamia, Bronwyn realized there would be no returning to sleep anytime soon.

Jamia insisted on cooking breakfast, to which Bronwyn was thankful. She was hungry and since she had been away for a majority of the past six months, there were no groceries in her condo. Within minutes Jamia returned with a basket of goodies. She brewed a fresh pot of coffee, poured ice cold orange juice, laid out a spread of croissants and muffins while she fried up some turkey bacon, and eggs.

Bronwyn yawned, sipped her coffee and went through her mail, while Falcon disappeared upstairs to take a shower, figuring Bronwyn was safe in the company of the militant Jamia.

"He sure is a handsome one." Jamia commented, refilling Bronwyn's mug. "He looks like he could beat the shit out of that pansy Ryan."

Bronwyn gave a slight smile in return, which prompted Jamia's next probing question. "He didn't give you that busted lip did he?"

Her question teemed with skepticism. Jamia was smart and attentive. Her discerning abilities always amazed Bronwyn and she knew she wouldn't be able to fake her way through this conversation without being found out. She continued to thumb through her mail so she wouldn't have to look Jamia in the eye.

"Come on Jamia, do you really think I would be with a guy who hits me?" "Definitely not, you'd kill him first. But you can't blame me for asking. He does look like a bad boy."

"That he does, but his bark's worse than his bite. He's rough on the edges but once you look past it…" her voice faded off as she came to an ivory colored envelope, addressed to her in aged Calligraphy. There was no return address, no stamp and no postmark, yet it was delivered with all her other mail.

Jamia kept rambling on but her voice seemed far away, the mysterious letter had captured her utmost attention. Grabbing her letter opener she slit through the envelope and pulled out an aging piece of parchment, unfolding it carefully.

Crossing the room, Bronwyn retrieved a Bible from the bookcase. Her hands trembled as she thumbed through the table of contents trying to locate the book of Habakkuk. Another cryptic message, just like the one she received the night of the ice cream festival. The message in the mysterious letter read; *Habakkuk 2:2-3.*

With trembling hands she thumbed through the pages. She wasn't much accustomed to the Bible, but knew from her childhood days in Sunday school that Habakkuk was in the Old Testament. Obadiah, Jonah, Micah, Nahum…Habakkuk. She turned to the second chapter, second verse, and with a trembling finger, underlined the words as she read.

Write the vision and make it plain, that he may run who reads it. For the vision is yet for an appointed time; but at the end it will speak and it will not lie. Though it tarries wait for it; because it will surely come.

Although the enigmatic message was from the Bible, she knew it was for her. She sat down hard in her chair, staring out over the patio, across the sandy beach, to where the ocean meets the horizon, lost in her own sea of thoughts. She read the passage again, dissecting each phrase.

Write the vision and make it plain. What vision? She hadn't had any other than a few nightmares and a couple of brief flashes of her and Travis standing in the falling rain. Was she to pen them down, or was there a foretold vision she was to see in the future?

That he may run who reads it. She was at a complete loss to the meaning of this phrase so she moved on.

For the vision is yet for an appointed time. Was this meaning the vision was yet to come or what she sees in the vision will be something that takes place in the future? She thought it was probably the latter.

But at the end it will speak and it will not lie. Though it tarries wait for it; because it will surely come. Something about the last phrase caused a dread to rise inside of her. The message was urging her not to give up hope, which meant only one thing…suffering.

She was so lost in her thoughts; she never heard Jamia go back into the kitchen, rattling on with endless advice and stories of past hurts in living with an abusive man. Nor did she hear Falcon return to the room and ask her what was wrong.

"Scribe!" His voice interrupted her thinking. "You alright?"

She nodded, handing him the envelope. He read the passage on the letter and as he looked back at her, she handed him the Bible, already turned to the assigned page. Taking the heavy book from her, he read the passage, and then with a nod of his head motioned her outside on the patio.

"You've had a vision?"

"No, nothing worth writing down anyway. Just some small flashes, mostly of Travis." She blushed at the confession, quickly turning her face toward the ocean, hoping he hadn't noticed the color flooding into her cheeks. He seemed surprised at the disclosure.

"Really? What kind of flashes?"

She leaned on the railing, continuing to watch the waves collapse on the shore. The breeze coming off the ocean moved her hair away from her face and cooled her burning cheeks.

“They’re always the same. He’s standing in falling rain, he looks distraught. Then I reach for him, and when I do I start to fall, and then it’s over.”

Falcon said nothing and she had no desire to turn and look at him even though she could tell he was watching her. She almost felt silly for telling him what she saw in the flashes, but he asked.

The delicious aroma of bacon and eggs tickled at her nose so she decided to trade the awkwardness of the patio for a satisfying breakfast inside. But as she turned to leave Falcon’s disclosure stopped her cold.

“He lost her.” His statement shocked Bronwyn, pulling her eyes from the incoming tide and onto him. Her heart leaped and she prayed it didn’t show in her face. He was referring to Travis’s love and she held her breath hoping he would continue.

“She disappeared when she went through the portal. No one ever saw her after. Travis searched for years and never found her.”

Bronwyn didn’t know what to say. She had a million questions but wasn’t sure which to ask first, or if Falcon would even answer them if she did. He looked at her so intently that she shifted her feet in the discomfort.

“She is beautiful, like you. In fact you resemble her in a way.”

Another shocking statement. For starters, she never knew Falcon thought of her as beautiful, which caught her off guard. His admission that she favored Travis’ love may have explained Travis’ attentiveness to her back in Moonshine. That, and the fact she was his ticket home.

“She was fearless, exciting, adventurous, kind, she had no enemies. Everyone loved her; even Abaddon.” Falcon paused and pulled a cigarette from his pocket. She watched him; wishing he would hurry and continue. He was revealing secrets and she desired to know them all. Holding the flame to the end of his smoke, Falcon inhaled, keeping his eyes fixed on her. He placed the lighter in his jeans before blowing a long line of smoke over the railing.

“In fact Abaddon loved her too much and couldn’t accept the fact she chose Travis over him. So to add insult to injury, he launched his upheaval on their wedding night, preventing them from marrying. Travis lost his brother, his love… his entire world in one night.”

Bronwyn’s heart thundered inside her chest, anguished at the thought. She remembered back to the night of the festival, being overcome, realizing it would have been her wedding night, had Ryan not broken off their engagement. Travis took her out on the lake to watch fireworks, comforting her. Yet her loss was nothing compared to his.

Falcon watched her as he exhaled another line of smoke.

“His greatest fear was that Abaddon’s men found her and took her back through the portal. If so….”

“Breakfast is ready.” Jamia announced, interrupting Falcon’s story, walking out onto the balcony with two plates of food. “Lets’ eat before it gets cold.”

Bronwyn sighed; her portal to information was closed for now.

CHAPTER THIRTEEN

Jamia cleaned up after breakfast, left a tray of muffins on the counter, and headed home leaving Bronwyn to sort through her belongings. It was pretty easy to decide what to take to Moonshine and what to leave behind. She and Ryan rented the condo furnished; only a few pieces actually belonged to her, and those items, she decided, could go into storage. The kitchen utensils such as plates, silverware, pots and pans, coffee maker, and the likes, all belonged to her. She would put them in storage as well, because as she remembered correctly, her cottage in Moonshine was completely stocked.

September was only a couple of weeks away. The weather in the mountains would be cooling off soon and she would need her winter clothing. Pulling out a suitcase, she began tossing her sweaters and boots inside. A feeling of excitement began to grow. She reveled in the idea of sitting in her mountain cottage, sipping hot cider, penning her amazing story, while watching the leaves turn shades of amber, bright orange and yellow, before saying their last farewell to the tree and falling to earth. As she thought of these things, her mind turned to Travis and she pictured him as a massive tree, speaking life into the people of his world. As their time passed without him, they would grow old, falling away from his nourishment, left to decay and die on the earth. Barak said they had three years left before they began to age and start the process of death. She wondered if her thought on this matter, was the vision she was to write down, but figured it wasn't. In her mind a vision should be something you see, like a huge movie screen, playing out a story that no one else is privy to but you. A vision wouldn't be a simple thought in the head; it had to be much grander than that.

With each suitcase she packed, Falcon took them downstairs, placing them in the truck, hastening their departure. He remained quiet most of the day and that disappointed her. She hoped he would continue the story he started on the patio before Jamia interrupted. However, he never picked it back up.

She sensed an anxious spirit in him. He kept his vigil, watching the beach, scrutinizing the people walking by, glaring at them if they ventured too close to the condo.

As the day wore on, her body reminded her she was going on only three hours of sleep. But she wouldn't stop. She was as anxious as Falcon to leave this place. Everything she touched was a reminder of her and Ryan's time together. True, she was no longer heart broke, but still she desired nothing more than to move on, burn the bridge and leave it in the past.

She took a break from her packing to enjoy a delicious meal Falcon ordered from a local restaurant. He set a nice table for them outside where they could dine and watch the sun set. Most of the beach goers already packed up and headed home for the day, only a few remained gathered around fire pits, roasting hot dogs, and s'mores. Bronwyn sipped at her ice water watching the sun disappear into the ocean, surprised Falcon hadn't opened one of the many bottles of wine in her kitchen. She guessed he wasn't kidding when he said strong drink wasn't for those who hold the lives of others in their hands. And come to think of it, she'd never seen him drink. Other than his chain smoking he seemed to be one of the most disciplined men she'd ever know. A warrior, always prepared, always one step ahead of the enemy and ready to run into battle. Ready to give his life for the cause, which meant he was driven by a passion, because all discipline is rooted in desire. And then, she had a thought, so she decided to voice it audibly.

"Do you have someone special waiting for you in Eden as well?"

He smirked, "Why? You interested?"

She laughed. She couldn't help herself; she'd walked right into that one.

"Hardly, I think we'd kill each other. Although, last night you did reveal a rather tender, poetic side."

He leaned back in his chair, "So you're sayin' I have a chance?"

Again, she laughed.

By the time they finished their dinner, the moon was high in the sky, reflecting its silver light upon the water. Falcon lit up a cigarette and perched himself on the railing keeping a careful watch over the surrounding area. The fire pits along the beach were ablaze leaving a line of small fires as far as the eye could see. Friday night beachgoers gathered around the warmth, dancing to the music flowing from their ipods. Couples walked hand in hand near the water's edge, a few straying near Bronwyn's condo, coming closer to the deck than Falcon liked.

Bronwyn looked out over the black waters.

"I love the ocean at night." She confessed. "It's so dark out there…so black…so mysterious; I always wondered if the roar was a lament, telling me of something I should know."

Falcon took a long draw from his cigarette, expelling the smoke slowly, studying her. The gentle breeze pushed her hair away from her face revealing a flawless profile with the exception of a slightly swollen lower lip. Unaware of his gaze, she allowed the ocean to hypnotize her with the rhythmic sound of crashing waves. Her heart ached for a reason she didn't know. There was an all-compassing emptiness enveloping her and suddenly she felt alone. True, she'd recently made a life altering decision, leaving her job and her best friends behind, not to mention rejecting Ryan after he came back. Still, the loneliness didn't stem from any of those things. Her soul felt as empty as the great black expanse she was staring into.

"Abaddon fell in love with Kenalycia too..."

Falcon's unexpected revelation captured her attention; bringing her eyes to his in an unplanned reaction. "...but Kenalycia's heart belonged to Travis and his belonged to her, and everyone knew it." Falcon took a draw, "I don't think there have ever been two people more in love than Kenalycia and Travis."

Bronwyn turned back to the ocean so Falcon could not see the pain of his statement reflecting on her face. Although she desired to hear more; any mention of Travis loving another, only resulted in a heaviness overshadowing her heart. Bronwyn hoped time away from him would ease the pain, putting things in perspective. But with each day that passed, she found herself longing to be near him. Now she must endure Falcon disclosing how much Travis loved another, and as much as it hurt, there was a desire to know more. Falcon paused and looked out over the black ocean before continuing the tragic tale. "They confessed their love for each other and set the date for their marriage." He took another draw, expelling a cloud of smoke. "In our world there is a week of celebrating that takes place before the actual wedding. The night before the ceremony is sacred and intimate. The couple meets at a secret location, and give themselves to each other for the first time. Sex, in our world is the ultimate gift, given only to the one person who truly holds your heart. We save our gift, and when it is presented in that way, it is the height of ecstasy. The pleasure never subsides because it has not been cheapened and used for selfish gratification. Neither do we give it to multiple people because then it loses its significance and desire."

Bronwyn could feel Falcon's gaze on her; and she wondered if he were intentionally accusing her with his words, knowing she had already given herself to Ryan. Her heart burned at the thought of Travis knowing that as well. She supposed he was still saving his gift for Kenalycia.

Falcon took another long draw and as he continued, Bronwyn noticed a distinct bitterness in his voice.

"Abaddon made his move the night Kenalycia and Travis were to give themselves to each other. His men were strategically placed all over Eden, poised and ready for his signal. One of his spies followed Travis to the secret location while some of his men kidnapped Kenalycia. Travis waited at the waterfall, but she never came. Instead, Abaddon showed up. As soon as Travis saw him he knew something was horribly wrong."

Bronwyn's heart raced; although the night breeze blowing off the water was chilly, it did nothing to lessen the heat flooding through her. And despite the intensity of the warmth, she shivered.

Pausing for a moment to take another draw, Falcon cut his eyes over to Bronwyn watching her unaware. His story was having the intended impact, so he smiled slightly, expelling another line of smoke.

"Abaddon showed Travis his knife, informing him the blood stain on the blade belonged to his brother Ariston. Travis flew into an uncontrollable rage and being a man of incredible strength he took out ten of Abaddon's men immediately. He overpowered Abaddon and was ready to kill him when Abaddon warned him that unless he surrendered he would give the order for his men to kill Brennun and Mavis. Travis surrendered. He was taken as a prisoner and escorted back to the citadel and placed with Brennun and the rest of the ruling royalty taken captive that night. Travis searched for Kenalycia only to find out she had been placed in Abaddon's care."

Swinging his legs over the railing, Falcon jumped down upon the deck. He crushed the butt of his cigarette and tossed it in the trash.

"Want to go for a walk?"

His invitation surprised her and she hoped he didn't choose to end the story there. He still had not disclosed what ever happened to Kenalycia.

"I will if you finish your story."

Walking along the shoreline, she wrapped her arms close around her body wishing she had thought to bring a light jacket. Falcon noticed her trembling.

"You okay?"

She nodded, "Just a little cold."

"We can go back," He said.

She nodded again, "It's alright. It's not as much from the cold…your story affects me, to where I tremble on the inside. It's intense…a very tragic tale, and I'm not sure why it's affecting me so, other than I know some of the people involved."

Falcon gave no comment as they walked in silence further down the beach. They stumbled upon an abandoned fire. Deciding to take advantage of its warmth, they sat on the cold sand, watching the burning bits of ashes rise with the breeze, and blow away from the pit. Falcon sat near her, silent, staring off into the dark expanse. She watched him, not caring if he noticed her deep inspection of him. As the dancing flames cast eerie shadows across his face, she wondered what he was remembering after all this time, and if the pain was just a memory or if his wounds still bled.

"Where were you when all this was going on?" Her question sounded accusing and when Falcon cut his dark eyes into her she wished she'd worded it differently.

"When Abaddon launched his revolt everything turned to chaos. No one knew who was siding with whom. Abaddon's inner circle was top secret and although he and I were very close he never included me in his elite, so the entire rebellion came as a shock. After the initial uprising he asked me to stand with him, joining his regime. He promised me a lot. I figured I could do more to help Travis and the others if I was on the inside. So I accepted his offer, making him think I gave him my allegiance. Unfortunately everyone else thought I had as well. Some even believed I was part of his elite and helped him plan the entire revolt. I could see how they thought such a thing seeing I lived in the main house of the citadel and had considerable authority. What Abaddon and the others didn't know was that I had plans of my own."

Bronwyn kept her eyes locked on him the entire time he spoke, captivated by his words as he recounted the wretched event.

"I saw Kenalycia every day because we were both living in the main house. She hated me. She, along with everyone else, assumed I was in league with Abaddon and had betrayed Travis. I knew Abaddon was planning on taking Kenalycia as his wife. I couldn't let it happen. I came up with a plan and tried to tell her but she refused to have anything to do with me. I finally caught her alone and forced her to listen. Once she heard me out, she realized my allegiance was still with Travis so she trusted me, agreeing to go along with the plan. I went to the prison and met with Travis. Following the plot, Kenalycia asked Abaddon if she could say her final goodbyes to her family who were being exiled through the portal. The darkness had not completely overtaken Abaddon so with a glimmer of good left in him, he agreed. Abaddon played right into my hand by asking me to accompany her to the portal. I secretly let Travis out of prison so he could meet us there. The plan was for him and Kenalycia to escape through the portal. When we arrived, I hurled a surprise attack on Abaddon's men. I was able to hold them back long enough for Travis to send Kenalycia through. He didn't go with her; instead he stayed back to help me.

Abaddon was outraged when he learned what happened. He had Travis severely beaten. Travis told me later he was able to endure it because he took comfort in the fact that Abaddon could not touch Kenalycia. Abaddon had me beaten for my betrayal as well, and when I was too injured to fight back, he sliced his revenge into my face."

Bronwyn was trembling almost uncontrollably now. Her teeth chattered, her jaw tensed and her head hurt. The images in her mind broke her heart. All the pain and loss endured during the betrayal enveloped her, swathing her spirit, piercing her soul. Vivid pictures of Travis and Falcons bloody, beaten bodies flashed through her mind while the sound of their anguish rang in her ears, overpowering the roar of the ocean. Falcon's story grieved her inner being with such a sorrow she'd never experienced before. It was almost too much to endure. Then suddenly the roar of the ocean was overpowered by the mournful cries of the oppressed. Falcon did not seem to hear the lamenting as she did; instead he sat starring out into the expanse, unresponsive to the pain searing a wound into her heart.

Just when she thought, she could not endure the weeping any longer, the song of the woman began to surface, overpowering the sorrowful howling. The peaceful haunting song infiltrated her soul and brought with it a renewed sense of strength, calming her spirit and empowering her with an unexplainable courage. The melody brought with it a realization that she was endowed with the power to write the redemptive story and make right all that Abaddon had wronged. This sanctioning filled her with great inspiration, destroying the blockage that had long since closed off her ability to write. Bronwyn felt it dissolving inside of her, freeing her imagination from its captive state. She lay back in the cold sand, starring at the night sky. The roar of the ocean became audible again as the song of the woman subsided. The salty night breeze, cradled her, cooling the intense burning heat.

Falcon's story ignited a passion inside of her, an outrage at the injustice, and a strong desire to love unconditionally. She realized the pain true love would bring. If she wrote the story the way it should be, then she would be reuniting Travis and Kenalycia. She would be sending Travis away, never experiencing him, but knowing he would experience all he ever dreamed. Her heart nearly broke with the thought, yet she knew it was what she must do. One single tear escaped her eye, rolling off the side of her face onto the sand and simultaneously, a star shot across the night sky, leaving a fiery trail. And at that moment, she felt the universe was grieving right along with her.

CHAPTER FOURTEEN

Although Bronwyn was existing on less than four hours of sleep, she had no desire to go to bed. After spending the past hour listening to Falcon unfold the events of Eden's uprising, her mind was alive. The inspiration that had been foreign for so long was back with a stimulating vengeance. So after a quick shower, she grabbed the leather bound book, unlocked the latch with the miniature key, and settled down to write. She didn't inform Falcon of her plan, so when he passed through the living area checking the doors before turning in, he stopped cold.

"You're writing?"

"I am," she smiled softly, confident in her ability to do so. "I know you're tired, don't feel like you have to wait up."

His face took on a respectful expression she had yet to see amidst all the sarcastic looks he'd thrown her way over the past couple of days.

"This is a sacred moment for me. What providence to witness the foretold story at its beginnings. To be in the very room as it is composed. Sleep can wait."

He took a seat across the room, and for the next three hours never removed his eyes from her. He watched as her hand moved rhythmically across the blank pages, filling them with life. Her body swayed as she wrote, as if her spirit was dancing to a melody that only she could hear. Every so often her lips would curl into a smile and a couple of times; a tear escaped her eyes and trickled down her cheek, splashing onto the dry parchment. She wrote for nearly three hours without stopping before laying her pen aside and closing the book; locking it with the small key. She looked at Falcon, her delicate lips forming a satisfied smile.

"It begins."

Falcon swallowed hard; his throat suddenly parched. He remained unmoved his eyes locked in on hers.

"You're pleased with what you wrote?"

"Yes, it begins well."

Standing from his chair, he extended his hand to her, "Then we best get our rest my lady scribe. We have an enormous battle ahead."

He was right, she needed rest, the lack of sleep combined with the intense emotion of the night was taking its toll and suddenly she couldn't wait to fall into bed.

Falcon escorted her upstairs and into the master bedroom. She placed the treasured book into her travel bag, zipping it shut."

"Should we set an alarm for the morning?" she asked, turning around. Before she could decipher what was happening, Falcon lunged for her, knocking her to the floor, blocking the shards of broken glass showering down around them, shattering the stillness of the room.

"Stay down!" He ordered, grabbing the small travel bag and pulling her toward the doorway. Terrified, she followed him, crawling on her hands and knees, feeling the jagged fragments of the shattered balcony door cutting into her skin.

Once in the hallway, Falcon pushed Bronwyn flat against the wall, shoved the bag into her hand and motioned for her to stay put. Her heart raced, panicked; surely he wouldn't leave her alone. He bolted down the hallway stopping at the top of the staircase, flattening himself against the opposite wall. To her horror she heard footsteps rushing up the stairs. Someone was in the condo! Riveted in terror, she watched as the dark outline of a man topped the stairs, entering into the hallway. Falcon stepped forward; with one swift move the man slumped to the ground. A slight shaft of moonlight drew a line across the hard wood of the hallway, illuminating a significant amount of blood, pooling from underneath the fallen man.

Bronwyn leaned against the wall unable to take her eyes off the gore. She grew dizzy, her stomach felt as if she would retch.

"Stay with me Scribe," Falcon was matter of fact, pulling her off the wall. She stepped over the corpse, shuddering and thinking she might vomit, as the sticky fluid oozed between her toes. Once they reached the base of the stairs, Falcon stopped and scanned the dark room. It was quiet and empty.

Hugging the wall as well as they were able, they made their way across the room toward the garage, stopping at the massive picture windows. Falcon pulled Bronwyn low to the ground as they inched their way underneath the glass panes. Taking advantage of their crouching position, a dark figure leaped from the upper loft taking Falcon down immediately. Bronwyn screamed at the unexpectedness of the attack drawing immediate attention to their whereabouts. The room came alive as shadowy figures manifest from the upper loft and dark corners. Within seconds, three men stormed the room. Falcon sprung to his feet, forcefully throwing the attacker off, tossing him through the plate glass window. Wasting no time, Falcon pulled his knife. Spinning around he kicked the approaching aggressor out of the way, while burying his knife deep into the chest of the second man. The front door burst open, splintering the hinges as another assailant bolted in heading toward

Bronwyn. Horrified, she stood frozen, watching everything unfold.

"Get out of here Scribe!" Falcon yelled jarring her from her petrified trance. The man dove for her as she whirled around heading back up to the bedroom. Hugging her bag close, she bolted up the stairs taking two at a time. With her adrenaline on overload, she dashed down the hall jumping over the slain man. Her bare feet slid in the sticky blood, still ebbing from the lifeless body, causing her to fall, sliding across the unyielding wood floor. She swallowed hard to keep from vomiting. Taking a quick glance over her shoulder, she saw her pursuer topping the stairs. Scrambling to her feet, she loped into her room slamming the door behind her, pressing her body against it in a feeble attempt to keep it closed. Her bloody fingers trembled, slipping off the latch, making it almost impossible to lock.

Please! She could hear the heavy footsteps of the ruffian moving fast down the hallway. She wiped her wet hands across her t-shirt hoping to dry them enough to grab hold of the lock without it slipping. *Please God*, she prayed again. The lock clicked into place just as the man slammed his body against the door. Excruciating pain spread through her body as the door shook violently, buckling under the force of the blow. She knew it would only be a matter of seconds before it was knocked completely off its hinges.

Dashing across the room, she knelt beside the bed, and with shaky hands, she lifted the heavy mattress. With one trembling arm she held it up as best she could and with the other she desperately searched the empty space underneath. *Please be here... Please.*

After hearing disturbing reports about psychotic fans stalking celebrities, Ryan purchased a handgun, despite Bronwyn's protests. He figured it might come in handy with his newfound fame. She hadn't thought of the gun until now and she hoped Ryan had forgotten about it as well and left it behind when he moved out.

Bam! The man threw his body against the door, intensifying her desperate search. The wood facing splintered, buckling the door. The next blow would surely force it open. She continued her blind search; the fear surging through her body, weakening her. Her wobbly arm wouldn't be able to hold the mattress up much longer. Then, her fingers touched cold hard metal. It was still there! She pulled the gun from its hiding place, hoping it was loaded, yet not at all sure she knew how to shoot it.

The sound of splintering wood drowned out her thrashing heart as the door came crashing open. Her hands shook uncontrollably nearly causing her to drop her only protection. Squatting down, she hid, crouching behind the king sized bed. Her heart smacked against her chest uncontrollably; the intense fear choking the breath from her throat. Her bedroom was a rather large suite; and she hoped it would take a few seconds before for the brute made his way to this side of the bed, giving her more time to familiarize herself with her weapon. The shadow moving across the wall however thwarted that idea. The man was rounding the corner of the bed. He stopped suddenly when he saw her but it wasn't the gun in her hands that immobilized him. He stared at her, giving her a curious expression before his lips curled into a smile. He laughed.

"As I live and breathe. They weren't kidding."

His random choice of words was puzzling. Reaching out to grab hold of her, he stretched out his brawny arm. "You're coming with me princess."

Scooting away from his reach, she raised the gun, aiming at his chest.

A deafening explosion pierced the quiet of the morning, as the handle unexpectedly kicked back into her face, knocking the gun from her hand. Extreme pain erupted inside her head, blurring her vision as blood began pouring from her nose. And despite her hazy vision she saw the man's eyes go manic as he lunged straight for her.

CHAPTER FIFTEEN

The explosion of gunfire upstairs caused Falcons heart to sink. Pulling his knife from the chest of his last attacker he rushed up the stairs, hurdling over the fallen man, nearly losing his footing on the blood covered floor.

Could it have ended so quickly? After all the years of waiting and anticipating their redemption, and with only one small section of the book penned, could all hope of deliverance be gone?

His heart ached as he thought of Bronwyn. He couldn't bear the thought of her dead. He believed her to be truly innocent, totally oblivious to what was really going on. A pawn in a game she didn't remember playing. True he'd been hard on her, giving her no slack, but his actions were for her own good. He knew the enemy well and must prepare her for the inevitable encounter. For all the good it had done. He would grieve later. Right now fury raged inside of him. He would find the one who took her life and mutilate him.

Replacing the knife in his jeans, he pulled his gun and stepped into the room. No need to kill in silence, the deafening blast had more than likely woken the neighbors. It would be only a matter of time before the police arrived.

Picking up on movement behind the splintered door, he kicked it off its hinges, and found himself starring down the barrel of a gun.

With a twist of his wrist he snatched the weapon from its owner, hurling it across the king sized bed. Grabbing Bronwyn, he buried her bloody face into his chest and kissed the top of her head.

"Let's get out of here." He whispered.

Stepping over the corpse one last time, they descended the stairs. Bronwyn glanced about her once peaceful living room, stunned. Four dead bodies lay scattered across the room each one's lifeblood splattered across the furnishings and draining from a gash across their neck or chest. Shards of shattered glass lay beneath the large picture windows. This time instead of stealing across the room slowly, they raced through it, heading to the garage.

Fortunately Falcon had already loaded the truck for departure. He grabbed the bag from Bronwyn, tossing it into the cab. Running over to the passenger side, she reached for the door. A dark figure jumped from the open bed, grabbing her hair. Yanking her head back, he placed the cold blade of his knife against her neck. Choking at the sting of it, she swallowed hard and closed her eyes. It would only take a fraction of a second for the blade to rip across her throat, ending her life. A small surge of air passed near her temples as a warm liquid splattered across her face. The man's grip lessened as he slumped to the floor. Falcon's aim was impeccable, missing Bronwyn by a fraction and landing directly in the forehead of her attacker.

"Get in." He yelled.

As they sped away, the peaceful sound of breaking waves was drowned out by barking dogs and approaching sirens.

CHAPTER SIXTEEN

Elam walked briskly through the beautifully landscaped corridor of the palace estate, making his way past the marble pillars. Lush floral vines snaked their way around the columns and up through the overhang, mingling with the massive ferns offering ample shade to cool him from his hurried pace. Making a sharp turn, he walked by the way of the sparkling fountain, making sure not to make eye contact with anyone. He had no intention of wasting time in idle conversation. Besides, he was of the elite inner circle and no one should dare engage in conversation with him unless invited. He wished to speak with only one man, the crowned head, Abaddon.

He carried news that would shake the very foundations of his world. He was certain to be rewarded even more. More than likely, he would be swiftly promoted within the elite to the position of Abaddon's right hand.

Rounding the corner, he pushed open the grand doors of the palace hall, purposely turning his head to avoid looking into the courtyard lying to his left. Despite his own malevolent ways, he feared the place. It was on the grounds of that majestic courtyard that the first blood was spilt. He witnessed what the dark desire for power could accomplish. To this day he could not relieve his mind of the image, of the fallen Prince Ariston. If by chance he dare to glance that way; he feared he would see the whole traitorous coup de' tat play out. It was his own fear that imprisoned him and lured his allegiance to the darkness. It was that weakness that caused the inhabitants of this earth to loath him as one of the most murderous traitors since the legendary Judas Iscariot. Today however, he felt a renewed sense of purpose and inner strength emerging, overpowering all doubt and fear plaguing him since that night. Times had changed, and the encompassing power was dark; you either embraced it or ended up merely existing hanging on to a feeble hope that could never stand against this certain kingdom.

Approaching the entrance to the secret room, he gave the attendant an arrogant nod. The guard immediately pushed open the door, allowing him entrance. His determined walk through the room accelerated his steps, pumping the adrenaline through his body. Just as he expected the inner circle was there, awaiting his return and the news of the capture of Prince Asa, and the death of the Scribe. They waited with great expectation, prematurely congratulating one another on the success of the mission. Confident they would be partaking from the tree of life soon, stopping imminent death, allowing them to continue living forever.

"You're alone?" Blaine taunted from the table, "Where are the others?"

"With war there are casualties," he spit his venomous words back on the viper. Blaine was resentful of his new position and would revel in seeing him demoted so he could slip into his position. He wasn't worth his time; it was he who was crossing the portal, taking the risk, doing all the work. It was his brilliant plan that was playing out; landing him the information he carried in his coat pocket. He focused his attention on Abaddon. The conversation at the oval table quieted as Elam approached.

"Your Liege," He bowed. His heart thundered inside of him as if it would suddenly leap from his chest.

Abaddon cast his fiendish eyes on him. A malicious calm gave expression to his face as he reclined.

"I only see you. I was expecting Asa and a corpse."

Elam swallowed hard more than anxious to deliver the news. He had no fear in not bringing Asa, for it was only a matter of time, considering the update on the situation, before Asa was in their midst.

"I am afraid it's only me at the moment. Nine fell and the others have remained behind for the time being. Asa is unaccounted for at the moment."

A roar of inquiry erupted from the oval table as the men hurled a multitude of questions upon him.

Abaddon raised his hand. A quiet hush fell across the room while Abaddon contemplated Elam's words. "I bestowed upon you the honor of guiding the council in how we were to acquire valuable information allowing us to locate the Scribe along with Prince Asa and the remaining heirs. In your scheming, you were to gain access to the second prophesy, as well as the location of the second portal, delivering the information to us before our adversary lay hold of it. So far, you have done nothing but lead our men to their deaths. I am pressed to believe you may be aiding our enemy more than us."

Elam's hand trembled with excitement as he pulled an item from his coat passing it to Abaddon. "Behold your Scribe."

Keeping his cold stare upon Elam, Abaddon took the item from his hand. "You offer a picture when I have asked for a corpse?" A rumble of laughter echoed among the men at the oval table, Blaine's was the loudest.

Elam could care less what the ignorant men thought. Once Abaddon looked at the photograph, he would be placed over their charge then they would suffer greatly for their insolence.

"Take a look my Lord. I believe you will be pleased with what you see." Abaddon removed his threatening stare from Elam and glanced down at the picture in his hand. A disturbing smile curled at his lips, and it seemed like an eternity to Elam before Abaddon lifted his eyes.

"Is she…"

Ordinarily Elam would never think of Interrupting Abaddon, but in this case it was absolute respect to do so, to keep him from having to ask the question in its entirety. "No, she is not"

Abaddon motioned to the coveted chair beside him. "You have served me well. Come and sit. We must talk."

Giving his attention to those gathered around the oval table, he addressed his elite. “Men your directives have changed. There is a new assignment. Listen carefully to Elam. He is your superior, take heed his instructions.”

CHAPTER SEVENTEEN

"Who is it?" Jamia asked, pressing her ear against the door, trying to hear over the three Bichons yapping at her feet.

"Police."

Sliding back the bolt, she opened the door, welcoming the two officers into her home.

"You the woman who phoned in the emergency?"

She nodded, pulling her robe tight, "I am."

"You said you heard gunshots?"

"Well at first I heard breaking glass. It woke me from a sound sleep. I was terrified. We're not talking about a few dishes; it was loud, like several windows shattering all at once. I jumped out of bed hoping it wasn't one of mine and that's when I heard what sounded like a gunshot coming from next door."

"Just one?"

"No, there were two. I'm really worried. I've called my friend several times but she's not answering. Please go check on her. She is in the company of someone she said was her boyfriend but I don't believe her. He's not her type. Plus, I noticed several bruises on her along with a fat lip."

"Okay we'll check on your neighbor. What's her name?"

"Her name's Bronwyn, Bronwyn Sterling."

Jamia peered through her window watching the two officers disappear around the corner, making their way over to Bronwyn's; hands poised on their holsters, their flashlights floodlighting a path.

Nearing the condo, Officer Robison pulled the radio from his utility belt.

"We've got us a homicide." He reported, his beam spotlighting a body lying motionless in the sand. "We're heading in could use some backup."

Drawing their weapons, the officers mounted the steps. Officer Robison rapped on the door. "Police!" All was silent. Keeping his gun held high, he tried the door with his free hand. It opened. He cast his light around the room and groaned. "My God, it's a massacre."

Back up arrived almost immediately. Officer Robison's superior along with several other big wigs, stepped from their unmarked cars, wanting a report.

"Seven body count, one outside, three in the living room, two upstairs and one in the garage. All males, no ID on any of them and no sign of Miss Sterling anywhere. We found a gun on the bed and a car in the garage. Ran the plates, the vehicle belongs to Miss Sterling. The neighbor reported a man visiting with Miss Sterling. I'm headed over there now to get some more information."

Jamia waited, taking a break from her nervous pacing to peek outside, hoping to see Bronwyn walking up her path. The continuous howl of sirens frightened her, as more emergency vehicles appeared on the scene, their flashing lights pierced through her curtains, pulsating inside her condo like a discotheque. The sound of a helicopter joining the madness filled her with alarm. What could have possibly happened? Pulling back her curtain, she watched its high beam searchlight sweep across the beach. Her heart fainted within her telling her something dreadful happened. Feeling helpless she sat quietly on her sofa, twisting her hands, and over petting her three dogs. Leaning against the soft cushions, she dozed off while she waited for news.

It was daylight when a quick rap at the door woke her from her restless sleep. She bolted to the door nearly tripping over the three dogs. She swept her hand across the room inviting Officer Robison inside while quieting her Bichon's. He took the offered seat on the floral sofa.

"My God it sounds like the end of the world out there," Jamia said holding her hand across her heart. "What happened? Is my friend okay?"

Officer Robison removed a small notebook from his pocket, "We're concerned about her safety. I need to ask you some questions, which might help locate her, if you don't mind?"

Jamia covered her mouth with her bony fingers, "She's missing?"

Officer Robison clicked open his pen, "Not sure if she's a missing person, however she wasn't at the condo. When was the last time you saw her?"

"Last night. She and her boyfriend, Dakota, I don't know his last name, were having dinner on the deck. I saw them walking down the beach, they got back home right before I went to bed."

Officer Robison scribbled down everything Jamia was relaying to him and nearly dropped his pen when she disclosed the information that the home was actually rented by the mega star Ryan Reese.

"Yes," her excitement grew; pleased to share the intriguing information that they were actually engaged and lived there together until Ryan broke it off last December.

Officer Robison looked skeptical, "I thought he was with Gabriella Mendez."

"I'm talking about *before* Gabriella." Jamia reveled in the fact that she was privy to such information. "He was engaged to Bronwyn. I can't imagine why he would trade such a sweet girl for the likes of that home wrecking whore Gabriella Mendez."

Officer Robison suppressed a smile, "What was the cause of their break-up?"

"Fame went to his bull head."

"Tell me about the man she was with."

Jamia began twisting her hands in her lap. "Between you and me, I didn't think he was her type at all. He sure was handsome enough, but there was something about him that didn't sit right with me. He was overly protective, and I noticed he kept his eye on her constantly. She seemed different too, like she was hiding something."

"What do you mean by that?"

"I don't know I can't put my finger on it but there was just something. Maybe she was hiding the truth about her boyfriend. She arrived with a swollen lip and bruises on her arms and legs. When I asked her about them, she blew me off." Jamia leaned forward and scooped one of her Bichon's in her lap. Her fingers trembled as she stroked the white hair. "She was going through her mail, and I noticed she became sort of overcome with a letter. We were talking and when she opened it she lost all train of thought. She headed for her Bible and then showed it to Dakota and they walked outside on the balcony and talked in private." Jamia blushed, "Now don't get me wrong, I usually don't read peoples mail, but I snooped some, you know, to protect her. The letter was a code of some sort. It was from the Bible, the book of Habakkuk. I think the letter may still be lying on her desk."

Officer Robison wrote fast, detailing all of Jamia's information while she sat patiently, stroking her pet, "So, can you tell me what happened over there?"

Clicking his pen closed, Officer Robison replaced it and the notebook back in his shirt pocket. "There was a shooting."

"Oh," Jamia paled, "Who was shot? Did she shoot Dakota? If she did it was probably in self-defense."

"That's what we're trying to figure out." Officer Robison paused a moment and then scooted closer to Jamia before delivering his next piece of news. "Actually," he said tenderly as not to upset her, "We discovered seven bodies in the condo."

"My God!" Jamia panicked, covering her mouth with both her hands. "Seven?" Her voice quivered with her words. "But I only heard one gun shot."

"The others had their throats slit," Officer Robison spoke softly attempting to downplay the grisly news. "If you feel up to it, I would like you to take a look at the bodies and see if you can identify any of them."

Jamia nodded. Grabbing a tissue from the box, she dabbed at her tears. She continued to fill officer Robison in, telling him of the troupe Bronwyn traveled with, and how she recently resigned. She mentioned the White Ram Pickup they arrived in, saying she didn't know the plate number, but remembered the tags being from North Carolina. When she finished, Officer Robison led her outdoors.

The scene outside astounded her. Red and blue lights flashed against the lavender of the early morning sky, calling attention to the myriad of emergency vehicles surrounding the scene. Several vans with news station logos sat parked nearby. Reporters gripped their microphones, attempting to get an exclusive interview from one of the uniformed officers, as well as one of the plain clothed detectives, who were busy entering and exiting the condominium. Yellow tape surrounded the exterior of the home barring entrance to the many onlookers standing around outside.

Jamia cinched the belt on her robe tighter and clutched officer Robison's arm as he led her, through the frenzy, to view the seven fallen men.

Jamia shook her head in disbelief, "My God, seven people murdered…who in the world could they be, and what on earth does sweet Bronwyn have to do with it all?"

CHAPTER EIGHTEEN

In the midst of the filth and grime of the service station restroom, Bronwyn tried to clean up. It was a futile effort, trying to remove dried sticky blood with thin paper towels and diluted liquid soap. Besides that, the only water temperature the dump restroom offered was ice cold. Glancing up at her reflection in the faded mirror, she nearly fainted. Blood from her busted nose covered half her face not to mention, the flesh and grey matter from the man Falcon shot. With her knees buckling beneath her, she grabbed hold of the porcelain sink to keep from falling.

Pulling clean clothes from her suitcase, Falcon glanced her way, and then bolted for her before she fell. Grabbing hold, he turned her to face him.

"Come on Scribe. You can do this, Stay with me here." He plucked off some of the remains of her assailant, flinging it across the dirty room. It was too much, she turned away hurling the remaining contents of last night's dinner across the floor.

Wasting no time, Falcon pumped a handful of liquid soap and smeared it across her face. He followed with the rough paper towels removing as much of the gore as possible. Satisfied for now he tossed her some clean clothes, her toothbrush and toothpaste.

"Change into these and brush your teeth. You'll feel better. Make it quick our ride should be here soon."

They'd driven for nearly two hours after leaving the condo, finally stopping at the deserted gas station. It had an outdoor restroom that could easily be broken into. Falcon grabbed her suitcase from the truck intending for her to discard her blood soaked garments in the trash. Into her travel bag he placed her phone, her wallet and the book. That was the sum of what they would be taking with them. The rest would stay behind along with Travis' abandoned truck.

Falcon respectfully turned away as Bronwyn peeled the blood soaked t-shirt from her skin. She shivered in the coldness of the restroom and quickly dressed in a pair of jeans, a clean tank and a hooded sweatshirt. Once Falcon heard the sound of running water, he turned back around, and while Bronwyn brushed her teeth, he pulled her hair away from her face, fastening it in a sloppy ponytail. They accomplished their tasks quickly, and then sat on the suitcase, to avoid the grimy floor, waiting for Falcon's men to arrive. They remained silent, both lost in their thoughts. The only sound shattering the stillness of the dismal bathroom was the constant ringing of Bronwyn's cell. Every call was from Jamia. Bronwyn eventually silenced her phone, but still felt the vibration of it against her skin.

"I killed a man." She broke the quiet.

Falcon leaned his head against the painted cinder block wall.

"You killed in self-defense. He would have killed you first."

She thought a moment, remembering the man's strange choice of words right before she pulled the trigger.

"I'm not sure he would have. He stopped his attack when he saw me. Then he said, *as I live and breathe, they weren't kidding.* Then he told me I was coming with him. I was terrified and didn't know what to do, so I shot him."

Falcon stood up fast, hitting the wall with his fist. She'd been around him enough to know when he was upset; something she'd said, agitated him. She knew better than to ask, so she shoved her hands into the pockets of her hoodie and watched him pull a cigarette from his jeans and light up. Aside from his impertinent ways and bad ass exterior, she was beginning to see a real person buried somewhere deep inside. Just a couple of nights ago, at the ram-shackled home, he'd revealed an insightful side. Tonight, she watched him fighting with a passion, killing to protect her, while the hunger for retribution burned in his eyes. When the man grabbed her in the garage, he didn't waste a second. His aim was flawless, his motive resolute. He was a true warrior, yearning for the battle. He'd shown no fear in the fight, yet now, he was anxious. What did he know that he was keeping from her? She decided to tip toe into the question.

"You weren't kidding about the enemy. Guess I finally saw them."

He remained standing, leaning against the cold hard wall, blowing his smoke toward a small rectangular window near the ceiling. He took another long draw, narrowing his eyes on her.

She shifted her weight on the suitcase, and stared back, deciding to give it another shot.

"I'm glad I didn't do this trip alone. You were right. I wouldn't have survived."

He didn't finish his cigarette. Tossing it into the open toilet, he crossed the small room, and squatted down in front of her. He seemed to be choosing his words carefully. "Scribe, we haven't survived it yet. We left a mess back at the condo. Now we're going to be running from the law as well as Abaddon's men." He paused a moment, as if he were engaged in an inner battle, fighting the urge to tell her something he shouldn't. Her pulse quickened, and for the first time, she thought maybe she didn't want to know. She'd heard and seen enough and if there was something even dire at play, then she chose the bliss of ignorance. He gave her a half smile as if he were reading her thoughts. Patting her knee, he stood. Her heart faltered a bit, he'd decided not to say anything.

"Ride's here. Let's move."

Outside the service station restroom, a black SUV sat idling, headlights off, waiting for its passengers. Falcon raised Bronwyn's hood up and instructed her to keep her head down. Pulling his gun, he grabbed Bronwyn's arm and led her out the door. She took in a deep breath, replacing the putrid air of the dirty restroom with the dewy morning breeze.

The passenger door to the SUV opened. All Bronwyn could see with her head down was brown leather boots stepping out of the vehicle. Falcon ordered the man to open the back door. Satisfied, he placed his gun back in his jeans and pushed Bronwyn into the back seat.

She sunk into the comfort of the soft leather seats, relived. She was spent, exhausted, not to mention extremely sleep deprived. Raising her head, she lowered the hood shadowing her face and surveyed the two men up front.

She recognized one of them instantly as the man in the garden with Barak and Falcon the night Travis kissed her under the willow tree. He was strikingly handsome as were most of the men she had met from Eden. Even the attackers at the condo had great physiques. She couldn't see the drivers face; only his light lavender eyes that continued to gaze at her in the rear view mirror. The blond man tossed Bronwyn a bottled water, "My name's Hawk."

She caught the water grateful for the drink, "Bronwyn, nice to meet you."

Hawk glanced at Falcon, communicating volumes through his eyes. Whatever it was Falcon was debating on telling her back at the service station was the unspoken elephant in the SUV. She didn't care, she was much too tired.

Hawk motioned to the driver, "This is Vulture."

He nodded, still looking at her in the rear view. Twisting the cap off the bottle, she took a long drink, wiped the dribble from her chin, and settled back for a much deserved rest.

Vulture drove for several hours stopping only for gas. Falcon and Bronwyn remained in the vehicle, keeping a low profile. Hawk brought snacks out to them along with the breaking news of the slaughter at Ryan Reese's condo. He said it was the subject of conversation everywhere. A wave of dread washed over Bronwyn. Up until now she hadn't dwelt on the repercussions of the attack. Her only thought had been escaping with their lives. Her phone vibrated all morning annoying her to the point where she had turned it off completely. Pulling it from her travel bag, she turned it on. It vibrated instantly with alerts of missed calls and text messages, she scrolled thru the list. There were seven from Jamia, ten from her mother, six from Bethany, four from Ryan, two from Trent, one from Marcus and several numbers she did not recognize. She could only assume they belonged to law enforcement. The phone vibrated while in her hand, the caller ID on the screen said *mother*. Her heart sank at the thought of what her parents might be going through. She sighed, showing it to Falcon.

"Can I answer it? She's gotta be going through hell right now."

Falcon took the phone, "Answer it. Don't tell her anything other than you're alright."

She agreed. He put the phone on speaker, placing it on the seat between them.

"Hello."

"Thank God!" Madison screamed, unaware her voice filled the inside of the vehicle, "Are you alright?"

"I'm okay."

"Where are you?"

"I'm okay," Bronwyn repeated.

"Where? Tell me where and I will come and get you myself!"

"I'm okay, momma."

"It's that all he'll let you say?" Madison's voice was in a frenzy. "This is all his doing isn't it? I had a strange feeling about him but I didn't want to say anything for fear of hurting you but now I wish I had. Can you get away from him at all?"

"Are you speaking with your daughter, Mrs. Sterling?" A masculine voice in the background interrupted Madison. There was a bit of static as the phone changed hands.

"This is special agent Betancourt, FBI. Am I safe to assume I am speaking with Bronwyn Sterling?"

Falcon pressed the key to end the conversation.

CHAPTER NINETEEN

It was early afternoon when the black Suburban exited the main highway, taking a secondary road for at least another eight miles. Bronwyn figured they were somewhere in New Mexico. She wasn't sure; she'd slept most of the day waking only for moments at a time when they would stop for gas, or when Hawk offered her something to eat or drink. She felt safe in the SUV, even relaxing to the point of resting her head on Falcons shoulder. However, she was anxious to leave the vehicle and be able to stretch having been riding in the same position for nearly twelve hours. Falcon informed her they were heading to one of the N.E.S.S.T's safe houses. She didn't know what to expect but hoped the place was big enough for her to shower and clean up the remaining gore, covering her legs and feet.

Vulture turned onto a narrow gravel road cutting across acres of lush pasture land. A herd of wild elk grazed nearby completely unaffected by the approaching vehicle. He drove another four miles before Bronwyn noticed a grove of trees directly ahead surrounding an adobe style estate. He stopped at a set of impressive iron gates, waiting for them to swing open. Once they bid him entrance, he followed the cobblestone driveway up to an extravagant two story villa; parking out front. Bronwyn emerged from her confined state stretching, thankful to be standing after twelve long hours.

The late afternoon sun greeted her skin. The heat felt wonderful, caressing her aching muscles and thawing out her numbness from the Suburban's overworked air conditioner. The cicadas and crickets composed a grand welcoming song, resonating into a deafening volume, as all of nature came alive with the hums and fragrances of the earth. The place provided a soothing calm, as if all of creation yearned to comfort her during this trying ordeal. She longed to remain outside and enjoy this rare euphoria, but Falcon was already leading her inside the manor.

Following, she stepped inside a spacious living area. The welcoming room offered a warm homey feel, also bringing a sense of calm. Rustic tile covered the floor, connecting to pale olive stucco walls. Dark leather furniture decorated the room, resting on plush throw rugs. A wide staircase led to an upper hallway, surrounding the open room on all four sides. Each side housed four doors all barring entrance to private chambers.

Hawk aimed a remote control at a piece of framed artwork above the fireplace. The scenic painting began rising, disappearing into the wall, revealing a flat screen television hidden behind it. Hawk switched the set on before leaning against the stucco wall.

Bronwyn's stomach dropped to her knees at the sight of her face plastered across the TV screen. An eager news correspondent stood outside the beach condo, clutching a microphone, informing all America of Bronwyn's personal affairs. Eagerly she spoke of Bronwyn's past engagement to mega star Ryan Reese and the miscarriage, which, in the reporters' opinion, was brought on by her extreme grief over Ryan's involvement with his alluring costar Gabriella Mendez. Just when she thought she couldn't be any more humiliated, the reporter spoke of a scandalous affair involving a married Inn keeper, Travis Colton of Moonshine. The correspondent continued to say that the Dodge Ram pickup registered to Mr. Colton was found abandoned near the Camp Pendleton Marine base in San Diego California, fearing the couple may have crossed the border into Mexico. That bit of news satisfied Falcon, seeing that was his modus operandi in driving south and abandoning the truck where he did.

Bronwyn and Falcon's faces split the screen, showing a picture of Bronwyn and a composite sketch of Falcon. Before ending her report, the correspondent stated Falcon was considered armed and extremely dangerous. Then, she passed her story over to a news conference where eager reporters stood poised with flashing cameras, anxious to hear what mega star Ryan Reese would say concerning the matter. He'd called a press conference in an attempt to clear any blight on his name concerning the massacre at his condo. Entering the building, Ryan approached the podium, surrounded by his manager and attorneys. Bronwyn's crossed her arms in front of her as he gave his opening statement.

"Good evening," he said, his voice seeped in grief. "It is with much sorrow, that I approach my public. I want to state that my deepest concern is with Bronwyn and her family during this difficult time. My prayers are that she is found safe and unharmed. My prayers also go out to the families of the seven men who lost their lives last night." He paused a moment, biting his lower lip, as if attempting to hold back an onslaught of tears. Looking directly into the cameras he positioned his face in utter distress. "Bronwyn if you can, please get away from this man who is holding you captive. I beg you." Sighing he turned his face away dapping at an unseen tear. His emotional pause had the desired effect, drawing longing sighs, sympathy from the reporters and a ton of flashing cameras.

"I still love you babe, I really do, and I told you that less than two weeks ago. I would die if anything happened to you. I will come looking for you myself if that's what it takes."

His final statement incurred a round of applause from his adoring public. Bronwyn rolled her eyes in disgust sickened that he would use this to play on the emotions of his fans, tying to heighten his already booming career.

His attorney stepped forward, in a show of taking

over for his grief-stricken client.

"I would like to state Ryan's complete innocence in the events that took place at the condo leased in his name. He has not lived at, nor been at the residence in over six months. He is presently working with law enforcement in their attempt to find Miss Sterling and apprehend the guilty parties. Ryan will now be happy to answer any questions that he is at liberty to discuss."

At that statement a roar rose from the sea of reporters.

"Were you engaged to Miss Sterling when you became involved with Gabriella Mendez?"

Ryan took over the microphone, "No. We had already broken things off."

Liar.

"Do you know the man, Travis Colton, who Miss Sterling is alleged to be having an affair?"

"No I do not."

"Do you know the man she is with now?"

"No I do not."

"Was Miss Sterling involved with drugs when you were with her?"

"Not that I was aware of."

Of course I wasn't, you of all people should know that!

"It was reported that you took a trip to the town of Moonshine, last week to see Miss Sterling. Any comment?"

At that question, Ryan's attorney took back over the mic. "His visit was strictly business, regarding a screen play co-written by Ryan and Miss Sterling. The visit has no bearings on the events of last night's massacre."

One last reporter overpowered the sea of voices.

"Authorities claim that Moonshine is nothing more than a ghost town, a modern day Roanoke. They found no one on their visit. Did you see a functioning town when you were there last week?"

They found no one? A modern day Roanoke? Feeling

as if she might faint, Bronwyn cast a glance Falcon's way. He was unmoved, still watching the report, unaffected by the disturbing statement of the reporter. And for a moment, she wondered if she might be crazy. How could an entire town of people disappear; unless, they'd never been there in the first place? She turned her attention back to the TV, anxious to hear his response. If Ryan had seen the town, it would prove she wasn't insane. Again, Ryan's attorney answered for him.

"Ryan was there for only a few hours. He never saw a town, just a small Inn where Miss Sterling was staying."

Her heart fell, her head began to swim as a sea of doubt began drowning all she'd been told. Just when she thought she might collapse, Falcon came to her rescue, for once disclosing a clear answer.

"After we left, Travis led the people underground, hiding them at the citadel. It's the only safe haven we have left."

So that's why Travis sent Falcon instead of accompanying her himself. The pictures in her mind of him leading the citizens of Moonshine across the placid lake to the safety of the citadel only heightened her desire to be near him again. The images in her head, taking her back to the night he rescued her from drowning, tenderly taking care of her needs underground in the dimly lit basement. Her heart grew heavy, forcing the yearnings from her mind. It was her duty to reunite him with Kenalycia; she could not allow her own desires to interfere with that blessed event. She turned her attention back to the television just as Ryan waved to his many fans as he was quickly ushered out of the room.

The story was promptly sent back to the news room desk. Two anchors, along with their expert guest, eagerly dove into the scandalous story, reporting their personal opinions and assumptions on whether Bronwyn was indeed a victim or a willing party in the whole ordeal.
Falcon aimed the remote at the TV turning it off. The

scenic oil painting descended slowly hiding the screen again. An unfamiliar voice interrupted their thoughts.

"No reason to keep her identity a secret anymore, is there Falcon?"

Bronwyn turned to the sound of the voice. A well-built man leaned against the far wall. He must have come into the room while they were engrossed in the news story. He too was extremely nice looking. His sun streaked hair was combed away from his face revealing russet eyes. A thin mustache lined his upper lip and his side burns grew far down his cheeks combining with his five o'clock shadow.

"Seems a lot of work for nothing, wouldn't you say?"

Bronwyn didn't like the way the man tauntingly spoke with Falcon. Walking up to Bronwyn, he boldly took her hand, kissing it gently as he bowed his head,

"And here she is in the flesh."

Bronwyn gave a slight smile as the tension beginning rising in the room.

"The names Macaw."

"I'm Bronwyn."

Macaw stared at her a few minutes a curious expression covering his face.

"My God she doesn't know does she?" His voice bellowed across the room giving way to an amused laugh.

"Watch yourself," Falcon's strict warning was quickly dismissed by the argumentative Macaw.

"I think we should tell her. She deserves to know. After all, she has put everything on the line for us."

"I won't warn you again Macaw, Travis' orders." Falcon's threat seemed final on the subject.

Macaw wasn't convinced, "Seems Travis may be allowing his personal feelings to interfere." He continued to examine Bronwyn, boldly stretching out his hand, stroking her cheek with his fingers. Feeling threatened, Bronwyn backed away, cutting her eyes over to Falcon. Macaw noticed and laughed, turning his attention away from Bronwyn and onto Falcon.

"I heard you found the second prophesy. Let's see it."

Falcon struck a match and lit the cigarette clutched between his teeth, "Can't, I burned it."

Macaw's anger revealed itself in his face as well as his voice.

"You burned it! Why? Information of that magnitude should be shared by everyone. What happened to accountability? We're supposed to be a team, remember?"

Falcon dismissed the reprimand, "True, but unfortunately I can't trust everyone."

"Is that why you murdered Oren?"

Falcon flicked his ashes in a nearby ashtray, unmoved by the accusation.

"Oren switched sides; he was dangerous and it was crucial to have him executed."

Macaw wasn't satisfied, "Switched sides according to you. The execution should've been approved by all, not the sole discretion of one."

Bronwyn felt the uneasiness growing in the room. There was an obvious distrust between the two. She wasn't sure who Oren was or where the other men's feelings lie on the matter. Hawk seemed to be irritated with Macaw as well. Vulture was harder to read.

Falcon took a draw, nodding toward Hawk. "I had Hawk and Barak's approval on the matter, as well as Travis'. Care to dispute it?"

"They approved it on your word alone." Macaw argued, narrowing his eyes on Falcon. "I for one don't think Oren turned. I think he found out some things about you, like where you were all those years you disappeared. I think you killed him before he could disclose the information. Just like I think you burned it because the prophecy had information about the treasure."

Falcon blew a line of smoke into Macaws face, "It's up to you what you choose to believe."

"I'm right aren't I?" Macaw wouldn't relent. "It had information on the treasure and you didn't want anyone else knowing so you burned it."

Falcon took another draw but remained silent.

Macaw inched his way closer, "It's hard to trust someone who keeps secrets, Falcon."

Bronwyn let out an involuntary laugh, "Welcome to my world."

"Then why do you do it Princess?" Macaw challenged. "Why put all your confidence in the hands of someone you don't know?"

He was right in a way but at present she knew more about Falcon than she knew about him.

She shrugged, "I know him more than I know you."

This time Falcon laughed which only provoked Macaw more.

"I think Oren discovered your secret. He found out where you were all those missing years and was ready to reveal when you had him executed."

"He was caught carrying information about the troupe," Hawk offered the information. "I was there, Falcon's right."

"You have proof to back that up?" Macaw challenged.

"Yes, we do." Hawk confirmed, dispelling the suspicion.

"And you never wonder where Falcon disappeared to all those years? He comes waltzing back and everyone accepts him, open arms no questions asked."

"He had Travis' trust. That's all I needed."

Macaw gave a sarcastic snort. "Abaddon had Travis' trust too, and look where that got him."

This time it was Hawk who moved forward in anger, "Watch yourself Macaw, you're bordering on disloyalty."

"Me, bordering on disloyalty?" He shook his head in disbelief. "You've all been deceived." He backed off the accusation for now, taking another route. "I want to know what the prophecy said."

Falcon eyed the others in the room while taking a long draw off his cigarette. Expelling a line of smoke, he began reciting the prophecy; smoke billowing forth with each word.

"*Draw you battle lines and prepare for war. The gates are opened and all dominions have been released.*" He looked at Macaw as he quoted.

"*Be diligent to know truth and do not be swayed from what you know to be right. For some among you will be influenced by the darkness and join forces with the enemy, threatening your redemption. The betrayers have crept in unaware and are living among you. Wolves in sheep clothing they are, eating at your tables, and then spying upon you when your backs are turned.*"

Falcon took another draw, this time cutting his eyes over to Bronwyn.

"*Be careful that you are not deceived. Their words will be convincing, they will offer pleasing and beautiful promises of knowledge and power, yet in the end, the only thing you will get for your allegiance with them is death.*" Bronwyn swallowed her mouth felt dry. The room was quiet as Falcons final words pronounced a sentence upon the guilty.

"That's it?" Macaw was skeptical. "I didn't hear anything about the treasure."

Falcon continued looking at Bronwyn, as if he were reminding her of the calling.

"*To the Scribe, pen your story. The beginning is yours. Follow your heart and you will preserve life. All depends on your ability to make the right choice. In time you will be led to the secret place. Enter without fear, it is there you will find the third book, and the third prophesy.*"

Then... "*He who holds these words in his hands and heart has the key to the second portal. The Scribe alone knows the location of the second portal."*

Macaw wasn't convinced.

"And what about you princess, did you read it as well or did Falcon burn it before you were able to see it?"

Bronwyn felt the stares of everyone. She didn't like the conversation and especially this Macaw fellow.

"Falcon read it to me. The language was unfamiliar."

Macaw's sarcastic laugh echoed off the high ceiling. "So neither you, nor anyone else actually read the prophecy, only Falcon? How do you know he interpreted what was on the paper?"

All eyes were on her again. Even Falcon cast his gaze along with the others as he casually leaned against the wall, taking another draw off his cigarette.

"Because I trust him." Her dislike for Macaw showed in her tone. Falcon gave a slight grin, watching the scene play out before him. His amusement in the situation angered Macaw. His eyes flashed as he took the conversation to a new level.

"And what has he done to earn your undying trust my sweet lady? Could it be that he too has fallen for you just as his brother did?"

"That's enough!" Hawk warned.

Falcon stood from his leaning position; his eyes flaming with anger. Vulture moved in on Falcon, while Hawk closed in on Macaw. Bronwyn's head began to swim.

Noticing her confusion, Macaw continued pressing his luck.

"Oh let me guess, Falcon didn't tell you about his brother either? Seems there is a lot of information he's kept from you my dear. It's no wonder you trust him. Seems like he makes his own rules just like his notorious twin."

Falcon was eyeing Macaw as if he would pounce on him at any minute. Bronwyn struggled for clarity midst the rubble of bizarre accusations.

Falcon has a twin? Who? The only person who'd fallen in love with her was Ryan, and he certainly wasn't Falcons twin.

Macaw read her face, "Are you intrigued my dear? I think she deserves full knowledge on the situation."

Falcon crushed the remaining piece of his smoke in anger, "She has no need of full knowledge when she doesn't have the wisdom to comprehend it. It could be disastrous, not to mention deadly."

"According to Falcon!" Macaw addressed his comrades as if they were the jury and he was delivering his closing remarks. "Falcon quotes from a prophecy only he has read. He chooses to keep certain information from our scribe, deeming her unworthy, criticizing her ability to discern. Why would she have been chosen if she was inept? He is purposely trying to control her for his own benefit no less. We all know his brother betrayed Travis and I believe Falcon is betraying us!"

Bronwyn paled at Macaws words. *His brother betrayed Asa?*

Macaw noticed her surprise, "Oh yes. If you've seen Falcon, you've seen Abaddon. They are identical twins. It's quite difficult to tell the two apart. They look exactly the same, except for Falcons nasty scar."

"I warned you." Falcon lunged toward Macaw. Vulture immediately moved in, positioning himself between the two, stopping an inevitable brawl.

Thoughts spun in Bronwyn's head like a whirlwind. Macaw's statement caused the peculiar heat sensation to wrap its hot fingers around her throat. She stumbled backward. She had been with Falcon for the past five days even sharing a bed while they slept, never knowing he was a blood relation to the man who was their mortal enemy. Why hadn't he told her?

"Falcon said Abaddon gave him the scar." Her voice rose above the scuffle. "Why would he do that if he and

Falcon were working together?"

"Abaddon did give him the scar." Macaw answered her. "I never said they were working together. Disloyalty is in their nature my dear. Falcon made Abaddon believe he was on his side. Made us all believe he was on his brother's side. Then he betrayed him. Abaddon feared he might try and do it again and deceive the people posing as Abaddon himself so he marked him. Now everyone knows the difference. Falcon is in this for his own benefit, he wants the same things his brother wanted."

She tried to soak it all in, muddling through the madness of it all. If information of this magnitude had been withheld, there was no telling what other shocking revelations would bombard her over time.

Macaw noticed her weakness, "Come take a walk with me princess and I will give you all the knowledge you need to write your story. I find it appalling that he has purposely held back crucial information. He fears you having full knowledge. He knows if you did, you might not cling to him as you do." Macaw offered Bronwyn his arm. "What do you say Princess? Take a walk outdoors with me. I have information that will shed quite a bit of light on everything."

The scuffle erupted again. Falcon's eyes narrowed in fury as he pushed against Vulture to get to Macaw.

"Don't go with him Scribe. You're not ready to hear what he has to say."

"No!" Macaw yelled, "Falcon is not ready for you to hear what I have to say. Beware of those who keep secrets and speak to you in riddles my love. They keep you confused so you will remain in their custody and place all your confidence in them." He extended his invitation again by nodding his head toward the glass doors leading to the patio. "Don't be afraid, it's just a simple walk my dear and you will know all."

Her mind raced with the possibilities; his invitation intoxicating. She looked around the room. Vulture stood poised between Falcon and Macaw, his eyes seared into hers, yet his face was unreadable. He remained silent while everyone in the room anticipated her decision.

Continuing to push against Vulture, Falcon looked as if he would attack at any moment. His eyes cut into Macaw like daggers and Bronwyn wondered what he would do if she took Macaws arm and headed outside.

"Why didn't you tell me Abaddon was your brother? You had plenty of opportunity. You told me so much of the story why did you feel a need to leave that out?"

His eyes flared and he looked at her in a way that took her breath away. "The pain in that confession is too much to bear. Death would have been a kinder separation."

She swallowed fighting the tightness in her throat. His confession resonated with her soul, evoking deep sorrow. She thought of the ram shacked house and how he'd seen it for what it used to be, and then she wondered if it was Abaddon he saw in the rubble.

"Clever answer," Macaw mocked, extending his arm to Bronwyn once again.

Pulling her eyes away from Falcon's gaze, she turned them on Macaw.

"I remember a story I learned as a child in Sunday school. A story of another Eden and someone offering a lady full knowledge. He promised her it would be to her advantage, and unfortunately she was convinced. It not only destroyed her but everyone else as well. As much as I want answers, I'd rather wait and discover them on my own. I have no desire to eat from your tree of knowledge Macaw, but know this, I trust Falcon with my life. What he tells me to do, I will do, and when he chooses to reveal a truth to me, I will listen. You would be wise to do the same. And another thing, never tempt me like that again and never speak about Falcon like he is not standing right here with us. He is your leader, and it's your responsibility to follow. He has fought hard and saved my life more than once. He has shared my bed and has been nothing more than a gentleman. You are wrong and you owe him an apology."

The silence in the room was deafening. Vulture released his grip and Bronwyn thought she saw him give her an approving smile.

"You're making a mistake Princess" Macaw growled exiting the room. "You're all making a big mistake."

CHAPTER TWENTY

After watching the special news report on TV, Bethany immediately packed her belongings and headed to the Sterling home. Since the troupe was performing only an hour away she decided to go offer comfort to Madison and Martin and wait with them for any news that surfaced. Now, she sat in the dining room, a small tape recorder between her and special agent Betancourt chronicling every word she spoke. First Detective Delane at the playhouse, and now Betancourt. She'd seen movies where people sat in a small room being interrogated by the police, but never imagined she'd be doing it herself. What could Bronwyn have possibly gotten into? Stating her name for the record, she proceeded to answer all the questions Agent Betancourt hurled her way, starting with how long she had known Bronwyn and ending with their last week together in Moonshine. The forced trip down memory lane only caused her to miss Bronwyn, and the deep friendship they'd shared since fifth grade. Her heart ached at the thought of her missing, hurt or possibly dead.

"When was the last time you spoke with Miss Sterling?"

His question evoked feelings of shame. Bronwyn had wanted to talk with her less than a week ago, before the troupe left Moonshine, but she'd refused. She was angry, hurt and at that time cared nothing for what Bronwyn had to say. Besides, she wasn't sure she could trust her, feeling as if Bronwyn had been lying to her about things for some time. Now, considering the tragic turn of events, she wished she'd accepted Bronwyn's offer to talk.

"About a week ago, before we left Moonshine. We

were on the front porch of the Inn, she took off. I thought she was going for a walk. She said she'd be back later and didn't return till five the next morning."

"Do you know where she went?"

Bethany took drink of her water. In all the years of their friendship, she'd never ratted out her friend, so to speak. They had covered for each other all through junior high, high school and beyond. In some way, she felt like a traitor revealing top-secret information. She had no desire to betray Bronwyn no matter how tense their friendship had become. Yet, if Special Agent Betancourt could use her information to help Bronwyn, it would be well worth her exposing some of her friend's deepest secrets.

"No, I can only guess. She'd become withdrawn and secretive recently. During our week in Moonshine she would disappear for long periods of time. She would leave and stay out all night. Then she just up and quit the troupe without any notice."

"She didn't give a reason?"

"She told our director Marcus that she wanted to leave the troupe to write her novel. But I think there was more to it than that. I think she wanted to stay in Moonshine because of Travis."

"Tell me about Moonshine."

Bethany sighed. She didn't know why the questioned bothered her but it did. Moonshine, she'd become lost in the place, enjoying an unexpected vacation in a forgotten little Norman Rockwell town. In some ways she felt conned, comparing Moonshine to a befriended stranger that you invite in, only to find out they robbed you blind while your back was turned.

"I'm not sure how to describe it. It's a strange place, that's for sure. We were all pretty apprehensive at first, but it ended up being one of the best places I ever visited."

"What did you mean by it being strange?"

"I don't know, we were the only tourist there…it's pretty secluded. Looking back on it, it seems like a storybook town, you know…too good to be true." She sighed again, longer and louder this time, trying to blow away the pain crowding into her heart. "Considering the turn of events, I guess it really was."

Betancourt smiled sympathetically, "How old would you say their eldest resident was?"

Bethany was taken aback by the randomness of his question. She unwillingly laughed. "I don't know. I never really thought about it." Her mind did a quick scan of the previous week. Travis, Mavis, that Falcon guy all looked late thirties, early forties, it was hard to tell. She thought of the days they were in town, and the people they interacted with. The manicurists, the waitress at the café, the people at the festival…

Her eyes met Betancourt's, "Come to think of it, there weren't any elderly people there. I'd say the oldest I saw was close to my age or maybe ten years older. That's kind of weird now that I think about it. Is that significant?"

Betancourt didn't comment, intending not to lose control of the interview.

"You said earlier you thought Bronwyn wanted to stay because she met someone. Tell me about him."

Bethany shook her head, "Travis Colton, he owns the inn where we stayed." Bethany felt dirty for the words she uttered but convinced herself she was doing Bronwyn a favor by exposing the ugly truth. "He's the towns' doctor too. He seemed pretty near perfect. You know the type, rugged, handsome, strong, quiet, mysterious…"

"You said she would stay out late and sometimes leave during the night. Was she with Mr. Colton during these times?"

"Yes. I think so"

Retrieving a picture from his coat pocket, Betancourt slid it across the table.

"Is this Travis Colton?"

Bethany picked up the composite sketch of Falcon, "No. this is Falcon."

"Do you know him?"

"I never met him, but some of the local women in town said he was some kind of secret agent. I only saw Bronwyn with him once, and that was really weird to me because he frightened her for some reason." Bethany sighed again, dropping her face in her hands. "She told me she saw him kill a man in the garden one night. She said he slit the man's throat with a knife.... I feel bad now that I didn't believe her."

"Why didn't you believe her?"

"I don't know...it all sounded so absurd and she had been acting so strange....I just don't know."

Bethany was angry with herself. Why hadn't she believed Bronwyn? She if anyone knew Bronwyn wouldn't lie about such a thing. Sure she did exaggerate the most mundane events, adding color and excitement, bringing them to life. It's the way she viewed life and she described its events the same way. That is, until six months ago, when Ryan broke her heart. After that, she'd lost her edge, lost who she was, and the dramatic flair she added to every occasion was gone. Bethany became so accustomed to it that when Bronwyn told her of the strange goings on in Moonshine, she ignored her, buying into Trent's philosophies about the human psyche.

"I heard on the news that the town is abandoned... The reporter compared it to a modern day Roanoke. How could that be? There were thousands of people living there. How could they all leave so quickly?"

Betancourt closed his small journal, replaced the pen in his coat pocket and turned off the recorder before summoning Madison and Martin back into the room.

"That's what I'm trying to figure out.

CHAPTER TWENTY-ONE

Madison and Martin joined Bethany in the kitchen, taking a seat at the table. Bethany's heart went out to the two. In all the years she'd known them, she'd never seen them looking so distraught. Madison was a wreck. She's been awake ever since the authorities called their home, relaying the dreadful news and asking for Bronwyn's whereabouts. From that moment on it had been nonstop phone calls and visits from the police, the FBI and the media, not to mention their many concerned friends. Bethany felt privileged in the fact she was able to be inside the home with them, seeing they had turned away so many people, asking for complete privacy. Even now, the yard out front was filled with media, and other curious folk, staking out the place hoping for a glimpse of someone or a chance for an exclusive interview.

Reaching out, Bethany took hold of Madison's hand, squeezing it in reassurance. Madison offered a feeble heartbroken smile and squeezed back.

Betancourt opened his briefcase and pulled out a soft leather bound book, laying it on the table. Madison gasped at the sight of it, her eyes wide with alarm.

"Where did you get that?"

"So you do recognize the book Mrs. Sterling."

"Yes, but how did you.....It had been locked away...hidden...."

"It was left behind at the crime scene."

Madison looked as if she were about to faint. "How in the world...." Then, the realization hit. "Bronwyn asked if I had any of her old writings, I never dreamed she was speaking of this one...she was supposed to have forgotten."

"Forgotten what Mrs. Sterling?"

Silence...Madison stood abruptly, leaving the table,

as if to put as much distance as possible between her and the book. Leaning over the sink, she dropped her face into her hands and sobbed. Martin left the table to comfort his hysterical wife.

Confused at Madison's sudden display of anguish, Bethany glanced at the cover of the handmade book reading the title: *Moonshine*.

Fear gripped her, she wanted to scream and wake up from his crazy nightmare. Better yet she wanted to give Walt a good beating for absent-mindedly getting lost and driving them straight into the twilight zone.

Betancourt didn't waste a minute, refusing to allow Madison's suffering to detain his investigation.

"Where did your daughter get this book?"

Martin took over for his distraught wife. "Bronwyn wrote it when she was ten."

Betancourt leaned back in his chair eyeing the Sterling's. No one said a word and the tension grew thick. Opening his briefcase once again, he pulled out another small book encased in a type of Plexiglas box and laid it on the table. The pages were yellowed, sticking beyond the border of the antique cover. The worn leather cover bore the faded title: *Moonshine.* Confusion masked their faces.

"What's that?" Martin asked guiding Madison back to the table.

"This is the original book of Moonshine, written by an unknown author over six hundred years ago. It's one of the oldest mysteries in the literary world, competing with the Voynich manuscript of the early 1500's. The author remains a secret to this day. The book is filled with cryptic passages identical to the ones in the book your daughter wrote."

He opened Bronwyn's handmade book of Moonshine. Madison gasped in fear when he did. He eyed her suspiciously.

"What frightens you about this book, Mrs. Sterling?"

Madison clutched the tissue in her hand. "You open the book and you unleash the terrors within it."

Bethany paled at her words. She'd met Bronwyn when she was eleven and never heard of this book. Neither Bronwyn nor her parents had ever mentioned it. She desired to skim through the pages but Betancourt kept a tight hold on it, thumbing through to the back cover.

Pulling back the soft leather binding he revealed an empty pocket.

"Do you happen to know what was hidden inside the cover?"

Madison and Martin exchanged glances.

"No, we don't," Martin nodded, "We never noticed that before. Bronwyn kept the book to herself."

Betancourt sighed and tapped the glass case protecting the antique book. "So, you tell me Mr. and Mrs. Sterling, how could a ten year old little girl write a book word for word as a six hundred year old novel she has never seen?"

"Bronwyn loved to read; maybe she had read it before." Madison's reasoning was far-fetched.

"Impossible. This is the only copy in the entire world."

Martin cleared his throat, "I know this investigation is not about plagiarism, so you wanna tell me what you're getting at?"

Betancourt's grin didn't quite set right with Bethany. "I think you already know Mr. Sterling. Now… do you want to tell me something about your daughter?"

Madison leaned into her husband for support, and closed her eyes. Tired and defeated she whispered, "Tell him Martin."

Martin held her close, kissing the top of her head. "Are you sure hon? We vowed to never speak of it."

Bethany' took a swallow of her water, hoping to relieve the tightness in her throat. What secret about

Bronwyn could they have vowed to never speak of? Fear gripped her and as much as she wanted to run out the back door, covering her ears screaming, another part of her knew she must hear what they had to say.

Tears escaped Madison's eyes, tricking down her cheeks along with the little bit of mascara still remaining on her lashes.

"That was before. I don't see how we can avoid it. Besides if it helps Bronwyn in some way, I think we should tell what we know."

Bethany finally found her voice, "For what it's worth, I think this is off the record. Agent Betancourt purposely left his recorder off. I think maybe whatever you say can't be held against you right now." She looked at Betancourt, "Am I right?"

Betancourt's eyes sparked at her observation, "She's right. Whatever we speak in this room will never be uttered outside of these walls."

CHAPTER TWENTY-TWO

After Macaw's confrontation downstairs, Falcon escorted Bronwyn up to the guest room so she could clean up. The room was nice, rivaling any five star hotel suite, complete with an adjoining balcony, a private restroom with a sunken bath and a separate shower. As much as she would love to relax in a tub of warm water and sooth her aching muscles, she decided on the shower. She would scrub off the blood and gore that had long since dried, and let the remains of the deceased disappear down the drain.

Grabbing a loofa, she emptied an entire bottle of creamy soap on her legs and with fury began scrubbing at the dried blood, not allowing her mind to dwell on the grisly events of the past twenty four hours. Neither would she think about Ryan's little press conference or the fact that her private life was now a public spectacle being scrutinized and judged by everyone. Tears rolled from her eyes mixing with the tepid water as she forced the mental pictures out of her mind. Instead, she had something new to mull over and the thought of it intensified her scrubbing. Macaw mentioned a treasure. That was the first she'd heard about it. Barak, Travis, nor Falcon ever mentioned a treasure; yet Falcon knew exactly what Macaw was referring to and that bothered her. She hoped this entire quest didn't boil down to a massive hunt for gold with everyone turning into aggressive marauders, killing for their share of the booty. If so, she was out. Even though she stood up to Macaw giving her allegiance to Falcon, there were still doubts, especially since the chilling disclosure of Abaddon being his twin brother. Why couldn't he or Travis reveal that piece of information? Something wasn't right, and with the doubt came the memory of Falcon's caution back at the diner.

"I know you don't trust me and I'm warning you now; there will come a time when you will trust me even less. If at that time, you react by what you see, all could be lost."

Maybe he was referring to the time when she would find out about him and Abaddon. Sighing, she rinsed the foamy soap from her legs. Trust was such a hard thing, especially when there isn't much evidence to warrant it.

After making sure there was no trace of the gore between her toes or anywhere else, she lathered her hair, clawing her head, so to remove any remaining pieces of gray matter left from the assailant's brain. She shuddered at the thought, nearly gagging in the shower. Following up with a creamy conditioner, she rinsed and then twisted her ebony locks, wringing out the water.

Shutting off the faucet, she opened the fogged door and reached for a towel, only to see Falcon standing in the doorway holding it. Startled she stepped further behind the cloudy pane to hide her nakedness, and there went the trust issue again.

Discreetly taking the thirsty towel, she wrapped her wet body and stepped from the shower. Her hair that usually hung softly to one side was pulled completely away, revealing the beauty of her face. Falcon's attention remained on her as she chose a sweet smelling lotion from the basket and then gracefully rubbed the creamy substance on her legs; oblivious of how sensual she appeared. Not allowing his mind to stray, he pushed away the forbidden thoughts, removing his eyes from her form.

"Put some clothes on, dinners waiting on the balcony."

A few minutes later, dressed in her jeans and a tank, and smelling like the sweet potions from the basket, she sauntered out onto the balcony delighted to see a hot meal. Falcon ordered the food from the kitchen while she showered, specifying certain foods so she could eat a healthy meal. She was glad he did; they still had at least two days to go before returning to Moonshine and the safety of the Citadel. She would need nourishment and ample rest if she were to make it back, dodging Abaddon's men, the authorities and a swarm of media.

Settling down in a comfortable lounge chair, she dove into her dinner of broiled fish and steamed vegetables.

"So there's a treasure?" She brought the subject up after taking a bite of her tilapia.

Falcon nodded while chewing, but offered nothing more than a shake of his head.

Cutting the tender fish with her fork, she asked another. "And you never mentioned it because?"

Shrugging he swallowed his water before answering, "Does it matter?"

"Maybe," she stabbed at her carrots. "It kind of puts a new twist on things. I don't mind aiding a cause that will put the proper people back in power, therefore saving the masses. However, I have no intention of putting my life at risk so someone can get rich."

Falcon popped a carrot in his mouth and grinned, "Money means nothing to me Scribe."

She eyed him closely, "Were there clues about the treasure in the prophecy?"

He grinned again but said nothing and she knew she wouldn't get any more out of him than that.

Frustrated she pushed her plate aside and stood. "I'm done, I'm going to bed."

Catching her arm as she brushed past, he pulled her down to his lounge chair, "I thought you said you trusted me."

She gave a sarcastic laugh, "I want to, God, I really want too but…"

"There shouldn't be any buts, scribe. Trusting is a choice, either you do or you don't."

"You seriously think you've earned it?"

He swallowed another drink of his water. "I'm not going to perform for you the way you want me to. I have my reasons for the choices I make."

"And I have my reasons for doubting."

"No you don't."

His audacity appalled her. "Put yourself in my shoes, Mr." Her tone was harsh. "My life has just been ruined. Talk about trust…I've more than likely lost the trust of my parents, my friends, the troupe, people I don't even know. Everyone thinks I've had an affair with Travis…"

"Did you?"

Painful self-consciousness blossomed in her cheeks, turning them a deep crimson; she felt the heat and knew he noticed.

"No, I didn't. I thought he was married to Mavis."

Falcon laughed out loud at that disclosure.

"So you would have…if you'd of known?"

Her cheeks continued to flame and she knew her eyes could not keep a secret so she pulled away from his clasp, grabbed her ice water and began chugalugging. She wasn't thirsty, but the glass made a great barrier, blocking her tale-tell expression from his view. Laughing, he rose from his chair removed the glass from her hand and wiped the dribbles off her chin. Amusement teemed in his eyes.

"So are you trustworthy? Did you act on your feelings?"

"No I didn't act on them, it wouldn't have been right."

His impish grin began in his eyes and continued across his lips.

"But Bethany thought you did."

"Bethany assumed. She should have trusted…"

She stopped cold, *should have trusted* her own words firing back at her.

Falcons grin went from impish to tender, "Assumptions can land you in a world of trouble. Money means nothing to me; there are other riches however, worth guarding. You, for example are such a prize. The prophecy did give another clue. It stated that only the Scribe can uncover the treasure, only you will know where to look." He was quiet for a moment and then locked his eyes with hers. "There is already a mark on you, can you imagine the heightened urgency to find you if that information was leaked?"

She lowered her eyes, ashamed until his next disclosure brought them back up even with his.

"When I read the prophecy to Travis, he told me to burn it. It was his idea…to keep you safe."

She felt ashamed, ignorant, and somewhat like Bethany, annoyingly demanding information and answers of things too complex for her to understand.

"I'm sorry."

He stared at her for a moment and she wondered what he must be thinking but she wouldn't let her mind make any assumptions this time. Giving her a slight wink, he escorted her back to her chair.

"Finish your dinner; you're going to need your strength."

Hawk joined them out on the balcony just as the sun dipped behind the horizon, painting the sky in hues of deep amber. He arrived with a second cart loaded with desserts and hot tea. As enticing as the pastry tray appeared, Bronwyn bypassed the sweets and offered Hawk her tea. Although it was still early she was tired and ready for bed. She hadn't gotten much sleep over the past few days, and now after taking a relaxing shower and having eaten a hot healthy meal she was ready to turn in.

"I'm going to bed, should I set an alarm?"

Falcon lit up a cigarette and took a swallow of his tea. "No, sleep as long as you like. We'll leave tomorrow after we're well rested."

Smiling she said goodnight and disappeared into the room, throwing herself into the welcoming bed. In a matter of seconds her body shut down in deep sleep.

Falcon watched her disappear in to the room. Macaw's little display had him on edge and although they were hidden at the safe house he couldn't lower his guard completely.

Hawk noticed his apprehension. "Don't worry. I'll keep watch tonight. You need your rest too or you'll never make it back."

Hawk was right and he knew it. He was tired, exhaustion setting in for existing on less than two hours of sleep in the past three days. If he didn't get rest he feared he might not be able to save the scribe should there be another assault. And, he knew there would be; it was just a matter of time. Being at the safe house with a few of his men enabled him to relax some, but still, his instinct wouldn't permit total rest.

"You think Macaw's switching his allegiance?" Hawk asked lighting up.

Falcon took another swallow of his tea, "No. Macaw would never switch sides. He lives for revenge, and hurts over Oren's death."

Hawk squirted a wedge of lemon into his tea, while clutching his cigarette between his fingers. "He just doesn't trust you and the rest of us for that matter. He's somehow got it in his head that we have started our own regime and that makes him dangerous."

"Falcon blew a line of smoke. "He's talking with someone; they're playing with his mind. Find out who it is."

Hawk agreed and they spent the next half hour finishing off the tea. Then smoking a few more cigarettes, they discussed the best possible way to sneak past the media and authorities and deliver Bronwyn safely to the

Citadel. The men in the N.E.S.S.T knew the woods well having survived in them for the past six hundred years. It would be no problem trekking through the Appalachians; the main concern was getting to that point.

Crushing the butt of his cigarette, Falcon swallowed the last of his hot tea. "I'm turning in. My minds too tired. We'll resume this discussion tomorrow."

Standing, he stumbled, bumping into the patio table, knocking over his empty tea mug. The trees in the distance began circling the patio like a fast paced carousel, throwing him off balance. Bracing himself against the railing, he tried focusing but his surroundings whirled around him and his vision began to tunnel.

"Damn it!" he gritted his teeth in anger, clutching the rail for support. This was not the result of sleep deprivation but rather a powerful sedative, no doubt, slipped in his tea. Still gripping the banister, he turned to face Hawk who'd brought up the dessert cart, surely…

The tea was having the same effect. He hadn't drugged him but that brought little comfort. Someone was working a plan and he feared the outcome. The only consolation was the Scribe hadn't drunk her tea. If she used her wits, she may have a chance. Trying to focus, he stumbled toward the bedroom. Teetering sideways, he bumped into the dessert cart, toppling it over.

"Sh-sh, quiet now or you'll wake sleeping beauty." A sarcastic voice taunted from the doorway. Falcon's lips snarled upward. *Elam!*

Falcon lunged forward and when he did, Elam pulled a gun, shooting Hawk in the chest. The effect of the tranquilizer numbed his senses but the sight of Hawk falling onto the floor, staring up in to the night sky, wide eyed in death sent a rage through Falcon rivaling the fury he felt the night his brother murdered Ariston. His rage fought against the sedative diluting the effect long enough for him to ball all his ferocity into his fist, striking Elam in the jaw. Recovering quickly Elam placed his weapon against Falcon's leg and fired. It was enough to send him to the ground. Two of Elam's men entered the balcony. One hoisted Hawks body off the ground and the other jerked Falcon to his feet, pushing him into the bedroom. Despite the sedative, pain detonated down his leg, shattering what little strength remained.

"Take them below," Elam ordered his men.

Falcon took a final glance at Bronwyn, sleeping peacefully in her bed. Her hair was swept away, fanning across her satin pillow, revealing the beauty of her face. Her long lashes rested high on her cheek bones and he wondered what dreams and visions were transpiring behind her soft lids. His lips formed a crooked smile. Behold their scribe; who'd of ever thought? She was not what they'd expected and the mystery surrounding her caused many suspicions. He'd had a few himself, but after spending several days with her he was convinced she was innocent of any treachery. Besides, he knew what it was like to be misunderstood. He was an enigma himself. True, he could spend countless hours defending himself, giving examples of his loyalty, releasing the secrets of his time missing in action, where he was and what he was doing, but he chose not to. He rather his life authenticate his character. Time would tell his true story and only those who walked shoulder to shoulder with him, looking past the facade would be able to read it.

Scribe's refusal to allow Macaw to enlighten her impressed him and her affirmation of his character was touching. Up until then he figured she loathed him, clinging to him solely out of fear and the need to survive. She was developing in her role of redeemer but in his opinion, still had a ways to go. She remained weak and fearful and completely oblivious to the evil ways of the darkness. She didn't understand the spiritual war that fueled the physical one and therefore was apathetic to its power. That, in his opinion was the most dangerous aspect of the entire quest. She was a good person yet she never spoke of God or any belief system of any kind. He knew from first-hand experience you can't remain neutral in a supernatural war. When the battle line is drawn across your soul, your heart will choose a side and that side depends on who you really are. Behind the skin, buried beneath the façade of her earthly personality, there was a persona that needed to surface. It would take cataclysmic events for it to emerge. He closed his eyes at the thought. Devastation reveals true character. The decisions a person makes under severe pressure screams of who they really are, and is the only thing that will start the transformation. He sighed; her identity was soon to emerge, because she would go through hell soon.

"Don't worry," Elam consoled Falcon. "She'll sleep through the entire journey."

Falcon struggled to stay conscience; he was fading fast. Even in his weakened state he could still best Elam yet he dare not try. Not with Elam's men in the room and one with the barrel of his gun pointing straight at Bronwyn's pillowed head. Elam sneered, noticing Falcon's contemplation in the matter.

"You make one move toward me or anyone in this room and she's dead. Abaddon will be disappointed but in the end I believe he would understand. There are casualties of war you see, and for a while her demise was the objective. Although, being who she is has changed things. Still, if victory demands a sacrifice, then a sacrifice she will be."

The arrogance in Elam disturbed Falcon; he saw the same pride growing in his brother over six hundred years ago. It is a fast spreading cancer, devouring humility, contaminating the mind and spirit until the person is a hollow shell of who they used to be. It is the prevailing weapon of the darkness. He could only imagine what the city of Eden was like now if that same arrogance was the pervading characteristic in the governance.

"You've changed Elam."

Falcon's accusation didn't set right with his betrayer. His dark eyes were daggers, cutting through Elam's pretense, exposing the cowardice that propelled his friend into settling for the best he could get from the darkness instead of having the courage to fight for what was right, even if it seemed to be a losing battle.

"Times have changed my friend. You either embrace it or you get swept away. It's a shame you couldn't adopt your brothers way of life, the two of you together would have been great. He wanted you as his right hand man, supporting his cause, ruling with him, governing the masses. You led him to believe you would, but in the end, you betrayed him and I don't think he'll ever recover from that pain."

The stare down between the two men was intense. Elam backed away first, having the most to hide and fearing Falcon could see into the depth of his tainted soul. Motioning to his men, he nodded toward the door.

"Get him out of here. We're wasting time. Let her sleep, she's not going anywhere."

Falcon kept his cold stare on Elam, all the while knowing it unnerved him almost to the point of remorse. Exposed guilt is a volatile weapon and can be used to your advantage or can backfire wounding the person aiming the missile. In this case Elam's final words on the matter caused it to backfire.

"He loved you once and maybe you could have stopped him before he went too far, instead you left…you left us all."

Elam's pronouncement of guilt hit hard. Falcon spent the better part of six hundred years reliving the *what if's* of the situation. He had done what he'd done. His objective was to remove Asa from Abaddon. If Abaddon continued to partake of the tree of life then he would live forever in his present condition, and that was something Falcon could not allow to happen.

Elam's men shoved Falcon into the hallway, he hobbled, the pain in his leg excruciating. Every agonizing step caused him to walk a tightrope between reality and unconsciousness. If the gunshot wound didn't take him under, the sedative would. Regardless of the haze filling his head he must think fast. He had one last idea. He'd tried it before but to no avail. He was going down and would no longer be able to protect the scribe. Now, with nothing to lose, he tried it again, praying it would work this time; and as the men shoved him down the hallway he summoned Bronwyn with his mind

.

CHAPTER TWENTY-THREE

"Bronwyn is adopted?"

Bethany's eyes widened at Martin's confession, "Seriously, she never told me that."

"Because she doesn't know." A look of guilt spread across his face, "We decided never to tell her."

"Why?"

Martin took a sip of his coffee before answering, "Because there is no record of her birth or birth mother."

Betancourt was intrigued. "No record anywhere?"

"No, and we searched for a long time," Madison interrupted her husband, trying to justify their decision.

Martin took his wife's hand, holding it in reassurance. "Thirty-four years ago we took a camping trip to the mountains. On our last night there, a deadly storm hit. It was terrible, unexpected and like nothing we'd ever seen. We hunkered down, in our motorhome, praying we'd survive. The next morning the campsite was nearly gone. We hiked around the area trying to retrieve as many of our things as we could."

"That's when I found Bronwyn," Madison interrupted. "At first I thought she was a toy doll, washed away by the storm. I reached over to pick it up, and to my astonishment she cried. She was naked, abandoned; there wasn't a blanket or anything. She seemed only a few hours old, but there was no umbilical cord, nothing. Other than being covered in mud, she seemed unharmed and healthy. We combed the entire area, it was abandoned. No one was searching for a lost child."

"Madison and I couldn't have children," Martin said, taking back over the story. "We prayed and prayed for a child but we never could conceive. We figured this was an answer to our prayers. We did an extensive search and still didn't come across any record of her birth or reports of a lost child. She was a mystery."

Bethany shook her head, "This is crazy! And Bronwyn doesn't know any of this?"

"No, we never told her because we didn't adopt her legally. We were afraid if she knew she might want to locate her birth mother and that could have caused us a lot of legal problems."

Martin refilled Betancourt's mug, "We were such a happy family. There wasn't a need to upset things. She was the light of our life, our gift from heaven."

Madison played with the tissue in her hand; and with her head bowed, continued the story.

"It wasn't long before we realized she was extremely gifted. Music came so easy to her. When she was very young she would sit down at the piano and play the most amazing pieces. I don't know how she did it; without any lessons at all. She was very creative and had a vivid imagination. She could tell the most amazing stories and would entertain us every evening with a new one."

Bethany smiled at the recollection. Bronwyn did have a special way in telling the most colorful stories.

"When she was ten she told us she wanted to write a book," Martin said. "We encouraged her endeavors realizing that she was truly a gifted child. But as she wrote she became consumed with the story, and in some strange way, it seemed as if the story began to devour her too."

Sorrow hollowed itself in Madison's face. Bethany had never seen her so distraught, and the thought of this family hiding such secrets all these years, unnerved her to the point of wondering if she knew the truth about anyone. All these shocking disclosures were taking their toll.

"She began having nightmares," Madison said still

twisting at the tissue in her grip. "She'd wake up screaming and crying. There was nothing Martin or I could do to console her. She kept insisting she was lost and needed to go home. She began to believe the characters in her story were real; people that she was responsible for saving. She began to withdraw from everyone and dwelt only on her story. Her grades started dropping and sometimes she would write in a different language."

Betancourt was leaning across the table now, "What language?"

"It was an unknown dialect. When we confronted her about it she said she didn't remember doing it, nor could she interpret what she wrote."

Bethany was stunned, not believing what she was hearing, "And you never found out what the language was?"

"Never."

Bethany's heart fell into the pit of her stomach as a haunting terror began growing inside of her. Just when she thought she couldn't take anymore Madison continued, adding to her anxiety.

"Things began to get much worse so we insisted she stop writing her story. She fought us over it and begged to finish it until other frightening things began to take place."

"What kind of frightening things?" Betancourt asked and Bethany wished he hadn't.

"She began sleep walking. We found her several times in the attic, in deep conversation with someone she referred to as Pravuil. Of course we didn't see anyone there, and when she woke, she didn't either."

"I did a little research on the name Pravuil, Martin said. "Get this; Pravuil is referred to as one of the seven highest angels. This archangel writes all the deeds of God, and is keeper of the books in heaven. He supposedly instructed Enoch of the Bible, and we all know what happened to him."

"I don't," Bethany confessed. "Although I'm not sure I want to know."

Betancourt smiled at her apprehension, "He disappeared one day. No one ever saw him again. It's believed God took him to heaven, like, beam me up Scotty."

Bethany sighed, "Great."

Martin reassured Madison, patting her on the arm, "We're going to find Bronwyn honey, don't you worry."

Shaking her head, she began to cry. "Martin, the entire damn town has disappeared. They're comparing it to Roanoke and to this day that mystery has never been solved. How are we going to find our daughter?"

Getting up from her chair, Bethany knelt beside Madison, consoling her. Betancourt allowed the women to grieve, aiming his words at Martin. "I know it's tough but we must continue; if we are going to find your daughter, I need all the information I can get."

Martin agreed, "There's not much left to tell. Bronwyn agreed things were out of control so she stopped writing. She gave the book to us but made us promise we wouldn't destroy it. And personally, I didn't think we should. For some reason, I honestly felt this was some sort of piece to the puzzle of the mystery surrounding her. Instead we locked it away."

"So she never actually finished it?" Bethany asked.

"No."

"So how does that compare to the other book? How does it end?"

Betancourt's eyes danced with intrigue, "They both stop at the exact same place. It was never finished either. That is one of its mysteries…how could a book that was never finished be published? And besides that, the publisher is unknown as well."

Bethany rested her face in her hands for a few seconds before speaking. "My God, Bronwyn never told me any of this and I met her only a year later."

Martin stood to retrieve the box of Kleenex for his wife.

"By then she had forgotten all of it. Honestly not less than two weeks after we took the book away she was back to normal and never spoke of the story. The nightmares and sleepwalking stopped. We got our life back. I honestly think she had forgotten all about it. She hasn't spoken of it since the day we locked it away."

Bethany shook her head, "Unbelievable. Wonder what in the hell caused her to remember?"

Betancourt replaced the antique book in his briefcase along with the one Bronwyn wrote. His actions implied the interview had come to an end.

"So what's next?" Martin asked.

Betancourt snapped his briefcase shut, "I'm headed to Moonshine to do some investigating." He pulled his card from his coat pocket. "I'll be in touch. If you think of anything, give me a call."

Standing, Martin shook Betancourt's hand. "I have a question if you don't mind me asking?"

"Go ahead," Betancourt agreed.

"If that's the only copy in the world, how did you get a hold of it? Where did it surface?"

"Off the record?" Betancourt asked.

Martin nodded.

"It's a family heirloom; I found it at my great grandmother's, buried in the spring house on her property. It belonged to my great grandfather, Haytham.

CHAPTER TWENTY-FOUR

"Scribe, wake up! Get out of here, now!"

Bronwyn stirred, waking at the command. The urgency in Falcon's voice warranted her sudden leap from the bed; fearing a reenactment of last night's harrowing escape. The room was dark except for the silvery glow of the moon filtering through the window. She looked around, all seemed calm; Falcon wasn't in her room. She must've been dreaming, reliving the events of last night. Her heart quieted. She looked at the clock, 10:46 PM, and wondered where he was. Last she saw him he was smoking on the balcony and drinking hot tea with Hawk.

Yawning, she opened the French doors leading out to the balcony, welcoming the gentle breeze. The stars were brilliant, scattering across the expanse, like jewels displayed on black velvet. Everything was quiet, peaceful; a chorus of croaking frogs, chirping crickets and the occasional howl of a coyote, in the canyon below, was the only sounds interrupting the calm of the hour. From where she was standing it was hard to believe she'd been a part of a massacre less than twenty-four hours ago. Yet in spite of the tranquility of the moment, she felt bedlam brewing not far away. Something wasn't right; she could feel it.

"Scribe!"

Startled she turned around but he wasn't there. His voice was loud. She hadn't been dreaming. Maybe he was yelling a warning from below. Considering the way things were transpiring on this trip, she thought it might be in her best interest to look. Leaning over the railing she scanned the area, it was empty. Making her way back inside, she peeked out the door, over the hallway railing, down into the living room.

"Falcon?"

The room remained dark and quiet, peaceful. Still, she couldn't shake the premonition and despite the calm she sensed a disturbance. Where was he? She'd heard him call twice now, both times with urgency in his voice.

"Scribe! If you can hear me, get out of here." Startled, she stopped at the bottom of the staircase, whirling around. Where was he hiding? "Falcon?"

Silence filled the empty room; no one was there. Her pulse quickened, dread screamed a forewarning, something was definitely wrong. What to do? Falcon's call was for her to get out of there, but where was she to go, and how? She wasn't leaving without him that was for sure.

"Falcon?" her voice was a whisper. Again, no answer. He had to be close by. His call was strong, why wouldn't he answer her? She stole across the room. The manor was immense and unfamiliar which put her at a disadvantage. To add to her handicap it was dark and she, unlike the others, did not have the benefit of night vision. It frightened her to think someone might be in the shadows watching her even now. Trying to calm her breathing, she contemplated her next move. The kitchen was visible from the living area; she'd go there and find a knife for protection…just in case.

Tiptoeing, she hurried into the kitchen. It too was oversized, restaurant style. The moon, high in the sky, shined its beams through the massive picture windows, illuminating off the two, spotless, stainless steel refrigerators, once again, giving a narrow pathway of light.

She snaked in between the countertops, quietly opening and closing utility drawers, searching for a suitable knife. Opening the fourth drawer, she discovered her prize; a small, but very sharp paring knife. It would be to her advantage to carry a little one that she could easily hide instead of a gigantic butcher knife that could effortlessly be taken and used against her. Closing the drawer, she clutched her defense and continued making her way across the kitchen. Fear gripped her, and she gripped the knife. The thought of having to use it caused her stomach to knot. She'd witnessed too many throat slicing's back at the condo and considering her abhorrence for blood, she wasn't at all sure she could actually plunge her knife into the soft flesh of someone, even if they were attacking her. She shivered, hoping it wouldn't come to that.

Slipping past the large island, she kept her back against the cabinetry as much as possible, remembering how shadows emerged from every dark corner back at the condo. These haunting thoughts kept her on edge.

A small puff of air touched her face as she reached the pantry. The door was open allowing her a peek inside. The food cupboard was quite large, extending deeper than she first realized. The corners were dark, the glow of moonlight unable to reach the far recesses. A shiver raced up her spine and as it did, she contemplated turning back but something in her spirit would not allow it. Call it intuition or plain stupidity but she had a hunch. She needed light however, and the further back into the room she crept, the darker it became. She slipped inside, inching her way past shelves of canned jellies, jars of honey, bags of nuts, beans and rice, and baskets of fresh vegetables along with homemade bread and pastries. The storeroom resembled an old time mercantile, stocked with supplies as well as food; and it wasn't long before she came upon a basket of candles and matches. Laying down the paring knife, she grabbed the necessary articles. Striking as quietly as possible, she lit the wick. Turning around, she held the light high, lighting the dark corners of the pantry. Grabbing her knife, she took a step forward. A gentle gust of air kissed her face, sending her small flame dancing before snuffing it out completely. Panic gripped her, yet she forced herself to stay calm; for some reason, she felt compelled to continue her sleuthing. Laying aside her weapon she ran her hand along the shelf searching for the book of matches. Re-lighting the wick, she cupped her hand in front of it, guarding the flame. Cautiously, she moved further back into the food cupboard, intent on investigating the source of the draft. The dancing flame cast twisted shadows on the walls, resembling gruesome faces, each whispering a warning not to venture one step further.

As she neared the end of the pantry, the cool puffs of air became stronger, raging a battle against the flickering candle. Arriving at the final shelf, she raised her candle illuminating kegs of molasses, maple syrup, honey, and agave nectar. The tap of the blackstrap molasses revealed a pregnant drip, ready to escape the spigot and fall to the floor. With the tip of her finger she rescued the drop, placing it on her tongue. Returning her finger to the spigot, she closed the tap to prevent additional leakage. As she did, the back wall moved slightly letting in another breath of air. Tugging again at the spout, the heavy wall swung forward like the massive door of a vault opening before her. Cool air wafted inside, reminding her of the moment in the rustic cabin when the rock wall slid sideways revealing the dark passageway to the citadel. She peered inside, her candle lighting the beginnings of what appeared to be another dark tunnel, leading to God knows where.

Looking behind her she contemplated retreating and heading back to the safety of her bed, yet her curiosity would not allow it. Besides, there was the mystery of Falcon's call, yet his warning instructed her to run and get out of there, not to go exploring. She remembered the words of the second prophesy, saying in time she would be led to the secret place and to enter without fear. It was there she would find the third book and the third prophecy. She doubted this was the secret place or the location of the third book, but at least it was a rehearsal for the real event. With that thought in mind, she stepped inside the daunting tunnel.

CHAPTER TWENTY-FIVE

Bethany stepped from the black Sedan and looked up at the inn. She'd left this place a week ago with no inclination she'd be returning so soon. But after Betancourt revealed his close relation to the story, and how he'd become obsessed, joining the FBI, and spending most of his life investigating the mystery, Bethany and Bronwyn's parents decided to accompany him to Moonshine. Each of them hoped to uncover more of the mystery surrounding Bronwyn's birth and disappearance.

The peacefulness of Sandalwood Inn was now replaced with the frenzy of a media circus. News vans, all displaying their stations insignia, were parked all over, littering the beautiful lawn, crushing many of the exotic plants growing in the fertile soil. Standing in front of cameras, clutching their microphones, reporters everywhere embellished stories, speculating of what may have transpired here in the hidden town; all renaming Moonshine the Modern Day Roanoke.

"This is the place," Bethany sighed, calling out to Madison and Martin as they climbed from the car. "This is where we stayed and the last place I saw Bronwyn." Tears burned in her eyes at the tragic disclosure

The familiar squeak of the screen door was the only welcome they received as they entered the lobby. Approaching the colossal desk, Bethany rang the small shiny bell, hoping Mavis would appear around the corner, missing tooth and all, welcoming her weary travelers.

Instead, a reporter, recognizing Madison and Martin, eagerly approached, ready for an exclusive. Once

Betancourt showed his credentials and demanded to be left alone, the reporter retreated.

Bethany gave her companions a private tour, starting with the room she shared with Bronwyn two weeks ago. Madison attempted to sort through some of Bronwyn's belongings but was stopped by authorities dusting for prints and collecting evidence. A particular item tagged and lying aside caught Bethany's attention, she hadn't thought about the mysterious vial with the puzzling verse until now. She mentioned it to Betancourt who examined the evidence, startling when he read the cryptic message, mumbling that Isaiah 42:9 was written across the first page of the old family Bible. Bethany took one last look before leaving the familiar room. She sighed, wishing she could turn back the time, heeding all Bronwyn's warning signs that went unnoticed.

Leaving the room, they took a stroll through the many gardens. The once serene healing grounds were now makeshift studios for the media, reporting their stories, hanging close to the elusive town in case any major developments transpired.

Bethany pointed out the garden where Bronwyn swore she saw a murder take place. It had all seemed so ludicrous to her at the time. Besides, Trent convinced her Bronwyn was on some sort of meds and was having a post break up crisis. Why had she believed him above her best friend?

Betancourt ordered the newly planted tree removed and soil samples taken from the spot where Bronwyn told Bethany the victim bled out. They continued on until they reached the last garden. Bethany admitted she hadn't been in this particular grove since it was always locked. Today however, the door was open. Following the shaded path, they came upon a group of photographers taking pictures of a lone tombstone; saying it was the only marker of death in the entire town which was quite peculiar. They went on to mention there wasn't a hospital either only a small clinic. Again, something so obvious yet went unnoticed the entire week she visited. Stepping forward she read the engraved stone.

"Brennan John Colton

Beloved husband,

Amazing father, brother, friend,

Prince of Eden,

On this world but not of it."

She glanced over at Betancourt who was reading the marker as well. "What does that mean; on this world but not of it?"

Walking to the headstone, Betancourt traced his finger over the engraving, and even though he said nothing, Bethany could tell the phrase resonated with him, more than likely affirming his investigation. She marveled at what an enigmatic incident they'd all inadvertently stumbled into. Yet, considering the new revelation on Bronwyn's adoption and the mystery surrounding her beginnings, Bethany had a gnawing suspicion that Walt's wrong turn two weeks ago had been a predestined event.

They left the gardens and continued on into Moonshine. The reports were right; it was abandoned, with no hint as to what happened or where the people had disappeared to. Eeriness walked along with her, shoulder to shoulder, mocking all those scurrying around, desperately trying to solve the mystery of the missing people. Every tree, every storefront gave a sneering smile, each knowing the secret of what dreadful thing swallowed this entire town.

They stopped at the café. Yellow police tape forbidding entrance, blocked the way inside the small restaurant and to the outdoor dining patio. Betancourt pulled the barrier aside allowing them admission. Littering the tables were plates of half eaten breakfast. Meals ready to serve out were abandoned on the cooling racks, while dirty dishes filled the sink in the kitchen. Betancourt tapped a table top with his fingers while scanning the patio; again, his eyes lost in a multitude of thoughts. He was impressive, attractive, and in excellent shape for a man in his forties. He had an air about him and although he seemed kind, Bethany was certain he was not the type of man you should cross. By his own admission he was obsessed with the mystery of his great grandfather and had been since childhood. He confessed on the drive up, that he'd never met his great grandfather, but was sure he'd caught glimpses of him from time to time, visiting the old homestead; even after it was rumored he had passed on.

The secret shrouding his grandfather was that he was immortal, never aging, and lived hundreds of years before marrying Betancourt's great grandmother. Betancourt's father used to tell him the stories his grandmother told him about her husband before her death, claiming he was from another world and one day would return to right all the wrongs of an evil ruler. He'd always considered them as the senile ramblings of a dying old woman, until one day when he overheard his grandfather and his great uncle trying to decipher the puzzle of their missing father. His grandfather swore he saw his dad hidden in the distance at his mother's graveside service. According to him he didn't look a day over forty, when in fact, if he'd lived, would have been close to eighty six.

After his great grandmother's death, the homestead became abandoned; there was no longer any reason to visit. The owner of the place let it go, not wanting to invest the money to modernize it and get it ready for new tenants. To this day it sits off the beaten path, somewhere in New Mexico, shrouded in mystery. Betancourt said he visits the place from time to time and on one such visit found the mysterious book, boxed and buried in the spring house. On other visits he's certain he caught glimpses of his great grandfather roaming the hundred acre property.

Bethany chilled at his stories.

"Bethany? What are you doing here?" The summons startled her, interrupting her inspection of Betancourt. Turning toward the familiar voice she was surprised to see Lillian and Trent making their way over. The troupe had come back, if only to see for themselves, if the reports were actually true. It was unnerving seeing the abandoned town when just a week ago they were milling around with the locals, enjoying their unplanned sabbatical. After offering their sympathies to Bronwyn's parents, Bethany introduced them to agent Betancourt. He asked them the standard questions and then enquired if they had observed anything out of the ordinary the week of their stay. They gave the same answers as Bethany but it was Trent who brought up the night hike to the waterfall. True, the place was somewhat mystical, like a hidden paradise right from the page of an exotic travel brochure. Definitely not your typical mountain waterfall, but other than that, she hadn't noticed anything out of the ordinary.

"What was so unusual about our hike to the waterfall?" Bethany's tone was accusing. She blamed him for this. She had become such a student of his ridiculous philosophies, believing Bronwyn was suffering from the effects of a broken heart, that she totally ignored her cries for help.

"I'm surprised no one else noticed." Trent's voice was condescending, a retaliation to her sarcasm. "When we headed to the waterfall that night Bronwyn had a nasty gash from the night before, when the canoe hit her in the head. On the return hike home, her wound was missing."

"My God you're right." Lillian covered her mouth with her delicate hand. "I'd forgotten all about her injury."

Bethany shifted her feet, suddenly feeling uncomfortable and wasn't at all surprised when Betancourt immediately asked them to lead the way to the spot. As gung ho as she was to solve the mystery and rescue her friend, she dreaded making the hike. The picturesque town, once resembling a Norman Rockwell painting, evoking comforting sentiments of God, home and country, now sat shrouded in a veil of secrecy. Now, a week too late, pieces of a very strange puzzle began taking a predominate place in her thinking.

Trent led the way to the falls, certain of the direction, admitting that over the course of the week he and Daniel had visited the place on three different occasions, and then made reference to having fun with a couple of the local girls. Bethany rolled her eyes disgusted and fell back a ways, walking alongside Madison. Lillian joined them and began recounting all the perplexities of their week in Moonshine. Unfortunately while they were in the thickest part of the forest, Lillian remembered Bronwyn making the claim that someone was following them on their way into town. That disclosure catapulted Bethany's thoughts to the night before the festival when Bronwyn fainted and later tried to tell her about cloaked men roaming the surrounding woods. Bethany shivered and even though they still walked by the light of the sun, she switched on her flashlight, bouncing the light through the surrounding trees, lighting the darker thickets. However, the forest was as empty as the town it guarded.

"This is quite peculiar," Trent voiced his observation to Betancourt. "We should be reaching the falls at any moment yet I don't hear the sound of rushing water."

He was right, it was quiet, peaceful, the only noise falling upon their ears was the repetitious chirping of crickets, cicadas, and a bullfrog in the distance, but no roar of a powerful rushing waterfall.

Just as she was about to suggest he might have taken a wrong path, they stepped into the clearing of the falls. She stopped suddenly at the sight, a sick feeling snaked its way up, wrapping around her throat and squeezing. Less than two weeks ago, Bethany witnessed these very falls dispense sparkling water in a powerful cascading downpour, now they stood before her dry and empty like parched stones in a desert.

"Oh my God, it looks so different, what happened?"

"It's a damn stagnate pond," Trent said stooping down to feel the water. Without the falls to stir and feed the steamy basin, the mountain pool grew stagnate; allowing a green slimy moss to blanket the surface, creating a film across the top of the water.

"It wasn't like this before?" Betancourt questioned them.

"Nope," Bethany sighed, "It was magical, like a fantastical paradise hidden in the middle of the forest. Now, it's more like an abandoned attraction at an amusement park, shut off and neglected."

“Like the rest of the town,” Lillian’s voice was soft… haunting.

CHAPTER TWENTY-SIX

Bronwyn tiptoed down the rustic wooden steps, vanishing into the blackness of the underground tunnel. Protecting her smoldering wick, she groped her way through the shadowy corridor. It was frigid and damp and smelled of wet earth. The further she descended, the steps changed texture beneath her feet, from crude wood to cold smooth rock, hewn from the underground hollow. She'd descended nearly fifteen feet before she sensed a presence in the tunnel with her. Something or someone was following, slinking behind her. Whipping around, she reacted to the presence, holding her candle high. A shiver crawled up her back sending chills more intense than what the frigid temperature brought.

"Falcon?" she choked out the word, "Is that you?" The only response to her call was the echo of a tiny pebble bouncing down the stairway, skipping past her. Leaning her back against the earthen wall, she took in a deep breath, trying to steady her breathing. It was then she saw the black hovering fog filling the passageway, snuffing out her feeble flame, leaving her blind in the foreboding darkness. The sudden loss of sight crippled her, leaving her defenseless. Fear bullied up against her, clawing into her flesh. The darkness invading the private chamber was more than the absence of light. It was a tangible presence rounding the corridor, watching her. She hadn't felt this frightened since she was a child.

The malicious vapor boiled toward her, intensifying the darkness and smothering any feelings of freedom. Had the air not been so frigid, she'd of thought she had descended into the very bowels of hell. The decaying presence hissed a warning to retreat; its breath reeked of sulfur, promising eminent death if she attempted one more step. Then to her horror, the passageway turned icy cold as the sinister presence manifest. Her back stiffened at the occurrence, and although she could not see in the thick blackness, she was certain someone was standing right behind her. Whirling around she aimed the paring knife into the blinding darkness; figuring whoever was standing so close would see and back away, or at least feel the impact of the dagger. The presence moved, hovering behind her again and then to her revulsion, an icy finger stroked the side of her face bringing a stinging pain. Spinning around, she backed away, planning her escape back up the stairway, but the darkness was suffocating, causing her to lose her bearings. The presence pushed up against her, forcing her backward, sending her sprawling down the hardened clay steps. Terrified, she plummeted into the dark abyss. Razor sharp stones tore into her skin, cutting her arms and legs. Desperate, she tried to grab hold of something, but there was nothing but wet, damp earth. She no longer felt the sharp edges of the steps and figured she'd slipped off the staircase and was now on a mudslide, falling with great speed, to God knows where. She'd read somewhere that underground caves could drop four or five thousand feet underground. The daunting thought paralyzed her and she wondered how long she could survive buried thousands of feet beneath the earth or if she would ever be able to find her way back to the surface. Then somewhere in the hostile darkness icy rain began to pour onto her face. Streams of water smacked against her as the mudslide submerged her into an arctic pool. Thrashing in the subzero waters she fought her way to the top, breaking through the surface, shivering and gasping for air. Then, a rapturous sight, light glowed in the distance. Bronwyn scrambled out of the frigid pool. Her muscles cramped from the freezing water, making it nearly impossible to walk. Shaking, she crawled on wobbly arms to the source of the light.

Considering the crudeness of the passageway that brought her here, she'd of never fathomed what lie beyond the colossal stalagmites. Peering around the limestone pillars, her eyes discovered a majestic room. Dumfounded, she tried to take it all in. A virtual mansion, rivaling any royal palace spread out before her. Grand chandeliers hung from an artistically carved rock ceiling, giving light to the underground fortress. Elegant furnishings spread across a white marble floor, and the arctic waters that engulfed her moments before provided a tributary, cutting along the far edge of the room. This delicate branch of the river offered a pleasing ambiance as well as piping fresh water to the other rooms. Intricately engraved doorways opened up to many other passages, all snaking off to secret locations. Marbled staircases spiraled upward, connecting to a higher level with an open hallway, surrounding the splendid room, much like the manor upstairs.

Still shivering, Bronwyn allowed her body to collapse; relieved she wouldn't spend the remainder of her life as a sightless mole burrowing her way underground. Now what to do? She needed to get warm. She was drenched and shivering uncontrollably. The temperature at this level was bitter cold and being wet only encouraged hypothermia. She must think fast while she still could. Obviously the place was a secret and more than likely off limits to her. Falcon had not mentioned it and felt compelled to leave her in the upstairs house. Should she be discovered down below, she'd incur his wrath again, and she wanted to avoid that at all costs. On the other hand, she'd heard him call her name upstairs, remaining hidden while telling her to run. Maybe she should have heeded his warning and made her escape. The thought caused her heart to fade. There was only one reason he would have warned her to run and that being he was in trouble. He'd instructed her earlier in their journey; to make her way to Travis should he go down. As much as she'd love to be near Travis again, she couldn't bear the thought of something dire happening to Falcon. Besides, how was she to find her way out of this place, and make it all the way back to Moonshine without being spotted by someone? Her face was all over the news and the authorities were looking for, her as well as Abaddon's men. The odds seemed overwhelming; still, she had no other choices. Either she continue on into the cavernous castle or retreat and make her way back up to the pantry. The decision was obvious. There was no way she was ready to face the formidable staircase of doom again.

Grabbing onto a stalagmite, she pulled herself to her feet. The shaking was almost uncontrollable now, as if she were trembling from the inside out. Abandoning her hiding place she stumbled toward the open room, staying as close to the rock wall as possible. A few more steps and her bare feet touched the smooth marble; leaving muddy footprints as she inched her way across the polished floor, a blatant announcement of her intrusion.

She was halfway across the room when she heard a frenzy coming from one of the hallways. Heavy footsteps, all rushing toward the open area, compelled her to dash for the shadows and take refuge in one of the many passageways exiting the room.

The scowl on the man's face, entering the chamber, was frightening and the men who followed at his heels seemed restless because of it. Bronwyn counted five and recognized none of them. Falcon was not with them, neither was Hawke, Vulture or Macaw. A seed of alarm took root; the men were dressed like those who launched the assault back at the condo, no doubt Abaddon's men.

"How could this have happened?" The angry man spewed forth his venom. "We take Falcon out and still we lose the scribe? I told you to sedate her!"

Bronwyn's stomach dropped, and she felt as if she couldn't breathe. *We take Falcon out...*Did that mean? No it couldn't, she wouldn't let that thought take root. Besides, she'd heard him call her name less than twenty minutes ago, he had to be alive. She couldn't make it without him and she knew it. Besides, as much as she hated to admit it, she'd grown quite fond of him, irreverent ways and all.

Clearing his throat in tension, one of the followers spoke up, "I put the sedative in her tea, and I used the most powerful one at that. I don't know what happened."

Their leader's eyes became daggers cutting into the man's defense. "How incompetent of you to put me in this predicament. This is the most important mission of my life and you were negligent, I no longer desire your service." With that final word on the matter he raised a gun, shooting the man point blank.

Jumping in shock at the unexpectedness of the execution, Bronwyn covered her mouth with her hands so not to make a noise.

"There is no place for inadequacy in my company," the leader said while putting the weapon back in his jacket. "Search the manor, she's not familiar with it, the rest of you take the grounds, it's dark, she won't be able to see as well as the rest of us. I want her found immediately."

Just as the men were leaving to carry out the orders another man stopped them cold. An evil grin tore across his face.

"No need to go above. She's not there."

To Bronwyn's horror, he pointed to the muddy footprints she'd left across the white marble floor. "The tracks are still wet, she can't be far. They lead over there."

"Find her now!" The leader growled his command. The men sprang into action. Bronwyn's heart seized leaping into her throat. Where could she go? The men were spreading out, taking every passage; with the leader himself heading her way. Taking off, she stumbled down the hallway. It was immense, seemingly running on for miles, with no place to hide other than taking one of the many doors lining the elaborate passage. She limped along, her bare feet numb from the icy cold marble. In a matter of seconds he would be in the hallway with her. Holding her breath she tried one of the doors, hoping she wouldn't barge right into more trouble. Her heart fell; the door led to yet another passageway. She wanted to cry. She was freezing and wet, her feet were numb and she couldn't stop trembling. She didn't want to think about the words the man used concerning Falcon, yet as hard as she tried, she couldn't keep them from echoing in her mind. He wasn't here to help her, he wasn't coming this time and she knew it. Slipping through the door she closed it quietly behind her as not to give her pursuer any inclination as to which exit she selected. Looking down at her feet, she was relieved to see she no longer left muddy prints. From here on out they would have to guess what door she chose. This should buy her a little time.

She sighed, doors lined this hallway as well; she wondered if she should take another or follow the passage and see where it led. She feared if she took to many alternate routes she would be hopelessly lost in the underground labyrinth. The passage snaked along, full of twist and turns and many covert doors all leading to the unknown. She'd had nightmares like this, being chased while lost in a network of doors and passageways each one leading to another with no end in sight.

Turning the corner she was surprised to see the hallway dead ending at another closed door. She feared opening it would only lead to yet another corridor.

Hugging herself, she tried to calm her shivering which was slowing her progress. Her movements were starting to get clumsy and drowsiness filled her head. She wanted nothing more than to lie down somewhere and sleep. She was tired and couldn't bear to think of trying to make it down another ice cold tunnel. The only thought that compelled her to turn the knob was that maybe there was warmth on the other side of the door.

The room was dark, lit only by the ray of light from the hallway. Slipping inside she ran her hand along the wall searching for a switch. As her fingers found the light something wrapped around her wrist, yanking her away from the wall and forcing her to the ground. Instead of hitting the hard floor she landed on top of a person, a still body. The glow from the doorway lit the face of Hawke. His eyes open wide, staring up at the ceiling in death. Before the cry of horror could escape her lips, a hand covered her mouth and pulled her from the body.

"Keep quiet," the voice struggled with the words. "They will hear you."

By now her eyes had grown accustomed to the darkness. Vulture lay dead near Hawke, along with a couple of other men she didn't recognize. Pulling away from the one who had hold of her, she turned to see Macaw. He too was bloody and seemed to be hanging on to life.

"Where's Falcon?" she nearly cried asking the question.

Macaw's expression reeked of shame. "I'm sorry, I was wrong, I should have…"

"Where is he?" She demanded, screaming the whisper.

Macaw, motioned to a bed on the far side of the room. Scrambling to her feet, she made her way over. Falcon's body was displayed on top of the satin coverlet, blood soaked through his clothing and onto the expensive fabric, he was beaten, like he'd put up a good fight.

Her trembling intensified and she struggled to breathe. "What…how'd this happen?

Macaw stayed lying on the floor, too weak to follow her to the bed; he closed his eyes, while coughing out the words.

"I gave Elam our location. I trusted him, he was a friend, I didn't believe he'd turned, I thought it was Falcon who had switched sides. When he arrived he brought an army with him. We didn't have a chance. They've launched a bloodbath… They killed everyone, they're all dead."

Bronwyn's heart crawled in her throat, "Who? Who's dead? Are you talking about the people in Moonshine?" Her voice quivered at the thought.

"No," Macaw coughed, exuding every effort to speak. "They killed the entire staff, everyone who lived at the manor, all shot to death in their beds. The women, the children, he killed them all." Macaw was crying now, choking on his own blood.

Bronwyn pitied him but she couldn't take her eyes off of Falcon. More than anything, she wanted to hear him give her a disparaging comment, flash his impish grin and then light up a cigarette. She wanted to cry, to scream, to crawl up beside him and die too, she was tired, cold and traumatized and not at all ready to fight her way to freedom. The past twenty–four hours had been nothing but sheer terror, death, and narrowing escapes. She was done, ready to call the authorities and turn herself and the entire bizarre story in. The tears escaped her eye, falling upon Falcons face. Wiping it away she rested her hand on his chest and noticed it rose slightly. She pressed harder, yes, she could feel it moving. He was breathing! Looking over at Macaw she announced her discovery.

"Falcon's not dead."

Macaw gargled and coughed up more blood, "Not now, but he will be." His voice was barely a whisper. "They're taking him back through the portal to be tried for treason." He grimaced in pain; and despite the frigid temperature, sweat poured down his face. "If you want to save him, then get out of here while you can. Make your way back to Moonshine. Find Travis, he can organize a rescue at the portal."

Trembling, Bronwyn crawled over to Macaw, her teeth chattered to the point where she could barely talk. With what little strength he had left, Macaw grabbed her wet t-shirt and pulled her face toward his, "Moonshine will be next. Elam knows where they are, when he's ready he'll launch his attack, but he needs you first. That's why you have to run now, go find Travis."

"How can I? I can't even find my way out of here. How am I to find Travis?"

Macaw laughed, and then choked a few more times because of it.

"He'll find you… he won't lose you again…"

Gagging, he coughed one last time and then closed his eyes. "Turn the shower head to the left… and hurry Abaddon's coming." His voice faded off to silence.

"What?" Bronwyn asked, leaning over him. "What did you say?"

Silence…he was gone. She bit back the tears. She was completely numb; drowsiness was overpowering her, the hypothermia taking its course. Had he said Abaddon was coming? He must have been delirious in death. Besides, he'd said to turn the shower head to the left; or was her thinking becoming muddled as well. Then a fleeting thought. A shower meant warm water! Slowly she crawled across the room to the adjoining bathroom, her wobbly arms scarcely able to support her weight. Exuding every effort she pulled herself up into the shower and turned the brass knob. Hot water poured over her, she cried out in pain at what felt like a million sharp needles piercing her frozen skin. Peeling off the oversized muddy t-shirt, she allowed the water to thaw her. She wanted nothing more than to sit under the warm water for hours. But time was of the essence; it wouldn't be long before the men came back for Falcon. The last thing she wanted was to be found wet; and naked at that. A soft terry cloth robe hung from a brass knob on the back of the door. She grabbed it to cover her nakedness, wrapped it around her and cinched the belt. Now, what to do? If she retraced her steps she could make it back to the main room but she was sure to run into Abaddon's men. Even if she did make it back undetected she was certain she wouldn't be able to find the staircase that led to the pantry. Besides she had no desire to put herself in that situation again. Then, she had a thought…it was worth a try anyway. Stepping back into the bath, she reached for the showerhead and turned it to the left. Nothing. Then she remembered the keg of molasses and how pulling on the spigot opened the door. She turned the nozzle again, pulling this time as she turned. The shower wall moved toward her opening up to a secret staircase hidden behind the wall. Thinking ahead she searched the bathroom and found a decorative candle and some matches. Darting back into the room, she leaned over the bed and kissed Falcon on the forehead.

"Initially I wanted to make this trip without you, I was wrong, I'm not sure I can do this by myself but you've left me no other choice. If you can hear anything I'm saying, hear this, hang on please, fight like the warrior I know you are…" she wiped away a tear, "Damn it Falcon I need you, I'm so scared I don't know where to go…"

"Run…"

Her heart leaped, "What? Did you say something?"

He continued to lay quiet, unmoving, yet she was sure…she heard his voice. Panic-struck she feared the hypothermia was worsening causing illusions.

"Run…down…"

Again his voice was loud and clear, but he said nothing…his mouth was still closed and his eyes remained shut. Hypothermia was dulling her thinking, *run down?* Run down where?

"Run down house….go to the run down house."

She whirled around. The voice was loud, like the one that woke her, yet no one else was in the room. Perplexed, she stood there trying to find the source of the voice. Falcon was unconscious and Macaw and the others were dead. Were her thoughts becoming muddled in the place somewhere between sleep and awake?

“Damn it Scribe run!” Call it premonition or whatever but at this point she didn’t care where it was coming from. Bolting for the bathroom she lit the wick and placed the book of matches in the pocket of the robe. Then, with great apprehension, she took the first step.

CHAPTER TWENTY-SEVEN

The staircase dead ended at a concrete barrier. Raising her candle Bronwyn scanned the wall looking for some sort of lever that would open the door. Bloody finger prints pointed to the device, a brass ring, embedded in a carved out circle in the middle of the wall. Grabbing hold of the ring, she hesitated. The bloody prints were fresh which meant someone had come this way not long ago. What if they were waiting for her right beyond the barrier? Entering could put her at risk of being caught. Still, the alternative would be retreating back down the staircase and into the room of death. She turned and pulled. The wall moved toward her, allowing her entrance. Cautiously, she stepped into another bath, this one familiar. The staircase led directly into her room, and it was empty. She wanted to cry tears of relief and fall into the soft bed and pull the warm blankets around her but there was no time to waste. If she were to save Falcon she couldn't waste another minute.

Grabbing her jeans and the hoodie, she dressed quickly. She would forgo the shoes not wanting to make any noise. Putting them in the travel bag, she snatched it up and placed the long strap around her neck before peeking out of the door. The house was still and as quiet as before. She figured they were still below searching every passageway in the labyrinth. Now was the time to dart outdoors and make her escape.

Tiptoeing down the stairs she made her way outside. She would follow the dirt road to the main highway and hopefully hitch a ride without being recognized. At this point however, she didn't care if she was turned over to the authorities. At least she would be protected from the ruthless men hunting her down.

The moon was high in the sky, giving ample light on this clear night. In fact, there was too much light and she figured she could easily be spotted. Hiding in the shadows of the manor, she strained her eyes, looking over the property. Macaw was right. Elam brought an army with him. Men were standing guard; intermittently positioned around the mansion, down the driveway and some in the open field. It would be easier to run through a mine field than to sneak past Elam's patrols.

Plotting a course of action, her eyes fell on the black Suburban that escorted her here only hours ago. Perhaps… it was a chance. Hunkering down she slithered along the shadows and made a quick dash to the vehicle. Crouching by the front tire she hid, waiting. Silence, there was no movement. She made it that far. Inching up, she peered into the driver's window. The glow of the moon reflected off the shiny keys dangling from the ignition. She slipped onto the plush leather seat, careful not to slam the door, it would only draw attention. Instead, she would secure it once in route. Pulling it close, she took a deep breath and turned the keys. As she expected, the sound of the engine pulled all attention her way. Black silhouettes moved from their frozen positioned all dashing for the vehicle. To her horror the Suburban, lurched forward and stalled.

"Damn it! She cursed, not noticing it had manual transmission. Unfortunately, she wasn't too familiar with stick shifts.

The men were closing in; she hit the power locks before starting the engine again. Pushing on the clutch she turned the keys, forced the gear in reverse, and stepped on the gas. Again, she stalled out.

"God please," she begged, while restarting the engine. Another stall; damn it, why couldn't she remember to step on the clutch? Three men leaped toward the vehicle. One tried the passenger door but to no avail, another jumped on the hood, while the other yanked opened the driver's door. She'd never closed it all the way! One last chance, with the clutch engaged she turned the keys and pressed hard on the gas just as the man's hand reached inside for her. The suburban peeled backwards, knocking the man to the ground. The front of the vehicle bumped upward as her front tire rolled across him, crushing his body as she backed away. Now to go forward; thinking fast, she kept her foot on the clutch while switching gears. Pushing the gas, the vehicle roared in protest, stalling out. What now? She'd mistakenly put it in third gear instead of first. By now two more men pounced on the suburban, while the man on the hood attempted to kick out the windshield. His boot came through; causing small round pieces of glass to shower in all around her. She had to get it right this time, it was her last chance. Turning the key she slammed the gear into first and peeled off, slipping it easily into second then third as she raced down the driveway. Jerking the steering wheel she turned onto the dirt road, knocking the man off the hood. She slipped the gear into fourth; she was flying now.

She checked her rearview, all was dark. Relieved she turned the heater on full blast and continued driving in fifth gear stirring up rocks and leaving a cloud of dust in her wake.

CHAPTER TWENTY-EIGHT

Bethany had been so mystified by the change of the falls that she failed to notice the effect the hike took on Madison. She'd turned ghastly pale and her knees buckled beneath her no longer supporting her weight. Holding her up, Martin searched the area for a place his wife could sit. Trent was the first to recognize the dilemma and as usual he came to the rescue, grabbing hold of Madison and helping Martin escort her to a nearby rock. One look at her and Bethany knew it wasn't the difficulty of the hike that was taking its toll.

"What's wrong?" She asked kneeling beside the rock.

"She's obviously suffering the effects of an altitude malady, exuding such effort at such a high elevation." Trent began waxing eloquent again; however, Bethany had no patience or interest in his diagnosis this time.

"What is it Madison?" She asked again, ignoring Trent.

Madison kept one hand over her mouth while shaking her head in disbelief. Anxiety flooded her eyes and Bethany figured she would faint at any minute. She looked at Martin for an answer. He didn't look any better himself.

"This is the campsite where we found Bronwyn." He whispered the information so Lillian and Trent wouldn't hear.

"Are you sure?" was all Bethany could say.

Martin nodded.

"So you've been to Moonshine before?"

"No, there's a campground probably seven miles down on the other side. We checked in there and then drove our camper on up. We never knew Moonshine existed.

"That was thirty-four years ago, how can you be sure it's the same falls?"

Martin smirked, "You don't forget things like that, besides it's only been twenty-four years. We came back every summer after that. It was on the camping trip when Bronwyn was ten that she started writing her book." Martin nodded toward the dried up falls. "She sat right over there, under the waterfall, and wrote its beginnings. We never came back after that trip because things just started going crazy."

Bethany was glad she was kneeling because at this point she didn't think her legs would hold her up any longer either.

"So in all the years you camped here you never hiked into Moonshine?"

"No," Martin was adamant in his answer. "We never hiked past the falls. There wasn't a trail back then, or at least not one we ever found."

Bethany looked up at Betancourt who once again was in deep thought; and despite Martin's intriguing revelation, she saw disappointment on his face.

"We better head back while we still have light." He tossed a stone into the stagnate pool breaking through the mossy film. "Whatever was here is gone now, no use hanging around."

The walk back was somewhat slower because of Madison. She appeared tired and sauntered along as if she were in a daze, which Bethany figured she probably was, seeing she felt somewhat confused herself. They made it back to Sandalwood Inn just as the sun was setting. Bethany headed for the black Sedan but to her dismay Betancourt said he wanted to stay at the inn, and do some more investigating in the morning light. The thought of sleeping in the new Roanoke unnerved her, so she thought of leaving the mountain with the troupe, but her plans fell short when she realized they were all staying up there too; due to various interviews scheduled for tomorrow.

Her old room was still secured pending the investigation so she took the room Anna and Karley had stayed in. Betancourt took Trent and Daniels old room, and Madison and Martin took the room Marcus and Wilbur had shared. The quietness of the inn had Bethany on edge and she feared the place might swallow her up during the night as it did everyone else. She had no intentions of being alone in the room so she asked Lillian to stay with her. Lillian was more than eager to accommodate her seeing her only alternative would be sleeping on the bus. They sat on the bed for over an hour discussing the strange turn of events and how they never would have imagined their Bronwyn getting caught up in a scandal of such caliber.

"You know," Lillian said, hugging her pillow as she spoke. "I remember Bronwyn asking a very strange question the day we got our pedicures. She asked Ashley if there was a secret society, a cult so to speak, roaming the woods in black hooded robes."

Bethany was intrigued, "How did the girls respond to her question?"

Lillian shrugged, "They didn't answer, it got quiet and uncomfortable so I changed the subject. Now I think she might have been on to something."

"No kidding," Bethany was sarcastic. "She was on to something alright. She tried to tell me about a murder in the gardens, but I thought she'd lost her mind. I can't believe she was telling the truth the entire time."

Lillian nodded, "What I'm wondering is what was it that compelled her to stay behind, especially since she was so frightened by everything? Do you think she was forced, you know, being black mailed by something?"

Bethany thought a moment, "The last we really talked was on the Sunday after the festival. She seemed normal, told me about watching the fireworks with Travis, later we cleaned up the room, did some laundry and then that evening after Mavis questioned her about the firework show, she took a walk. She didn't come to the room until five the next morning."

"I remember," Lillian picked up the timeline. "When we got back from breakfast she was gone and then showed up later with Falcon. That was a big surprise seeing she was terrified of him."

"You're right, it made no sense at all; but nothing does…"

"Then Ryan arrived and we all found out about her pregnancy." Lillian shook her head, "Unbelievable she kept that such a secret. She must have lost it right before we started touring. No wonder she was quiet and distant all the time."

Bethany felt ashamed. She's been a bad friend, becoming angry and pulling away just because Bronwyn kept her secret shame to herself. She sighed, "She left with Ryan and that was the last I saw her until right as we were leaving. She wanted to talk but I was so upset I told her no…I didn't know she wasn't coming with us until we were well on our way down the mountain…you're right Lil, what could have possibly compelled her to stay?"

They sat in silence for a few moments, both lost in thought trying to imagine what could have possibly been transpiring right under their noses. Bethany stood from the bed breaking the silence, "I'm starved. Wanna go raid the fridge?"

Lillian yawned, "No I'm too tired to eat; besides it's too late, anything I eat now just turns to ugly fat. I need to get to bed anyway. My interview is early in the morning."

Bethany shook her head, "Why did you agree to an interview?"

Lillian grinned, "We're talking Good morning America here Bethany. I'm an actress, I could use the publicity."

Bethany rolled her eyes, "I'm getting some food."

Betancourt was in the kitchen making a sandwich. He offered to make Bethany one as soon as he saw her. His looked delicious, so she agreed. Laying out two more pieces of bread he motioned to the coffee maker.

"I made a pot, but I better warn you, it's strong."

"Just how I like it," she said grabbing a mug from the cabinet and filling it. "As tired as I am, I doubt anything could keep me awake."

She sipped her coffee, he was right; it was strong, a little too strong so she made her way into the pantry looking for the creamer. It was quite large and much deeper than she first realized; ample size for stocking everything you need to run a small bed and breakfast, even the back wall was lined with kegs of maple syrup, honey and black strap molasses. Bethany smiled remembering the amazing waffles Mavis served up every day and thought it might be a nice gesture to make Madison some in the morning. Locating the creamer she joined Betancourt back in the kitchen. She watched him spread egg salad across the bread, then layer it with fresh cut tomatoes, lettuce, onions, and pickles. He tossed in a few jalapenos before closing it with the second piece of bread. Placing the sandwich on a plate he carried them outside on the porch, offering her a seat on the swing.

"Thank you," she said and then bit into her late night snack. "I was starving. I've been too upset to eat and didn't realize how long I'd gone without food until a few minutes ago."

He smiled, "Well there's a lot of food in this kitchen, and it'd be a shame to let it go to waste."

Bethany nodded and swallowed, "Mavis was a great cook; I had a lot of delicious meals here." She sipped at her coffee, "You know, agent Betancourt, people who plan on going away usually clean out their fridge. By the looks of it, Mavis never planned on leaving, neither did the people at the café. So what's your take on it all? Where do you think they disappeared too?"

Betancourt smiled, "My name's Jacob, you can drop the agent Betancourt."

Bethany tried to suppress her smile, she was glad he felt comfortable enough to be on a first name basis with her but she didn't want him to know it. Instead she tried acting indifferent and continued on with her question.

"Alright Jacob, what do you think happened to everyone?"

He sighed, "I wish I knew. I have my suspicions, but that's all they are. Years of investigating, and the more I find out, the more mysterious it gets."

"How long you been investigating?"

"Since I was a kid, but started it seriously at the age of nineteen. That's when my great grandmother passed and my great uncle swore he saw my great grandfather in the distance at the graveside. Since he was supposedly dead I became curious."

Bethany sipped her coffee and wished she'd put in more creamer, "What do you mean supposedly? Wasn't there a funeral when he passed?"

"Yes, but the casket was sealed. No one ever saw the body."

She was intrigued, "Ever think of exhuming the casket?"

Jacob took a swallow of his coffee. "Of course I did… it was empty."

She shivered at his blunt confession. "Whoa, why would it be empty?"

"Because he's not dead. They just wanted us to believe he was."

"Who ordered a sealed coffin?"

"My great grandmother, she said he'd been burned badly in an automobile accident. She wanted him to be remembered for the way he was before. No one questioned her at the time."

"So she was in on his secret?"

Jacob nodded, "They say she loved him with a passion and he loved her too, that's why suspicion began sometime after his death. She wasn't that shook up over it. Then there were reports of them spotted together. Of course she denied it, and it was a touchy subject since he was gone. What got me interested was a picture of a man in the distance, at her graveside, standing in the trees. It was too far to make a positive ID but my uncle swears it was him. Not long ago I had the picture blown up and analyzed. It was him alright; he hadn't aged a day, when in fact he'd of been eighty-seven."

Bethany shook her head, marveling at the mysteries of the universe. And at that moment, just when she wondered how many inexplicable secrets go on all around us undetected, the lazy tune of the dulcimer began wafting through the trees. She sat up straight.

"Someone's still here…whoever is playing that dulcimer…they're still here!" her voice trembled at the eerie thought. "Someone played that same tune almost every night the week we were here."

Jacob laid aside his coffee and walked off the porch, Bethany shivered, staying close on his heels. Reporters, and law enforcement officials came out of their campers, and tents; all milling around, looking up past the tall pines and into the starry night sky, spooked by the song.

Jacob ordered some men to take to the hills and investigate the source. The group immediately armed themselves, like soldiers, taking off into the woods.

"Tell me about the song," he asked.

Bethany rubbed her arms to keep from shivering. The night was warm but still a chill stroked at her skin. "Not much to tell. It played almost every night, it was soothing. I always pictured some mountain man sitting on his porch, rocking and playing his dulcimer while smoking a pipe. I never thought much of it."

Jacob looked up into the sky, "It's a signal. They're communicating which means they are close, and I have a suspicion they are hiding right under our noses."

Bethany trembled and looked around, wondering if Bronwyn was close by too, watching her. "So what are your suspicions?"

He grinned but didn't answer the question. "They say my great grandfather played a dulcimer."

Bethany forced a smile, the eeriness of the night taunting her. "Really? So, you have a picture of him? Maybe I should know what he looks like just in case I see him walking around here in Moonshine."

Jacob reached in his shirt pocket, pulled out a photograph and handed it to her.

"Meet my great grandfather, Haytham Elwell."

Bethany paled, "Oh my God, that's…."

He smiled, "I know."

CHAPTER TWENTY-NINE

Bronwyn had been driving for half an hour when she took the exit, pulling off the main road. As far as she knew she wasn't followed and that surprised her. However, she wasn't going to waste time worrying about a run of good luck. Making a left hand turn she pulled onto a narrow country road. She was following her instincts; and being good at directions she could usually find her way back to a place if she'd been there at least once. A half a mile further and she'd succeeded. The headlights illuminated the ram-shackled home. She wanted to keep them on but feared she was only drawing attention to her whereabouts if she did. Sighing, she killed the engine and shut them off. She kept the doors locked; however, wondering what good it would do, seeing the windshield was gone.

The place sitting before her was intimidating, like an old haunted house that everyone avoided because of the harrowing stories told about the residents and how they had been murdered, and walk the halls not knowing they're dead. She shivered trying to control her vivid imagination and then remembered Falcon's take on the place, and how he'd seen the beauty of what once was. She forced herself to think of it in that light.

Taking in a deep breath, she removed the keys from the ignition and tossed them into the travel bag. Rummaging through the glove box she found a flashlight and a book of matches. She put the matches in her pocket and grabbing the flashlight, she climbed from the safety of the driver's seat.

The front door was locked so she entered in through a broken window, being careful not to cut herself on the remaining shards. Switching her flashlight on, she bounced the beam around the open room. Several pieces of furniture remained, faded and soiled from being subjected to the elements, due to the broken windows and leaky roof. The cushions on the couch were torn, the fluff pulled out, revealing rusted springs; no doubt the work of squirrels and other wildlife burrowing to find material to make a nest. A thick layer of dust carpeted the hard wood floor, along with scattered dried leaves, sticks, and broken glass.

She refused to think about her situation, alone inside the old house, out in the middle of nowhere. It was like the beginning of a horror movie, nothing about it seemed right at all. The only reason she had come here was the voice back in the caverns had said, *run down house.* She wasn't sure if it meant to run back to the house, or if it was telling her to make her way to this God forsaken place. No matter, she was here, and as harrowing as it may be, it offered a place to hide for the rest of the night or until she could figure out how to make her way back to Moonshine without being spotted.

Taking every precaution, she tiptoed up the staircase, making sure each step was secure. The condition of the second floor was much like it was downstairs, covered in dust and dirt. A branch from a nearby tree had long ago crashed through one of the bedroom windows, offering a passage inside to all the woodland creatures that cared to relocate. Searching the room, the beam of her light caught the glowing golden eyes of an owl sitting high in the ceiling rafters, staring at her. His inspection stopped her cold and she gasped at the eerie sight. It made her think of the red glowing eyes in her nightmare which did nothing to ease her fearful mind. Retreating, she quickly made her way out of that bedroom and into the next.

This one surprised her. It was in much better shape than the rest of the house. The room was well-kept, as if someone tended to it, much like a person would a grave side. The thought caused her to wonder if whoever preserved the room was close by, possibly in the house now, watching her intrude on the sacredness of their sanctuary.

Scanning every corner as a safety measure, she made her way over to the four post bed and ran her hand over the beautiful hand-stitched quilt lying on top. The bed faced a stone fireplace and two large portraits hanging above the mantle. She cast her beam on the pictures, ready to see who once inhabited the run-down house. If the hidden owl hadn't stolen her breath away, one of the two faces staring at her from the vintage photographs did. Casting the light on the mantle she noticed a smaller framed picture of the same two people. Flipping the frame, she tore off the back cover, removing the old-fashioned wedding photograph. Turning it over, she read aloud, "Haytham and Carleene Elwell 1925. Falcon's real name must be Haytham Elwell. She sat hard on the bed, dumfounded. The picture was nearly a hundred years old, and other than the clothing, Falcon still looked the exact same. He was right; they didn't age, not like everyone else anyway. Walking around the room, she collected more photographs noticing Falcon hadn't aged in any of them but the woman had. In the last picture of her, she looked to have been in her sixties.

Exhausted, Bronwyn lay across the bed. Despite the crudeness of the place she felt safe in this room. Perhaps it was because Falcons face stared at her from the wall making her feel as if he were still protecting her. She sighed, wishing he were with her now, so she kept the light on his face; it made her feel better. She wanted to sleep but the urgency in what she should do kept her from it. She needed to make her way to Moonshine, find

Travis, so he could intercept Falcon at the waterfalls. But how was she to get to Moonshine? The Suburban had a busted out windshield, and she couldn't make the two day drive without one. Neither could she stop to have it fixed or she'd be recognized. Then a thought, perhaps there was a car in the detached garage. It was possible, after all someone or something had instructed her to come here. It was worth taking a look, yet, she had no desire to leave the safety of the room and venture out in the dark of night again. Besides, if a car was indeed in the garage, would it even run? Still, the thought of Falcon unconscious and bleeding compelled her to swing her legs over the side of the bed and get to moving. As her light left the old brown and white portrait of Falcon, it highlighted a particular stone in the fireplace jetting out a little further from the others. Curious, she crossed over to examine the crude rock. Running her hand over the stone she grabbed the protruding corner and jiggled. It moved at her interference. Stopping, she looked around. No walls were moving and if they were, she definitely had no intentions of following another passageway down into hell. She pulled at it again, this time it began sliding out of its home, revealing a hidden compartment somewhat like a safe, but with no combination lock. Lowering the heavy rock to the ground, she aimed her light into the cubby hole. A single box lay inside accompanied by a lone envelope. Grabbing the letter, she opened it and shined her light on the paper. It was a death certificate. According to the document, Falcon passed away in the year 1949. Lifting the antique box out of the hole, she opened the lid and discovered several old journals, all belonging to Falcon. Fascinated, she carried the crate over to the bed. Finally, an introspective look inside the life of the cagey man. Settling onto the mattress, she positioned the flashlight for perfect reading and lifted the first book from its hiding place. She opened the cover and read the handwritten words on the first page.

The adventures of Abaddon and Haytham

My memories of a beloved brother, who once walked in the light of peace and was good.

Bronwyn read through pages of stories about Falcon and Abaddon; some were humorous while others were tender and compassionate evoking tears. She was impressed, Falcon was excellent at penning the stories and she thought maybe he should have been chosen as the scribe instead of her.

His deep admiration for his identical twin was evident, but as she switched journals and began reading his memories of Abaddon's treachery, the esteem he held for his brother switched to contempt. The pain in Abaddon's betrayal had taken its toll on Falcon as if his very soul had been ripped from his body, leaving a hollow cave inside of him, filled with echoes of his hatred. The devastating disappointment in what Abaddon had chosen turned to bitterness. This bitterness became a cancer, eating away at him, transforming his own character into an insolent rogue with an ill regard for his own life. The fruit of his resentment produced a dangerous rebellion that if he wasn't careful would catapult him into a world as dark as the one his twin inhabited. The last page in the journal was Falcon's final say on the matter.

And so with part of me missing what then shall I live for if not revenge? My passion is not to destroy my brother because of his wickedness, for even though it pains me to admit, it was his weakness that allowed the invasion of the darkness. I cannot fault him for this flaw for it dwells in every one of us. It's the fissure in the resolute wall of our convictions. This tiny crevice is the key hole that the enemy unlocks with promises of fulfillment; and yet we are not fulfilled. So, in time the tear in our spirit divides, separating us from what is good until the gap is so wide we can no longer return. Is there a way back? What then will fill this void so we may cross back over?

Bronwyn closed the journal, much more educated about Falcon and her nemesis. Yet, with the knowledge there came great sadness. Abaddon was no longer the evil ruthless ruler, but the brother of a friend, taken captive by a much darker adversary. Did this wickedness have a name; a face? What were her chances in going against the pervading darkness? Could she in her quest rescue both Abaddon and Falcon? And what if this impious spirit knew of her weaknesses? She had many. Could she too unknowingly fall prey to its promises?

Outside, the crunching of tires moving into the gravel driveway signaled the approach of a vehicle, interrupting her thoughts. Quickly, she gathered the journals, placing them back into the box. Looking out the window, she saw a car approaching without the use of headlights. Her heart fell, whoever it was intended on a surprise attack. Scrambling, she placed the crate back in the cubby hole and with trembling hands lifted the heavy stone, securing it back in place. Killing the flashlight, she crept back into the bedroom where the owl sat in the ceiling rafters. If critters could use the tree branch as an entrance perhaps she could use it as an exit. Besides, now would be an excellent time to check the detached garage for a car. Placing the strap of the travel bag around her neck, she climbed on top of the hefty limb, inching her way down and stopping where it made a Y shape, connecting to the trunk. Maybe she should just wait in the tree; she doubted they'd look up there, but she wasn't going to take the chance, especially remembering what happened back in Moonshine when she hid in the tree from the cloaked man. Climbing down another branch, she made the jump. She was on the far side of the house and either needed to make her way to the Suburban or the back yard where the garage sat, several feet behind the house. Crouching in the overgrowth, she crawled toward the front. The Suburban was out of the question. A burly looking man stood guard; preventing her from escaping that way again. To the garage it was; staying hunched down she crept to the back.

"She's been inside!"

The announcement coming through the broken windows made her heart skip a beat.

"Her footprints lead upstairs, check it out."

Forcing herself to stay calm, she took in a deep breath for momentum and then dashed from the bushes, darted across the back lawn and slid up against the side of the garage and peered inside. Empty. Now what to do? She needed to move, the garage would be one of the first places they looked should they search the grounds. With nowhere to go but the surrounding woods she made her escape. Fortunately, there was a crude little path, not too overgrown, so she was able to make her way down it, picking up the pace, separating herself from the thugs looking for her. Without much light she wasn't able to see the change in the surface of the footpath and suddenly felt herself slipping, sliding in ankle deep mud. The unexpectedness of the change threw her off balance, sending her falling into shallow water bubbling out from under the rustic wooden door of a turn of the century spring house.

"Damn it!" she cursed again, this time out loud. How many times in one night could she fall off a path and land in frigid water? At least the temperature outside was warm, for that she was thankful.

The spring house resembled a wooden shack. It had a weathered roof, a barricaded door in which the pieces of plywood had been pried away, and one small window near the back with glass so filthy it would be impossible to see through. The place looked as if it hadn't been used for years. Switching on her light she examined the door, looking for the best possible entry and was unnerved to see claw marks scratched into the weathered wood. What kind of animal would make such hideous scrapes? The area didn't seem conducive to grizzlies… mountain lions perhaps. Great, just what she needed, something else to add to the terror of this long night.

Prying open the door she held her breath hoping she wasn't barging in on a family of wildcats. Waving the light from wall to wall she saw the spring house was empty save for the rising water bubbling up with such force that it created a wading pool in the bottom. Before fully committing to entering the moist hideout, Bronwyn flashed the light into the water looking for snakes. Not finding any she slipped on inside, closing the door behind her. Safe inside she kept her flashlight lit while wading across the frigid pool and then took a seat on a concrete slab. She would wait here until they gave up and left. They may have been able to follow her tracks on the dusty floor inside the house but there was no way they would know she had taken off into the woods. She felt safe at least for now, or at least until her light began to fade.

"No, not now, stay with me… please don't do this to me." she whispered her protest; but despite her coaxing the light dimmed and then faded out…darkness.

She was too tired and frustrated to curse this time; besides, she had a suspicion the batteries hadn't simply died but that a force beyond her control extinguished her light. For the first time in several days, the intense heat sensation invaded her body, a warning signal that something wasn't right. She dropped the flashlight and rummaged through the travel bag until her hands touched the cold metal of her cell phone. Pulling it out she turned it on, notification bells began sounding immediately, deafening in contrast to the silence surrounding her. She quickly put the phone on vibrate and the contemplated her next move. She had one bar left before the battery died, she could call 911 and tell them her location. When the police arrived they would have Abaddon's men to deal with, giving her a chance to escape. She would wait in the springhouse until the ruckus was over and then hike her way back to the main road. It seemed like a good plan until her phone went black; this time she cursed and the darkness became tangible, crawling upon the concrete slab with her, blowing its scorching sulfuric breath against her neck. She bristled at the presence, she'd sensed it before. It was the same evil existence that manifest in the passageway, tearing its finger into the side of her face and sending her tumbling into the murkiness of the underground cavern. The same presence swept through Moonshine her first night, tossing her into the angry waters of the lake, trying to drown her. It was this all compassing evil that stole the virtuous spirit of a much loved brother, enslaving him to do it's bidding as a murderous, malevolent enemy. This was her adversary, and what her book of redemption must annihilate.

The angry marauder beat against the door shaking it, demanding entrance. Holding her breath Bronwyn pulled her legs up on to the concrete slab, hugging her knees. The fear was overwhelming, ravaging her body and at this point she'd rather face a thousand of Abaddon's men than this heinous apparition.

A gust of wind blew through the room blowing open the weathered door allowing the sinister wraith to enter. The moist chamber continued to shake, rocking from the foundation upward as a vexed howl filled the room, screeching its hatred for her, hissing its intent in words she couldn't comprehend. Her desire was to run from the dark tomb yet her body wouldn't move. Whether it was intense fear or a force the demonic spirit inflicted upon her, she was paralyzed. Her eyes searched the darkness for a glimmer of hope. What could she do? Her mind went back to the night at the falls where she had a similar experience but this time she knew Travis was not coming to her aid.

Taking in a deep breath, she closed her eyes, trying not to panic she desperately searched for peaceful thoughts to counteract the fear and slow her accelerating heart rate. "Please," she whispered. "I am so lost in all of this. I have no clue what to do. I need some kind of guidance. I am willing, but lost." The heat continued to rise within her as the faint voice of a woman began to sing. The voice was soft and melodic. The music flowed delicately from the unseen woman's mouth directly into Bronwyn's soul. The lyrics of the song were in the unknown tongue yet they somehow stirred the spirit within her. A brilliant white light invaded her thoughts bursting through all the confusion and panic. Rays of blue and lavender burst forth from a magnificent sphere, making her think the room was aglow with fireworks; yet she kept her eyes closed for fear of interrupting the vision. The woman continued her haunting song singing as a mother would to her child. The white ball of light burst, exploding into tiny fragments, each miniscule piece spiraled upward. Bronwyn felt her innermost being soaring through the atmosphere beyond the confines of the dilapidated roof. A gentle breeze tenderly pushed her along, as the glow of the moon cradled her body. The tiny orbs of light encircled her as she flew across the great expanse. One by one the orbs collided with her body, exploding, each having a unique effect on her. Some calmed her, some empowered her, some filled her soul with longing, some offered courage and inspiration, and some offered feelings of emotion she could not comprehend. The explosions became addicting as she anticipated each encounter. Then, a memory; it came suddenly, flashing across the screen of her mind and in that moment she saw it all, everything she'd forgotten, everything that had been stolen from her. At the vision an anguished scream tore from her lungs, coming head to head with the vexed howling of the sinister spirit. Her spirit rose into battle with the opposing force. She screamed again and again, her torment colliding with the vicious rage spewing from the darkness. When her voice could no longer scream she fell into the cool dark water. In the distance she heard the weathered door swing open and heavy footsteps enter the darkness. The small building shook as another vexed howl filled the room and then suddenly faded away as the threatening presence dissipated. A euphoric feeling of love surrounded her. This love empowered her giving her more inner strength than she had ever experienced. The enraptured feeling consumed her, filling her with peace. The orb of light began to fade, the song of the woman drifted off to silence as the bubbling waters swirled around her. Someone was splashing their way toward her. Lifting her from the waters, they carried her outside.

CHAPTER THIRTY

Bethany woke early and joined Lillian in the adjoining restroom to get ready for the day. Even though she'd stayed up pretty late, talking with Jacob, she had no problem getting out of the comfortable bed. She had incentive; Jacob had asked her to meet him at sunrise for a hike back to the falls. He said he had a suspicion and since she was dying to know what it was she agreed to go with him. Besides, he was handsome.

"Where are you off to so early?" Lillian asked while putting a second coat of mascara on her lashes.

Bethany applied a thin layer of gloss over her lips before replying. "Just doing some investigating with Jacob, I mean agent Betancourt."

Lillian lowered the wand and stared at Bethany in the mirror. "So we're on first name basis with the man now are we?"

She grinned, "Well, Agent Betancourt is a mouthful; Jacob is so much easier to say."

"Uh huh," Lillian was sly, "Bethany Betancourt is a mouthful too."

She laughed and then felt guilty for her giddiness. She had only met Jacob because of the tragedy that had befallen Bronwyn. Lillian's next observation didn't add any comfort.

"You're like Bronwyn was a couple of weeks ago, staying out late and then venturing off with a mysterious man. Maybe it's the magic of this place." Grabbing her purse she headed out the door, "Be careful Beth," She gave a haunting whisper, "We wouldn't want you swallowed up in the secrecy of the unknown."

She left the room and Bethany shivered.

Jacob was waiting for her on the front porch; he looked much more approachable in jeans and a t-shirt than he did in his intimidating black suit. Tiny lines creased around the corner of his mouth when he smiled, and she thought it added to his attractiveness, and that when he grinned he favored his great grandfather. He was sporting a backpack, which he informed her carried their breakfast and a thermos of hot coffee they could enjoy once they reached the falls. Her heart skipped a beat at the thought.

They made the hike to the falls in record time; making small talk about the beauty of the place. Bethany told Jacob detailed stories of her stay last week and how, other than the fact that no one else was visiting the hidden town, everything seemed normal. It was when she mentioned *normal* that he chuckled.

"The best disguise," he said, "Is appearing normal."

She'd never thought about it that way, but he was right. Whatever secrets the town was hiding were veiled in the ordinary.

"Not one of us noticed anything unusual the entire time we were here, except Bronwyn." Bethany sighed, "She wanted to leave right away, went hysterical on us during lunch our first day, saying she'd was being stalked by men in hooded robes roaming the woods… no one believed her."

Jacob moved aside a low branch blocking the path. "If she was so frightened what caused her to willingly stay behind when the rest of you left? She must have found something enticing, something worth staying for."

Bethany laughed, "She did, and his name is Travis."

Jacob disagreed, "Then why is she with my great grand-father?"

Bethany stopped walking and looked at him. "I don't know. That is the question of the hour. She was afraid of him, or so she said, and then she shows up on the back of his bike like they're dating or something. She takes him to her parents' house in Texas and introduces him as someone named Dakota, calls him her boyfriend and then fabricates some story about him having her on contract to write a book. Then a blood bath happens at her condo and they disappear into thin air. You tell me, you're the FBI investigator here."

Jacob smiled and motioned for them to continue walking. They'd reached the clearing and he pointed to the rocky staircase leading to the top of the falls. "Let's have our breakfast up there."

Bethany wasn't used to rock climbing and became a little winded with the intensity of the climb. Jacob however, was in excellent shape, scaling up the rocks like a deer with hinds feet, moving easily across the uneven terrain of this mountainous landscape. She felt somewhat embarrassed for tiring so easily and her inability to maneuver through the stony path. The climb was steep but not too treacherous and without the water cascading off the rocks, there was no fear of slipping. Still, she was grateful when they finally reached the top.

Opening his backpack he pulled out a thermos and two mugs. The aroma of the coffee, combined with the scents of spruce and pine, was the perfect morning blends; invigorating her senses. He uncurled a paper bag and retrieved two large egg and cheese biscuits.

Bethany was surprised, "You cooked?"

He grinned again, "I was too excited to sleep so I got up early."

Bethany wondered if his excitement stemmed from the investigation or meeting her for the walk. She hoped it was the latter.

"Okay Jacob," she said biting into her biscuit. "Don't keep me waiting. I wanna hear your suspicions."

"It's simple really," he said while chewing. "You got a town of people who never age, hiding out up here for hundreds of years, with a deep secret."

Bethany grinned this time, "You think they have the infamous fountain of youth?"

He shook his head, "No."

His answer surprised her, "No?"

He took a swallow of his coffee, "If they had access to the fountain of youth, my great grandfather would have shared it with my great grandmother. They loved each other dearly, why would he continue to stay young and allow her to age?"

Bethany shrugged, "Maybe she didn't want to live forever."

"Maybe," he said, "But then I think my great grandfather would have refused the potent water and aged with her. What's the good of immortality if you live alone?"

Bethany nodded, “True.”

“Besides,” Jacob continued, “A group of random people who discover buried treasure is more than likely to turn on each other in time, or at least one member of the group will spill the beans, leaking the secret. So what is it about this assembly of people that allow them to exist up here for years in unity and pull off this facade flawlessly?”

Bethany shook her head, “I don’t know. You got me there.”

He smiled and took a deep breath. “My suspicion is they are guarding the Tree of Life.”

“You’re serious?” She laughed. “You mean the Holy Bible Tree of Life? The one Adam and Eve wasn’t supposed to eat from?”

This time it was Jacob who laughed, “You need to study your Bible more young lady. That was the tree of knowledge, not the tree of life.”

She blushed at her ignorance, “Sorry I’m no Bible scholar.”

He grinned at her and that caused her to blush even more. “Well let me give you a little Sunday school lesson then. Once they ate from the tree of knowledge, they were banned from the Tree of Life. The serpent had told them the truth, and once they had eaten, they had all compassing knowledge and not necessarily knowledge of evil alone. And now, God could not allow them to eat from the tree, and live forever with that knowledge. So he made them leave the garden and then he put the tree in another dimension.”

Bethany's eyes were wide now. "You think God put the tree here?"

Shrugging, Jacob leaned back against a rock and sipped his coffee.

She thought a moment, "I wonder why? Why would God not want them to have knowledge?"

Jacob sat aside his mug and wiped his mouth with his arm. "It's not necessarily the knowledge of evil. I think it's all compassing knowledge that he didn't want them knowing. It's not always expedient to know everything. Wisdom however, is different from knowledge. With life comes wisdom, so eating from the tree of life must have given wisdom and wisdom is better than knowledge. You can have all the knowledge in the world but if you do not have the wisdom to use it, then that's where you become dangerous and maybe what God was trying to prevent."

Bethany shook her head in disbelief, "Wow, and I never took any of that as literal."

"Most people don't."

"So things like that really exist?"

Jacob took a deep breath, "Bethany my dear, I work for the FBI. We not only investigate terrorist, gangsters, mobsters, and serial killers, but we have a special branch devoted solely to incomprehensible mysteries. I'm just saying; nothing is impossible."

She sighed, "As adventurous as I thought I was; I think I'd rather exist in normalcy. There are some things I'd rather not know."

Pouring the last of his coffee out on the rocks, he began loading the back pack, "That's too bad. I'm leaving today, heading out to the old homestead; there's something there I need to check on and I was going to invite you to come. But if the mystery is too much for you…"

She smiled, intrigued at the invite, "I'd love to come."

CHAPTER THIRTY-ONE

Bronwyn stirred in her sleep, too tired to open her eyes. Her head throbbed and when she swallowed it felt like a million pins were sticking in her throat. She tried to think but her mind was cloudy. She'd been so many different places in the past week, existing on hardly any sleep, her rest always interrupted by a desperate run for her life. Was she in danger? Should she run now? Where was she? Think…

The fog filling her head moved aside just enough for her to remember the ram shackled house…Falcon's journals…the springhouse…the footsteps!

She sat up fast and looked around. The room was dark giving her no clue as to where she was.

"Hello?" her voice was hoarse and it hurt to speak.

Someone stirred in the far corner. A dark silhouette moved from the shadows making its way toward the bed. Then, the sound of a striking match echoed across the room, the tiny flame dispelled the gloom of the dark chamber. Bronwyn took in a quick breath, "Falcon!"

Relief flooded over her, he was alright. He'd escaped Abaddon's men and come to her rescue once again which was pretty amazing considering the condition he was in the last time she saw him.

"I thought you were dead. How'd you…"

He smiled, turning up the wick of a small lantern. The calm she felt only seconds ago shattered. Something wasn't right… something about his smile… No, that wasn't it…She gasped again, backing away, the scar beneath his eye was missing!

"Please don't be frightened of me. That would distress me so."

The voice was different too. It was smooth, polished, and eloquent; and even though he'd asked her not to be frightened, terror gripped at the realization.

"Where am I? Where's Falcon?"

His smile didn't grow but remained the same. His eyes however skewered directly into her, demoralizing her to the point of where she had no other choice than to look away. Her eyes fell upon a strange vial hanging around his neck. The sight of it brought added unrest. Icy fingers touched her chin, lifting her face back toward his.

"You are safe, in the city of Eden. Haytham, or Falcon as you know him, is being well taken care of; I can assure you."

Eden? His declaration paralyzed her. Terror numbed her to speechlessness and although she longed to question him profusely her body would not allow it.

"I am no one for you to fear," he continued, "And yet no one to trifle with as well. Contrary to what you have been told by those who plot my demise, I am not your enemy."

He poured water from a pitcher into an ornate goblet and handed it to her. She didn't reach for it so he sighed and sat it back on the table.

"You are very lovely, by what name are you called?"

"Abaddon?" pain stabbed at her throat as her voice choked out the words. This time Abaddon held the goblet to her lips forcing the drink.

"What a coincidence, that is my name as well." He grinned and she swallowed the water. It felt heavenly against her parched throat and his playful response lifted some of her fear.

"My name's Bronwyn," she said wiping the dribble from her chin. "How did I get here?"

His eyes impaled her once again and she knew by his silence he wasn't going to answer the question, not the way she wanted him to anyway.

"You located the second portal my love, transportation was quite simple after that."

"So what happens next? Are you going to kill me?"

His smile faded and she wished she hadn't asked the question.

"It grieves me that you think so ill of me. As I mentioned before, you need not fear me. If it was my intention to kill you, I would have ended your life when I found you lying helpless in the shallow pool. Besides, I usually do not make it a habit to slay the innocent."

"Then why did you bring me here?"

"Because my dearest Bronwyn, you are being deceived. The stories Haytham and his cohorts have told you are not entirely the truth. They have painted a grim picture indeed and I fear have misled you. So, before you begin to pen your oeuvre, I hope to expose their false charges and in a sense exonerate myself. I simply request you give me the honor of allowing me to clarify my side, and why I felt the need to execute the man I knew to be a threat to our world. Afterwards you are free to make your choice. "

She listened. His words were convincing and his motives seemed fair enough but she wondered what the consequences would be if after hearing his argument she continued to give her allegiance to his enemies.

"And if I still decide to write the story, after I hear your defense, you will permit that?"

Abaddon stood from the bed and she watched him make his way to the door. He looked identical to Falcon minus the scar and the clothing choice. He was dressed casually yet elegant in dark linen pants, a light gray pirate type shirt, opened in the front revealing the strange vial. He accessorized with a scarf draped once around his neck, the fringed ends hanging open and a wide leather belt cinched tightly around his waist. His pants were tucked into knee high soft suede boots.

Stopping at the door he pivoted on his heels, facing her once again.

"I will send my personal attendants in to care for you. They will honor any request except the one to leave. You are confined to the castle and the surrounding gardens for your protection."

"Protection?"

He shook the hair from his eyes, allowing them to bore into her one last time.

"Beautiful Bronwyn, there are many in this world who do not wish your book to be written. Given the chance, they will kill you."

CHAPTER THIRTY-TWO

Abaddon's personal attendants flooded the chamber only seconds after his departure which made her believe they had been hovering outside the door waiting to do his bidding. There were seven altogether, five women doing the serving and two men standing guard. All were silent as they went about their task of drawing a bath, brushing her hair, laying out clothing and serving her refreshment. They only spoke if spoken to, and then used the least amount of words possible.

After a tranquil bath in milky sweet smelling waters, she received a relaxing manicure and pedicure. Halfway thru the foot massage she began feeling somewhat anxious knowing Falcon was lying in prison, hurt and possibly hanging on to life. Even though she needed the bath and relished the pampering, she felt it was an extreme waste of time considering the urgency of her situation. She longed to see Falcon and planned on asking Abaddon on their next encounter. The terror she felt for Abaddon earlier was gone, replaced by wild curiosity and a spark of adventure.

She would not allow her mind to mull over the fact that she was in another dimension. It was too much to take in and she knew dwelling on it would only bring on extreme anxiety and handicap her judgment. Her best defense would be to remain sharp and alert to her surroundings while gaining all the knowledge she could. That, she felt, would be the key to her return.

The ladies finished off her nails with a pink gloss and then dressed her in a strapless, pale yellow, Athenian style gown. She gazed at her reflection wearing the form fitting bodice and thought the attendants must have performed some kind of magic; transforming her into a tantalizing goddess. For the first time, in a long time, she felt beautiful.

They slipped a pair of ankle strap sandals on her feet and then stood back to survey their work. It was then one of them spoke without being prompted.

"Dinner is being served in Abaddon's private dining room. He has requested your presence. Hamza and Conall will escort you there."

The beefy guards gave a slight bow of their heads acknowledging their assignment and swiftly escorted her out of her isolated chamber, down a broad hallway, and then descended a wide spiraling staircase. They made their way across the floor of an exquisitely furnished sitting room and through a set of double French style doors. Stepping outside, her delicate sandals clicked along a cobblestone walkway bordered by flowering bushes, hedges, hanging ferns and moss covered trees.

The sun, hanging low in the sky, radiated its warmth, while birds scattered across the soft violet expanse finding their rest in the massive branches of nearby trees. Other than her unfamiliar surroundings, this world proved no different than her own. The manor grounds resembled a small renaissance city, quaint and simple yet surprisingly modern all the same. Many people scurried about, all staring at their infamous visitor, much like the citizens of Moonshine on her first day in town. These people however did not share the same excitement as the Moonshiners. In fact, Bronwyn noticed her presence seemed to bring a much different emotion and it was difficult to discern whether they were saddened by her arrival or angry. In any case she was grateful for her guards.

Her escorts led her to a neighboring structure with enormous wooden doors. Grabbing the brass handle, Hamza swung open the heavy gates allowing her entrance.

The place was breathtaking, and in all of Bronwyn's travels she'd never witnessed anything as lavish. Cathedral style, stained glass windows surrounded the room, the top of each pointing high to the third floor dome ceiling. Plush sofas, divans and soft rugs littered the floor of the colossal area. Rectangular tables, no higher than a foot, formed a three sided open square in the center of the room, allowing the waiters easy access. Lush decorative loungers, surrounded the outside of the low lying table allowing the diners to recline while eating. Ornamental fountains occupied the open area as well, offering a soothing ambiance to the reclining guest along with a small band of musicians pacifying the listeners.

Unsure of the situation, Bronwyn took in a nervous breath. She was the last to arrive, all the other diners were already at the table lounging and drinking from ornamental goblets. At her entrance the idle chatter dissipated giving way to curious stares. One of the servers quickly made his way over to her, promptly escorting her to the settee nearest Abaddon. His stoic expression melted into a pleasing smirk as Bronwyn took to the comfortable couch, reclining on her left side.

Leaving the others, the servants congregated around her, tending to her alone. Dipping her hands in a bowl of warm water, they washed them and then wiped them dry with a soft cloth. A servant filled her goblet with drink, while another brought her large portions of food laying out a spread of broiled fish, rice, cheese, nuts, fresh fruit, a variety of bread and creamy sauces for dipping. Once they'd served her they brought food to the rest of the guest. There were no utensils on the table; everyone used their hands dipping into their own personal bowls. Bronwyn watched the others eat, spellbound by the eccentricity of it all.

The musicians continued playing, their melody evoking a greater sense of lonesomeness, and although Bronwyn was the obvious guest of honor at a prestigious dinner party, she felt isolated. Each note of their heart-rending tune brought with it suffocating thoughts of being trapped in another dimension far from Travis, never being near him again. She wondered if he had any way of knowing her situation and figured he didn't since she had no idea where he was either. Her heart nearly ruptured at the thought and tears burned at her eyes with every stirring note the orchestra played. She wished they would stop or at least change the dirge to a livelier tune.

A cold substance touched her lips, breaking her trance and interrupting her mournful thoughts. Abaddon held a piece of bread covered in a cold creamy sauce to her mouth. "Eat, beautiful Bronwyn. Tonight's banquet is in your honor, each dish prepared specifically for you and while you are a delicate specimen of true loveliness, I fear you have become somewhat emaciated. Tell me, when was your last decent meal?"

Her mouth accepted the offered morsel, leaving a trace of pottage on her lips which Abaddon promptly wiped away with his fingers. Her stomach tightened at his touch and she tried not to shudder as a new dread began manifesting inside of her. Quickly dipping into her bowl, she began to eat so he wouldn't feel the need to feed her again. And although she kept her head bowed, concentrating on her food, she felt his gaze upon her and her cheeks burned hot because of it.

After a few minutes of painful silence the dining guest began chatting again and even though they spoke in the foreign dialect their body language was easy to understand. Each one trying desperately to outshine the other while attempting to gain the favor of their esteemed host. Abaddon however appeared apathetic to their triviality concentrating only on Bronwyn. She tried keeping her eyes low but every now and then they would glance up, and each time, she found his eyes fixed on her. She tried looking at the other diners but received in return, scowls from the women and looks of distrust and loathing from most of the men. There was one lovely woman however, who kept silent during most of the meal. She too seemed disgusted by the showy antics of the group and offered Bronwyn a soft comforting smile when their eyes met. The meal continued on for what seemed like hours and sometime during the whole of it, the sun set, and no longer filled the colorful stained glass with light. The room grew dim and soon the attendants began lighting the dozens of candelabras sitting in various locations around the room. The orchestra continued playing, the diners continued to gorge and chatter, and Abaddon persisted his unrelenting inspection of Bronwyn. She sighed, in all the tumultuous events of the past week; this occasion was proving to be the most torturous.

With the main course finally over, the servers cleared the table making way for trays of delectable desserts. The platters they laid on the table were laden with puddings, custards, fruit tarts, cakes, and an assortment of pastries.

Abaddon spoke and when he did, the room resonated with his voice. "Before we bring our next guest into the room, I request the language of choice be English as to accommodate the lovely Bronwyn. I will now dismiss the musicians and the servers, and all the women except Bronwyn of course. Your desserts will be served in the starlight chamber.

Her stomach knotted at his announcement and the seed of fear attempted to take root once again.

The room cleared quickly, the chatter gone leaving an unnerving silence. This time Bronwyn kept her eyes on Abaddon. His composed demeanor seemed to change and as he drank from his goblet, she wondered what malevolent thoughts were invading his consciousness. He poured more into his chalice, savoring the drink, moving his tongue across his lips, like a serpent sniffing into the air. His pupils darkened as his eyes stared into the open room, focusing on nothing. The pencil mustache outlining his lips pointed downward framing his frown.

The heavy doors clattered opened. Bronwyn gasped at the sight. Two brawny guards shoved Falcon into the chamber. Blood oozed from his nose and lips. The eye above his scar was bruised and swollen shut. His hair was matted, sticking to the front of his face and a bloodstained bandage was wrapped around his right thigh. He wore a brass collar fastened tight around his neck with chains clasped around his wrist and ankles. His clothes were gone, only a loin cloth of sorts covered his nakedness.

Standing from her reclining position, Bronwyn intended to make her way over to Falcon but a harsh command from Elam stopped her. "I'd stay put if I were you sweetheart."

She turned to face the arrogant man who gave the unwanted advice. She'd seen him before; in the underground cavern, leading the revolt. He was the man who easily gunned down one of his own; no doubt the one who ordered the massacre, killing Vulture, Hawke and Macaw.

"Well you're not me," she bit back, her anger for Falcon's condition fueling her courage. With determination she made her way toward Falcon. Elam's pride interfered once again.

"Stop her!" he gave the order directly to Hamza who moved away from the wall and caught her by the upper arm, pulling her back away from Falcon. Appalled, she attempted to yank loose but his tight clutch would not allow it.

"Sit!" Elam ordered as if she were a misbehaving dog. Her disgust for him would not allow her to sit, so she stood in defiance, staring at him with eyes like daggers. Elam nodded to Hamza who with one effortless tug slammed her back onto the plush divan. Fury boiled inside, giving way to a spirited rebellion. In retaliation she grabbed the edge of a dish filled with warm custard and hurled it toward Elam; the contents splashing into his face and covering his expensive attire. The room grew deathly quiet, the tension hung thick in the air, all eyes on Elam and Bronwyn. Even Abaddon sat unmoved watching the battle of wills. Not to be shamed in front of the men Elam stood abruptly, and in one swift move pushed her flat on the settee then clinched his hand around her delicate neck. His fingers circled around her throat much like the brass collar Falcon wore, and then he squeezed enough to steal her breath. She gasped for air and he climbed on top of her pressing his face close to hers.

"The plan was to kill you on sight. Your life has been spared due to unforeseen circumstances. Still, you're better off to me dead so I wouldn't press the limits anymore. You understand?"

She couldn't swallow let alone make a sound, and for the first time since her arrival she suffered. The wickedness of the enemy was now set in motion and the seed of terror began to grow.

"You understand?" Elam asked again, tightening his grip around her neck. He wanted her submission and she refused to give it. From where he was positioned she could easily raise her leg and knee him, but wasn't sure if she could get enough momentum to do any harm. If she made the attempt and it fell short he might end her life right there. He tightened his choke hold again and she wheezed. The light in the room seemed to dim and in a distance she heard Falcon say, "Submit for now Scribe, it's your only chance."

Before she could acknowledge Falcon's request and give in to Elam, Abaddon's voice resonated across the room.

"Enough!" at his command, Elam loosened his grip but finalized his disapproval with a hard slap across her face. Against her unyielding resolve, she rolled onto her side, gasping for air and cried out in pain.

Leaning forward, Abaddon cupped her head in his hand and fed her drink from his goblet. The sweet nectar mixed with the copper taste of blood oozing from her split lip. She stifled at the taste of it. After drinking a few swallows, Abaddon again wiped her lips, cleaning the blood with his fingers. Expressionless, he stared into her eyes and then licked the blood from his fingers. Shuddering she looked away, horror flourishing inside of her.

He faced Elam, "We've wasted enough time and I needn't remind you that time is no longer on our side." He picked up his chalice and returned to his reclining position, "Give your report."

Elam wiped the custard from his clothing the best he could before turning to the table. He glared at her and in some strange way she almost feared him more than she did Abaddon. His arrogance fueled his ambition, and a prideful man desperately trying to advance his influence is dangerous; especially when there is no integrity or morality to channel his lust.

He cleared his throat, but not in nervousness. “My strategy for the most part has been quite successful. However, as in all best laid plans, there are unforeseen circumstances that slow the progression of the operation. I was able to cast suspicion in the hearts of a few of Haytham’s men. They unwillingly gave up his location and as I suspected he had the prophesied scribe in his keep. The identity of the scribe however was one of those unforeseen circumstances and my directives were changed because of it. I complied with our Lord’s wishes and now we have in our possession, the scribe and Haytham. What we still lack is Asa, and the book of redemption which was unfortunately left in the other world. However, we have the Scribe and a wordless book without the author is useless.”

For the first time since her arrival she thought of her travel bag and the book of redemption. Where was it? Had she left it behind in the spring house? Her heart raced at what she had already written and the consequences if anyone were to read it.

“It’s not wordless.” She interrupted his report, inciting alarm on the faces of the men.

“I began the story already.” Abaddon’s eyes cut over to Elam no doubt reprimanding him with his mind and in the deafening silence Falcon raised his eyes and flashed her a concealed grin.

Elam made light of her announcement, "What does it matter? So she began the story, she couldn't have written much. They've been on the run for the past week; at best she penned two or three pages." He gave a confident smirk. "I'm right, aren't I? You were only able to pen a couple of pages?"

She returned the sneer, "It matters not how many pages were penned, what's important is the power of the words written." She lifted the chalice to her lips, carefully avoiding the painful split. "Ever heard of the Latin term In medias res?"

He hadn't and so she swallowed the sweet nectar before enlightening him.

"It's a literary narrative technique where the story begins at the conclusion, rather than the beginning and then backtracks." She smiled savoring his pained expression.

"I'm quite good at it; I adopted that writing style some time ago. Who knows, I may have begun the book of redemption in that manor, if I did, then I'd say your fate has already been sealed."

There was a silence for the space of about ten seconds before the room turned to chaos. Elam's voice rose above the uproar, "She's bluffing."

Raising her eyebrows, she challenged his accusation, "Why would I make that up? The second prophesy said the beginning of the book was mine and if I followed my heart I would preserve life…so I did."

At the mention of the second prophesy the clamor intensified. Elam tried to regain control but when Abaddon stood the bedlam stopped.

"It sickens me to see the elect become rattled and lose all restraint at the slightest hint of hostility. If our fate were already sealed would we be here at this hour with two of our most notorious enemies as our prisoners? It's a disgraceful regime that accepts defeat in their hearts before the war is finished waging. Any of you who accept subjugation on circumstantial evidence will be executed immediately. Am I clear on this?"

The men shifted on their chaises, self-conscious of their esteemed leader's disapproval. Even Elam wore a shameful expression, which switched to bitter hatred when he looked Bronwyn's way. She'd humiliated him in front of Abaddon, and his own men, knowing somehow, someway he'd make her pay. Abaddon was her only chance of escaping Elam's wrath. For whatever reason he seemed to like her, but then again that could be to her detriment as well.

Abaddon returned to his chaise, resting on his left elbow. He patted the open space next to him, and then extended his arm to Bronwyn. Her heart thundered against her chest, she'd displayed amazing nerve going up against Elam in a battle of wits but feared her spunk might take a beating under his heinous plotting.

Swallowing hard, she remained frozen on her personal sofa. She had no desire to cuddle next to Abaddon; he'd touched her lips twice already, even licking her blood from his fingers and the thought of his unwanted advances turned her stomach.

His eyes bore into hers, then tilting his head; he patted the area beside him once again. She remained frozen yet made the mistake of glancing toward Falcon. She didn't know why she did but wished she hadn't. Abaddon noticed, and a slight nod was the only instruction needed for the guards to club him in the back of his legs; sending him to his knees. It was then she noticed the deep lashes cut into his back. It was when the guard lifted his club again poised to strike that Bronwyn made her move, jumping from her settee and joining Abaddon on his. She didn't recline but sat in the offered space which seemed to please him. Leaning high on his elbow he stroked her hair, while touching the softness of her cheeks.

"Don't hurt him...please. He doesn't deserve to be treated that way."

Laughter erupted from around the table followed by opinionated comments of the legends surrounding Falcon. Elam's sarcastic voice launched a pathetic rebuttal.

"The punishment for high treason is death and I believe that holds true in the world you come from as well."

"If that be the case then all of you should be sentenced first. For it is my understanding, that Abaddon led the rebellion that dissolved the allegiance with the three governing princes of Eden."

At her words a hush fell across the room, the silence so stark that the sound of the trickling fountain seemed like a massive waterfall. No one spoke, not even Bronwyn, although her mind raced with a million reprimands, she dare not utter another, not yet anyway. Her candor surprised her. It had been sometime since she'd been this gutsy. The break up with Ryan had changed her, stripping her of her spirited personality and sense of adventure. Bethany had been right; she had changed and hadn't noticed it until now. Maybe it was traveling through the dimension, or the fight to save her life that jolted her back. Whatever the case, there was a sense of freedom in being herself again.

Rising to a sitting position, Abaddon put his arm around her, drawing her close. Avoiding her swollen lip, he placed a lingering kiss on her neck before whispering in her ear. "Do you love Haytham?"

Her stomach constricted at his touch and she fought to stay calm. She didn't want to display fear, for if Abaddon knew of her faintness he'd use it to his advantage. She turned her mouth to his and whispered back her disparaging answer.

"I suppose if I did, it would help me get through this. Since you two are identical I could always pretend you were him."

He laughed and his eyes danced. Then standing abruptly he headed for the exit.

"We're done for tonight." With those words he stormed out through the massive doors leaving everyone baffled… everyone except Bronwyn.

CHAPTER THIRTY-THREE

The soft rap on the chamber door startled Bronwyn. Had she been sleeping she'd of never heard it. But ever since she returned from the dining room, sleep would not come. She'd laid in the regal bed for some time, contemplating her situation, the sexual advances of Abaddon, Elam's loathing of her and Falcon's physical condition. She figured he was alright emotionally; he was strong-willed, determined. Besides, the grin he'd flashed confirmed he was still his wayward self; no doubt planning his escape and the criminal beating of the guards holding him. She'd spared his life for now anyway, insinuating to Abaddon that she didn't love him. She did love Falcon, but not in the way Abaddon was referring. There was only one man she truly loved and he was worlds away. Her heart burned at the thought of him and she wondered if he was thinking of her, and if he was concerned that she was missing in action. He probably figured out by now that Abaddon's men had captured her, and she hoped he didn't think she was dead. She'd been away from him for as long as she'd known him, and she wondered how she could love a man she'd only known for such a short amount of time. It was crazy, but she couldn't help it. The love she felt for him was like nothing she'd ever experienced before. And just as traveling to the new dimension had renewed her self-awareness, it had also heightened her longing to be with him.

The rap at the door sounded again and her stomach tighten, hoping Abaddon wasn't coming in with certain intentions. Maybe she should feign sleeping and her clandestine guest would go away. Another soft knock and she figured Abaddon being who he was would just enter and not wait for an invitation. Whoever was outside was knocking softly as not to call attention to themselves. Figuring it might be important; she climbed out from under the silk sheets of the magnificent bed. Unlocking the door, she opened it just wide enough to see the beautiful woman from dinner with the soft smile.

"Please may I come in?"

Curious, Bronwyn bid her entrance.

"I do apologize for waking you from your slumber."

"Actually you didn't. I haven't been able to sleep."

"I can empathize with that," that woman's words were tender. "It's not surprising considering the dramatic turn of events after dinner, still the hour is late and for that I apologize."

Bronwyn wondered how the woman knew what happened after the evening meal since the lot of them had been sequestered to another room. "So you heard?"

The woman smiled. "News like that travels fast, even if it does transpire during a covert meeting. Bedside's Elam's soiled clothing sort of gave it away." She laughed delicately and touched Bronwyn on the hand. "You've got spunk honey, hang on to it and keep your wits about you, it will help you survive."

Bronwyn relaxed, finally a friend, possibly someone to confide in, and enlighten her on how to stay alive in this dimension until she could find a way to return home. And as if the woman could read her mind she offered just that. The expression on her face grew serious as she moved close to Bronwyn and motioned to the outdoor veranda.

"Have you smelled the fragrances of the evening? They're quite delightful and therapeutic. The aromas will aid in relaxing you so you can sleep."

This was her secret way of luring Bronwyn onto the balcony so they could talk without the fear of being overheard, which suddenly made Bronwyn paranoid, wondering if there were listening devices or cameras hidden in her room.

The night air was balmy, a soothing breeze stirred through the trees, mixing the fragrances of the flowering plants, delivering the pleasing aroma onto the upper balcony. Bronwyn inhaled and smiled. The perfume brought a euphoric feeling; she'd smelled this bouquet before and recently, where? The scent desired to take her back to a particular event, a blessed memory that she had forgotten. Her heart skipped, longing to unlock the memory, it was there, close, within the reach of her fingertips. She inhaled again and her mind went to Travis.

"Smells heavenly doesn't it?" the woman interrupted her dreaming.

"It does."

The woman moved in closer and spoke in hushed whispers.

"Time is not on our side so I will get to the purpose of my late night call. I do apologize for my ill manners. I have yet to introduce myself to you. My name is Kenalycia and they say you know my Asa."

Bronwyn's cheeks burned a crimson red and although her heart dropped into her stomach it raced while doing so.

"Is he well?" Kenalycia asked, tears burning in her eyes at the question. Bronwyn's throat tightened preventing her from speaking so she shook her head instead.

Kenalycia sighed, and then took in a deep breath. "Has he waited for me or does he love another?"

Bronwyn forced a smile, holding back the tears that were pooling just behind her eyes. Her heart thundered and suddenly she felt extremely exhausted. The first time she saw Ryan on the cover of a magazine with Gabriella could not begin to compare to the way she felt now. Swallowing hard, she bit back the emotion. She didn't want to cry, not in front of Kenalycia but she wasn't sure how much longer she could keep her tears at bay.

"The rumor is his heart belongs to only one person." She worked hard at keeping her voice from quaking. "He's waited faithfully."

Kenalycia dropped her face into her hands and began weeping. She was a beauty, ivory skin, ebony hair and emerald green eyes. Her lips were full and her lashes fanned wide across her lids, giving her such an innocent look.

"It was such a wicked thing that happened. We were robbed, separated by evil, never having the chance to live our life together. Abaddon led the revolt the night of our union. He kidnapped me and had me confined to the palace. After Haytham helped me escape through the portal, Abaddon's men found me right away and brought me back. My recovery was top secret, Asa never knew. The day he went through the portal without me was the day I died inside. After Asa was gone Abaddon made me his wife. I've survived only with the blessed hope that I will be with my dear Asa one day. And now…you're here and it seems possible again." She hung her head, "I hope he will have me even though I've been with Abaddon."

Looking away, Bronwyn let the breeze dry her misting eyes. She took in a deep breath, "I'm sure his love for you far surpasses that."

"Will you take me to him?" Kenalycia's question surprised her. Her first reaction was to say, "*Not on your life sweetie, finders keepers, I have the key to the portal and I'm heading back alone".* Instead, she thought of the joy it would bring Travis if she showed up with his love in tow. But, could she do it? She loved him herself with a strong powerful love and although she couldn't explain it, she knew it wasn't a lustful crush. There was a painful depth to it. But then again, wasn't that the true love Travis had defined for her so beautifully that night in the garden? Could she give him away, knowing she would never experience him, but he would experience all he'd ever dreamed? She could if her love was for him and not herself.

"I'm a prisoner here, same as you. I am not allowed to leave."

Kenalycia moved in closer, "For years I have been plotting my escape. The one problem was that Abaddon controlled the portal. Now you control it, so with your help I will be able to put my plan into action."

Bronwyn offered her second excuse, "I don't know how to use the portal and for that matter I'm not sure I'm the one who controls it."

"Yes, you do control it, you came through it alone. Abaddon found you here, lying in the shallow pool at the falls."

She came through alone? Bronwyn fought through the haze of that night. She remembered hiding in the spring house. The rest was a blur. Concentrating, she faintly recalled something terrifying coming into the darkness, scratches on the door, then the song of the woman, the intense heat, the moon, the tiny orbs of light…it was all coming back! There was a memory…something she'd forgotten about, something very important, what was it? And just as the memory began to take root, Kenalycia touched Bronwyn's shoulder, interrupting the revelation, leaving the events of the night just as hazy as before.

"Are you alright dear? You seem perplexed."

"It's all just a tad bit overwhelming," she said, frustrated at her intrusion. Kenalycia's wide eyes locked in on hers, "I understand completely, but we must make haste if we intend to make it to the portal before sunrise."

"Leave now?" Kenalycia's anxiousness was understandable but Bronwyn never fathomed she meant to escape immediately. She seemed somewhat pushy and it didn't set well with Bronwyn and she wondered if her irritation stemmed from jealousy.

"Yes, now. My dear take it from one who knows, by tomorrow night you will be in Abaddon's bed. He is quite captivated with you and he has no qualms in taking what he wants. As a matter of fact I am somewhat surprised he hasn't had you escorted to his bedchamber already."

Bronwyn shuddered at the thought.

Noticing Bronwyn's fear, Kenalycia gave another warning, "And it gets worse. Some of the women here are ruthless. They all desire to be intimate with Abaddon.

Given the chance they will hurt you. You should have heard their plotting during desert."

Leaving sounded like the thing to do but then there was the matter of Falcon. It didn't feel right leaving him behind.

Excuse number three, "I can't leave without Falcon."

Kenalycia looked puzzled, "You have a pet bird?"

"Haytham…I meant Haytham. I can't leave without him, especially since Abaddon plans on executing him. He saved my life so many times, it wouldn't be right to abandon him."

Again Kenalycia's lips melted into the soft smile. "You are so lovely, no wonder you were preordained to be the Scribe. I can imagine the stories you have penned are filled with sacrificial love. It's beautiful really, something so foreign to our world, especially during these days of Abaddon's rule."

For a moment it seemed Kenalycia had disregarded the urgency in her mission as she gazed across the veranda, staring into the starlit sky, as if she were reliving cherished memories once forgotten.

"No matter," she said breaking her own trance. "Rescuing Haytham at this point is suicide. But don't be troubled, Abaddon will not kill him anytime soon. He'll need him. Like you, Haytham also has the key to the portal. With you gone, Abaddon won't be able to access it without him."

Kenalycia's knowledge on the matter seemed reasonable; still it seemed cruel to leave him behind.

"Please," Kenalycia was losing patience, "if we're to accomplish this we must leave now. The two men guarding your door are my friends. They will accompany us there safely; but we must make our escape now, otherwise it will be too late."

"And what will the punishment will be if we're caught?"

"We won't be caught," Kenalycia was adamant. "I believe it's mine and Asa's destiny to be together, we were stopped before; we won't be again. You have arrived and now the promises are being fulfilled. Besides we have Hamza and Conall with us. They are the two highest ranking guards in the entire city of Eden. No one will question us, if we are seen with them."

Heavy hearted, Bronwyn sighed and tried to think of another excuse to delay their expedition but there wasn't one.

"Okay, let's go."

She dressed back into the Athenian gown wishing she had something more appropriate to wear, but the servants had taken her clothes, leaving her with only the dress and the silk nightgown she was wearing. Of her two choices, the dress seemed the most appropriate. When she finished changing Kenalycia gave a soft rap on the door. Hamza opened it and nodded acknowledging all was clear. Kenalycia squeezed Bronwyn's hand and together they tiptoed behind Hamza and Conall down the splendid spiraling staircase across the sitting room and out through the double French doors.

Once they'd made their way out of the main castle and across the grounds, it was only a half hour walk to the portal. They didn't talk much; and when they did, it was usually in the other language. Bronwyn didn't care;

she didn't have a lot to say anyway. She purposely kept her mind off the subject at hand; but as hard as she tried to not think about it, she found herself unwillingly rehearsing what she would say to Travis.

Hi honey, I'm home and I brought you a souvenir from Eden.

That wouldn't work; he probably would be offended that she referred to his lifelong love as some kind of vacation knick-knack. Maybe…

Hi Travis, I'm back and would you look what the cat drug in.

No that seemed too disparaging, like she was comparing Kenalycia to a disheveled dead rat. How about bearing her soul?

*Hello Travis, I went to Eden and met Kenalycia and I brought her to you because I know having her back will make you happy. Even though it kills me to hand her over to you, I will do it because for some reason I love you. I can't explain why my heart is so drawn to someone I've only known a week. It makes no sense yet the first time my eyes looked into yours that stormy night on the bridge, my soul connected to your soul and it has not rested since that moment. It longs to be near you, aches at the thought of you, yearns for your touch and tries to remind me of something I have misplaced and need to find. To be honest, I feel adrift without you and I never realized how lost I was until I stood before you that night, and for a brief fleeting second I felt as if I'd come home after having been gone for years…*Tears pooled in her eyes, spilling over and trickling down her cheeks. She was glad the early morning hour remained dark; that way no one would notice the pain etched in her face.

The morning air was heavy with dew, soaking the tall grass; and even though Bronwyn held the hem of her dress high, it still absorbed the water. The misty air wreaked havoc on her hair as well as the luscious curls the servants put in the night before; now, her tresses hung limp, sticking to her neck. She glanced over at Kenalycia who resembled a fragile goddess; her perfect lips were pursed in an anticipated smile, no doubt conjuring up the romantic welcome that awaited her. Her thick mane of hair seemed to come alive with body, and the tiny dewdrops clung to her ebony locks like miniature stars in the midnight sky. Bronwyn no longer felt beautiful in her Athenian dress.

Abruptly, Hamza, stopped and spoke to Kenalycia and Conall in the foreign tongue and then retreated back a ways, disappearing into the trees.

Bronwyn wished they'd clue her in without her having to ask, and again she felt annoyed and hoped it didn't show in her voice.

"What's' going on?"

"My apologies for our rudeness, I forget you do not speak the language. Hamza is making sure no one is following. It is possible for hitchhikers to sneak into the portal making the trip through the dimension. Once the portal opens, it remains accessible for a good seven minutes allowing easy access for any stowaways. That is what happened during my escape. Everything turned to chaos. Haytham and Asa were so engaged in fighting off the enemy; they never saw the men jump into the portal and come after me. I was apprehended in no time, and brought back through the vortex." She sighed, "We're trying to keep that from happening again."

Bronwyn had a desperate idea that would keep her from the pain of seeing Travis welcome back his love.

"Why don't I open the portal and send you through with directions on where to find Travis. That way I could remain behind and guard the door so no one follows you."

And if it were possible, Kenalycia's eyes widened even more, "Oh my, you are such a dear. I'm overwhelmed at your kindness to a complete stranger. Forgive my emotion but it is a rare find these days. To be honest I haven't had a real friend in years, not one I could trust anyways."

Shame punched Bronwyn in the face. Her offer wasn't birthed from kindness but rather from her hearts self-preservation. In any case it didn't matter, for Kenalycia would not hear of Bronwyn remaining behind. It was much too dangerous. Hamza returned, barked a few words in the unknown dialect, and they continued on.

The portal site had been transformed into some sort of a shrine. A giant ornamental structure had been fashioned around the entrance. Two soldiers guarded the entry to the underground waterfall at all times. Two burning torches stood at the opening giving the passageway to the underground portal a primeval look. Hamza went on ahead and spoke with the two guards. After a few minutes he motioned for them to come. Following Hamza they descended the steep decline into the underground cavern. Beautiful lights had been placed into the rock walls, illuminating the shallow pool and falling water, giving it a mystical appearance. The waterfall looked almost identical to the one in Moonshine. Bronwyn sighed at the memory of that night and the supernatural encounter she'd had at the top. The recollection of Travis touching her face and placing her hand on his chest was now almost unbearable. She forced the thought from her mind and as she crept along behind the falling water, nervousness clawed at her stomach. She was anxious to see Travis, there was no doubt about it; but the eagerness was crowded out by knowing she was not the one he'd be thrilled to see. Tears burned in her eyes so she kept her head down so Kenalycia wouldn't notice. She'd hate to explain how much she loved her Asa. She took a deep breath as she stepped on the polished rock behind the falls. Kenalycia moved in beside her and when Hamza and Conall crowded in on both sides, Kenalycia gave an affirmative nod.

"I'm sorry; I don't know what to do." Bronwyn admitted.

"You simply say two words. They can be any of your choosing."

Before she could say anything, somewhere in the distance the haunting song of the woman began ever so softly. She paused to listen; the melody summoned her heart, trying to remind her of something long forgotten. It was the same with the opulent scent on the veranda; it too tried to unlock a forgotten secret. What was it she couldn't remember?

"Please," Kenalycia seemed anxious, "We must leave now, I was followed once before and do not wish for it to happen a second time."

Bronwyn nodded and closed her eyes, "For Travis." It was a whisper, but still she said it. And then… the vision. Under the falling water Travis reached for her, and just as she reached out to him, she fell into the blackness.

CHAPTER THIRTY-FOUR

The only turbulence during the flight to New Mexico took place in Bethany's stomach. The fact that she agreed to accompany Jacob to the homestead after knowing him for only a few short days surprised her. It wasn't like her to take off in reckless abandon without sitting down and making out a plan first; let alone with a man she hardly knew. And to make matters worse, he was kin to Falcon and as far as she knew, it was Falcon who had put Bronwyn in peril. Or maybe Lillian was right and the peculiar town of Moonshine had a strange effect on unsuspecting women; luring them into surreptitious relationships with shadowy men who enticed them into precarious situations. Now, sitting thirty thousand feet in the air, jetting toward an abandoned house, shrouded in secrecy, she wondered if she hadn't lost her mind somewhere in the fallout of what happened to Bronwyn.

August was winding down, September would be here soon. A month ago she would've never imagined all of this. It's funny how life will take a drastic turn without giving any warning at all; and suddenly you find yourself catapulted into situations beyond your control. Like the time her mother picked her up from school, and instead of driving home, they hit the interstate and drove for hours until they arrived at a rundown motel in Texas. It's hard for a fourth grader to understand why her mother would leave her father and put that many miles between them. It was also difficult to fathom why she wasn't allowed to say goodbye or even go home and get her favorite things. Her mother had packed only what she thought was necessary, leaving behind Bethany's most treasured possessions. It was that turn of events however that eventually allowed her and Bronwyn's paths to cross…a treasure she had no intention of leaving behind this time.

Swallowing back the tears she looked out her window. The earth below resembled a green and brown checkerboard, with each square of land perfectly measured and set with boundaries. Even the streets intersected at precise times, all life controlled by the human mindset of parallel lines and boxes. This pattern continued on for miles, repeating itself until a river snaked its way through the checkerboard, interrupting the plan with beautiful twist and turns.

The picture below reminded her of a blog she read once, titled; *Because We Are Beautiful.* In the article the writer mentioned this very scenario; comparing it to how we as humans live our lives, spending our time and efforts trying to put the whole of life and God in our little boxes of understanding. "Little by little," she said, "We create a world without the beauty of mountain ranges or rivers; and although the flat land is boring to us, we prefer it because it's safe and seems to make sense." And as Bethany's eyes followed the river she wondered if this entire turn of events was God's finger, interrupting her carefully laid out plans. And if that was the case, then maybe some good was to come out of this too. With that thought, the turmoil of her mind gave way just enough for her to settle back and sleep the remainder of the flight.

The plane hit the tarmac just as the sun hit the horizon. Since it would be futile to try and investigate after sunset, Jacob suggested they go out to dinner instead and get an early start in the morning. He chose a nice restaurant, requesting a table outdoors so they could dine under the starry sky.

Through the first half of dinner they talked about his career and the fact that he had never submitted to holy matrimony. He confessed he was pretty much married to the job; and that, combined with having to keep secrets of his whereabouts and activities, usually ended up running off all the women he dated. Then he complimented Bethany on her sense of adventure, saying the fact she dropped everything to accompany him to Moonshine and then on to New Mexico impressed him. She relished the compliment but thought the impulsive decision was birthed more from her innate curiosity than a daring spirit.

"Bronwyn always sparked my sense of adventure," She admitted to him. "I probably wouldn't have done half the things I did, had it not been for her prodding me along."

Jacob sipped his wine, "She's been a good friend to you?"

Bethany nodded, "The best. I love her, she's like the sister I never had."

Taking another sip of his wine, he narrowed his eyes on her. "How far would you go to help her?"

His question unnerved her and the look on his face added to the alarm.

"What do you mean?"

"Exactly what I said, How far would you go to help her?"

This time it was Bethany who grabbed her glass and drank. The wine warmed her inside, relaxing the panic stricken butterflies in her stomach. What was he up too? Clearing her throat, she tried to keep composed. "Why?"

Resting on his right elbow, Betancourt leaned over the table, "Because Bethany, Bronwyn is part of something that will be hard for you to wrap your mind around. What you learn could change the course of your life forever."

She must have looked bewildered because he continued on. "I'm not sure what belief system you subscribe to, or if you believe in God. All I'm saying is if you have any faith at all, what you learn during this investigation will test it. I just want to make sure you're ready for the challenge?"

She laughed brushing the warning off, "My mother got upset after reading The Da Vinci Code; said it shook her faith. I read it. So what if Christ was married. Marriage isn't a sin? Would being married make him any less the messiah? I figure, if a fictional novel could shake your faith, well it wasn't that strong to begin with."

"True," Jacob said, "But what if the information has the opposite effect. What if it not only proves the existence of God, but of other entities as well?"

"Are you implying that Bronwyn is an extra-terrestrial? If that's the case why doesn't she just phone home?" Bethany laughed at her own joke; hoping humor would lighten the anxiousness she was feeling.

Jacob didn't miss a beat, "Not extra-terrestrial my dear, but extra dimensional. Do you realize that almost all paranormal activity is caused by breaks into other dimensions?"

Bethany squirmed in her chair feeling as if she'd just entered the twilight zone. She'd never been one to delve into the paranormal, the subject frightened her.

"What are you saying? You think Bronwyn is in another dimension right now?"

"She could be, I don't know, but I do believe she came from one. How, or for whatever reason I don't know."

Bethany took another sip of her wine. Martin admitted there was no record of her birth, no missing child report, nothing. Then there was the strange language… it was all so bizarre. To think her best friend was from another dimension was too much to take in. And if she hadn't heard enough he continued.

"Bronwyn's special Bethany. I think she was hidden here, on our earth, for a purpose."

Goosebumps tickled her skin, racing up her arms and stirring her hair.

"What purpose?" and as soon as she asked the question, she wished she hadn't. True sometimes it was better off not knowing things, but not knowing didn't make it any less real. The issue was; could she handle the knowledge she was soon to receive? And then, there she was, standing at the tree of knowledge, wondering if she should take a bite of Jacobs's apple.

The dinner conversation robbed her of sleep. Lying in the hotel bed, she watched the news, listening to eerie stories of Roanoke and Moonshine. The latest accounting coming across the wire was that the whole thing was a publicity stunt for Ryan's new movie. It was amazing what some people chose to believe. Speaking of believing, she'd pulled the Gideon Bible from the drawer but didn't really know where to begin reading. After skimming through Genesis, and trying to make sense of

Revelation, she closed the book and muted the TV.
Picking up her cell she aimlessly hit Bronwyn's speed dial number. As she figured, it went straight to her voicemail. She let it play, enjoying the sound of her friends cheery voice. At the tone all was silent, and as the light emanating from the TV cast shadows across the room, she mulled over Jacobs answer to her question and finally drifted off to sleep.

CHAPTER THIRTY-FIVE

Hamza jimmied open the springhouse door, it was early morning, the sun just beginning to rise in the late August sky. Bronwyn had no clue as to what day it was, or how much time had passed since she'd been away. The days switched over in a blur of confusion; her only hope was that things had calmed down and they would be able to make it back to Moonshine undetected. The authorities were no doubt still searching for her and Falcon. The thought of him chained and in prison, worlds away, caused her heart to feel sad and she wondered if he would approve of what she was doing.

Bronwyn led the way down the long crooked path to the ram shacked house. The Suburban was still parked out front along with the car that arrived the night she sat upstairs reading Falcon's private journals. Fortunately Elam had left the keys in the ignition, so at least their transportation problem was solved. The recollection of the journals spawned an idea so before climbing behind the wheel, she left her companions with the car, and went inside to retrieve the books.

The front door was ajar so she entered that way, thankful she didn't have to climb through the broken window in her evening gown. The early morning sun pierced through the shattered panes casting a golden glow across the dirty floor. The rays filled with floating dust created a haze, obscuring her vision; but a creak on the steps brought her attention to the form of someone standing on the decaying staircase.

"Bronwyn?" Her heart raced at the familiar call. Shielding her eyes from the glowing rays she stepped past the light. Her vision cleared for a moment until the tears pooled blurring her ability to see once again.

Travis bit down hard on his jaw, closing his eyes and then reopening them like he did the first night she met him on the bridge. He stood still, gazing at her form outlined by the golden light. She smiled at him through her tears, thrilled to be in his presence yet sickened at the thought of passing him over to Kenalycia. Pushing her voice through the emotion, she choked out a greeting.

"What are you doing here?"

His voice was quiet yet determined, "Falcon said I would find you here."

She laughed through the tears, "Well you did."

He stared at her, taking in her form, "You've been to Eden?"

She nodded, "I have."

He smiled at her again and when he did she thought her heart would literally rip right in two. Taking a deep breath, she motioned her head toward the front door and although she'd rehearsed what she would say nearly the entire trip, she could think of nothing other than, "I brought you back something."

He stepped off the staircase, making his way toward her, and as much as she desired his touch she stopped him by nodding toward the front door.

"Go ahead, take a look."

Giving her a lingering gaze, he stepped into the glowing rays of dust where she could no longer see him and headed out the door.

No matter how self-sacrificing the act, she couldn't bear to watch. She had to leave. Rushing out the back door she bolted down the porch steps, tore across the overgrown yard and headed toward the crooked path. She no longer held back the tears stinging in her eyes, but rather allowed them to pour down her face. Once deep in the woods, far away from everyone, she stopped running, squatted against a sturdy tree and sobbed.

She cried without stopping, her heart mourning the extravagant loss; and while she gave into the pain of sacrificial love, she neglected to hear the footsteps skulking down the path, stopping directly behind her. Yet in the face of her inner grief, she sensed the opposing spirit, a manifestation so sinister, her skin chilled in the warm morning sun. Turning around slowly she jumped to her feet, terror pulsating through her veins at the sight of Elam's manic smile.

CHAPTER THIRTY-SIX

Bracing herself, Bethany grasped the door handle while Jacob sped into the front yard of the run down house. Bumping across the lawn, he drove over the broken sidewalk, stopping only a few feet from a dead man lying in the grass. Blood marked the path of his demise, splattering across the porch and ending in the puddle where his lifeless body lay. Two men were engaged in an intense knife fight, tumbling over the two parked cars and across the overgrown yard while a beautiful woman watched the battle. At their arrival Bethany watched her disappear into the darkness of the abandoned house

"That's Travis," Bethany gasped, recognizing one of the men, while bracing against the intense bumping.

Jacob slammed on the brakes and then pulled a gun from his jacket, inserting a round in the chamber. "Call the police."

Pulling her cell from her purse, she dialed 911; her fingers trembling with each punch. While she waited for the operator, Jacob jumped from the car, aiming his gun.

"FBI Freeze!"

Paying no attention to the command, Travis continued his fight, slashing his razor-sharp knife across the chest of his latest victim. Weakened, Hamza stumbled, giving Travis the opportunity to grab him, and with the same prowess as Falcon, slit his throat and tossed him in the dirt.

Horrified, Bethany screamed into her phone, telling the operator what she had witnessed.

Travis turned to Jacob, peering at him through the tatters of hair sticking to his face, wet with perspiration. Bethany shuddered; she'd never seen such ferociousness in Travis; he'd always appeared as such a gentleman, she never figured him to be the blood soaked savage standing before them.

"Drop your weapon now!" Jacob ordered cocking back his gun.

"There's no time Jacob," Travis panted. "Bronwyn's in trouble."

Guarded, Jacob kept his gun aimed but softened his tone, "How do you know who I am?"

"Your great grandfather is my friend."

Travis' disclosure confirmed Jacob's suspicions. He grinned pleased for now, "So he is alive."

Travis' agitation rang in his voice, "Alive yes, but in serious trouble and needs my help. The longer you detain me you seal his and Bronwyn's fate."

Jacob narrowed his eyes in on Travis, contemplating the situation. "This is a high profile case Mr. Colton. I can't in good faith just let you walk away. It's my duty as an agent of the Federal Bureau of Investigation to take you into custody."

"I'm sorry but I can't let you do that," Travis was resolute, his eyes burrowing into Jacob's.

Jacob grinned, somewhat amused. "Pretty bold words seeing I'm the one holding the gun."

"True," Travis agreed. "But I'm the one holding the secrets you've been searching for all these years. You want to know where Haytham Elwell is, I'll tell you, but only after I have Bronwyn safe with me. Now I'm going after them, shoot me right here, right now or bring that gun of yours and help. It's up to you." Travis didn't wait for Jacob to make up his mind. He took off running around the back of the house faster than Jacob had ever seen anyone run. He couldn't have shot him if he wanted to.

Jacob took off after him. "Here goes fifteen years of faithful service."

CHAPTER THIRTY-SEVEN

Grabbing a fist full of her hair, Elam pulled Bronwyn's face up against his. "You didn't really think I'd be so lax as to let my most valuable prisoner escape her first night in captivity did you?" His scalding breath burned against her skin as he laughed. "I do want to thank you for leading us right to Asa. What you thought was an act of true love will imprison him for the rest of his life."

In spite of the pain, she struggled against his grip, hate for her captor fueling her fight. Then to her anguish she heard the sound of footsteps rushing down the path.

"Trav….."

Elam's hand muffled her warning.

"Bronwyn!" Travis called out, urgency ringing in his voice. Her heart heaved with sorrow. In her eagerness to see him again, and reunite him with his long lost love, she had inadvertently sealed his demise. She struggled against Elam, stomping on his foot, and then tried landing a backwards kick to his groin. He shoved her into the constricted hold of one of the two burly guards who accompanied him through the portal.

"Keep her quiet!" At his command, the beefy man slapped his thick hand over her mouth covering her cries of caution.

"Be prepared," Elam instructed his men. "Asa will be ours today. We carry this out and you will live in extravagance for the remainder of your lives."

As the footsteps grew closer, Bronwyn screamed muffled warnings. Her captor pressed his hand harder across her mouth, worsening her split lip. Agonizing pain, mingled with sticky blood, oozed from the fresh wound.

Elam pulled his pistol, pulling back the trigger; but instead of aiming it at the sound of approaching footsteps he burrowed the barrel into the side of Bronwyn's head. Poised for victory, he sneered delighted to be in control. Travis stopped at the threat.

"Make a move and I'll kill her."

Bronwyn's heart thundered against her chest as once again she faced Travis. He was alone, Kenalycia wasn't with him, and his blood stained clothes gave reason for her to believe something dreadful happened. The cold barrel pressed into her temples didn't frighten her as much as the ferocious look emanating from his eyes. And if it were possible, she felt his glare alone would annihilate every living thing around him. The man holding her must have sensed the same for he slowly released his hand, unveiling her blood stained face and an oozing split lip. "I'm sorry Travis," she mouthed the words despite her pain. "I didn't know…I would have never…"

Tightening his jaw, Travis glared at Elam, his eyes detonating in rage. "You've caused her much pain today; I will kill you because of it."

Elam smirked, but fear revealed itself in his countenance. Bronwyn remembered Falcon's accounting of the night of the revolt, and how Travis went into a rage taking out ten of Abaddon's men with ease. The only thing that stopped him from killing Abaddon was his threat of the immediate execution of Brennun and Mavis. She figured the story of that fight had spread over the years, no doubt inciting fear in Elam. And now, seeing Travis standing before him, soiled with the blood of his fallen men, was proof he'd singlehandedly taken out Hamza and Conall, two of the fiercest guards in Abaddon's militia.

A strong wind stirred out of nowhere, pushing through the forest, bending the trees and flattening the tall grass. Looking up through the thick branches, Bronwyn watched ominous clouds boil across the sky, snuffing out the sunlight; until the wind whipped her hair into her face obstructing her view. A chill fell into the air, threatening the warmth of the August sun, bringing a sudden end to the morning serenade of the birds and cicadas. An eerie silence hung like an omen that something was about to go terribly wrong.

The sound of approaching footsteps seemed deafening in contrast to the unnerving stillness. Elam's attention left Travis for the moment and focused on two people running toward the standoff. Not able to use her hands to brush away her hair, Bronwyn tossed her head, clearing her view and was stunned to see Bethany running behind a man carrying a gun. How in the world had Bethany ended up here and for the matter, who was she with?

"FBI, Freeze!" Jacob stood poised, ready to shoot. "Drop you weapon now!"

Elam sneered in defiance.

"I said now!" Jacob ordered pulling back the trigger.

Ignoring his demands, Elam directed his words to Travis. "I could care less who this man is, or what organization he's with. I'm in control here and I will kill her unless he drops his weapon."

Raising his hand, Travis signaled Jacob to back off but kept his eye on Elam. "Abaddon will kill you if you end her life and you know it."

"True, Abaddon wants her alive for reasons I am sure you well know." He taunted as a sensual perversion glow in his eyes. "However, it's my opinion that we all would be much better off if she's dead, so I have no qualms about killing her. Abaddon would eventually get over the loss and be better for it. She produces a weakness in him that results in poor decision making."

"Is that so?" Abaddon stepped past the trees, joining the group. His unexpected appearance tore a look of horror into Elam's face. Thunder echoed in the distance, applauding his arrival, adding to the ominousness of the moment

Bronwyn shivered at his presence, as an abominable dread manifest, filling her spirit with imminent doom. She feared for Travis more than herself. It was no secret Abaddon demanded she be kept alive, Travis however, was Abaddon's key to eternal life and would be taken alive as well. But what worried her, was Travis not succumbing to the demands of his mortal enemy. This would result in unspeakable acts of brutality that she couldn't bear to witness.

"Behold, the long sought after prince Asa," Abaddon said, leering at Travis. "It's been a long time my friend; and may I sincerely say it's good to see you."

Travis didn't respond to Abaddon's greeting and revealed nothing in his expression. His dark eyes burned into his enemy, searing a mark of vengeance on his betrayer's soul.

The wind whipped through the trees, wailed a heinous dirge, circling the confrontation. Dead leaves blew up in a small whirlwind spinning across the dirt path. Again Bronwyn's hair became a blindfold, hindering her view of what was soon to transpire between the two. She twisted her arms, hoping to free herself from the thug's tight hold. Annoyed with her struggling, the guard yanked her arms, nearly pulling her elbow out of socket. She cried out in pain and when she did Travis cut his eyes into the man; the strength of his stare intimidated him to loosen his grip.

Abaddon however, stared back, unmoved and unafraid; and with an attitude of superiority grabbed Bronwyn from the guard. Stroking her hair, he brushed it away from her face; continuing on with his heinous plot.

"Well done Elam, your plan played out just as you suspected it would."

Elam gave a nervous smile, hoping his last comments would be forgotten in the midst of their victory.

"Thank you my Lord, it is my pleasure to carry out the task. Might I add your presence is a welcome surprise?"

Ignoring the phony gratitude, Abaddon surveyed the group, his eyes stopping on Jacob. "Who are you?"

"I'm your great grandson," Jacob introduced himself still poised to shoot. "And I want to know what the hell's going on here."

Abaddon laughed, "My great grandson? Now that is interesting. You no doubt are mistaking me for my disreputable twin, Haytham."

"I'm with the FBI, and I've called for backup, the police will be arriving any minute and this place will be surrounded; you'd do best to surrender to me right now."

On the heel of his announcement, sirens sounded in the distance accompanied by the low rumble of thunder.

Bronwyn had been dodging the authorities for days now; however being taken into custody would be a welcoming event in light of their present situation.

White lightning dropped from the sky, ripping its way down the grey canvas, falling somewhere near the old house. A deafening pop echoed across the property, immediately followed by an explosion, shaking the ground, vibrating up through the soles of their feet. Abaddon's lips pulled into a fiendish grin, as if he'd directed it where to go. "Looks like we have a direct hit."

Fire roared from the decaying house as the wind whipped the flames high in to view. Not intimidated in the least with the threat of police thwarting his plan, Abaddon turned his attention to Bronwyn, lustfully stroking her hair, "Clean up Elam, it's time to leave."

In one swift, unexpected move, Elam removed his gun from Bronwyn, immediately shooting Jacob in the chest. He slumped to the ground as a horror-stricken Bethany screamed. The split second incident was all Travis needed to throw his knife, sinking it into Elam's throat. Elam's hands curled around the blade as he collapsed to his knees, gurgling, struggling to pull it out.

Abaddon kept a tight hold on Bronwyn, unmoved by Elam's misfortune. A sinister calm resonated in his voice as he continued to call out orders, not once contemplating the possibility of defeat. "Use the tranquilizer on Asa, get him to the portal, I have help waiting on the other side." One of the guards pulled a handgun, aiming it at Travis, just as Abaddon yanked Bronwyn onto the dirt path pulling her toward the spring house.

She fought hard against him, but his strength was too much for her. The sound of an exploding firearm caused her heart to plummet into her stomach. Straining her neck, she tried turning her head to see what had become of Travis. Abaddon jerked her head back, but from the corner of her eye she saw him; dashing directly toward her, madness burning in his eyes. Lunging, Travis took them both down. The three collided with the hard earth, knocking the wind from her lungs. Pain invaded every inch of her body as she struggled to catch her breath under the men's crushing strength. Travis regained his footing first, pulling Abaddon off her and slamming him up against a nearby tree. Using his elbow, he forced a punch to his gut. Abaddon doubled over, taking the blow and then retaliated by pulling a knife and charging toward Travis. Like a possessed man, Abaddon flew through the air, his eyes white with rage. Bronwyn screamed, cringing at the sight.

Spinning on his heels, Travis kicked the knife from Abaddon's grasp; sending it flying into the air and then catching it with ease. Six hundred years of indignation discharged from his fist as he brought the blade down slicing into Abaddon's face, cutting deep beneath his eye. Stunned by the blow, Abaddon stumbled backward, losing his balance. Travis lunged forward kicking him in the jaw, sending him sprawling to the ground. Abaddon moaned struggling to hang onto consciousness.

The sirens were deafening, most of the vehicles having arrived at the ram-shacked house. Fire engines pulled onto the property, the fire was raging now; consuming the dried overgrown grass. The wind tossed the burning embers into the trees igniting them like torches.

Leaving Abaddon writhing in pain, Travis turned his attention to Bronwyn, helping her to her feet, "You okay?"

She didn't think she was but she nodded anyway.

"We need to move, fast." He made his way to Bethany who was sobbing while holding Jacob's gun and leaning over his lifeless body. Travis pulled the gun from her hand, and then grabbed the one lying next to Elam. Placing both guns in his belt, he grabbed Bethany by the elbow. "Let's go."

Bronwyn's heart went out to her. She knew firsthand the terror she must be feeling. All her previous annoyance melted into compassion for her distraught friend.

Just before making the dash to the springhouse, Travis pulled his knife and sliced through Bronwyn's dress leaving the hem line high on her thighs. Then he made a quick stop, kneeling down beside Abaddon who was struggling to stay conscious.

"I won't kill you, not today; instead, I'm leaving you here, just as you did all of us. I'm going back to rescue Haytham and then reclaim Eden. I will bring the royalty from Moonshine back to their homeland while you remain here and pay for Haytham's crimes. I will secure a place in Eden for the story of redemption to be written, sealing your doom. I will eventually come back for you, so you better hope you die in prison; it will be a better fate than what I have in store for you."

Having said his peace, the three bolted for the spring house just as the rain began falling in torrents, extinguishing the blazing trees.

Ignoring the authorities command to freeze, they dodged bullets and striking lightning, running blindly through the rain, veering between the trees and leaping over fallen limbs and debris. All the while Bronwyn wondered where Kenalycia was, and why she wasn't coming with them.

Lightning struck just yards in front of them, the bolt splitting a tree in two, sending half of the trunk to block their path. Bethany screamed in fright, the expression of her face revealing sheer terror.

"This way," Travis said pulling them both on a quick detour to the other side. The rain was falling in torrents now. The worry of being consumed by the jumping flames was now extinguished by the downpour; her only concern was being shot or being burned to death by a powerful bolt of electricity. The rain pelted her so violently that sometimes she feared she'd been hit by the flying bullets.

A few more feet and they arrived at the portal. Travis kicked open the door to the spring house and the three darted inside, splashing through the ankle deep water and heading toward the cement slab in the back. It was then she noticed her travel bag partly submerged in the water, hidden in the far corner. Grabbing it, she ripped it open, and pulled out the precious book and held it close. Taking Bronwyn's hand, Travis pulled her to him, "Abaddon has men on the other side, armed and ready to attack. You and Bethany stay down, take shelter behind the rocks."

She nodded, wide eyed.

The wind howled, shrieking through the forest, shaking the distressed wood of the spring house, ripping the worn roof from the walls and tossing it through the air like cardboard. The small shack collapsed around them like dominos. In the distance she saw Abaddon, hobbling toward the spring house, blood poured from his wound, mixing with rain, giving him the appearance of a possessed mad man. Shuddering she reached for Travis, and although she could barely see him in the driving rain, his face indicated the severity of their situation. As she reached for him, the heat sensation exploded inside of her. This was her vision. The one she had since she first met him. And as she fell into the blackness of the portal something told her this wasn't the first time it had all happened.

CHAPTER THIRTY-EIGHT

The men were waiting, just as Travis predicted. What Elam had hoped would be an ostentatious escort through the city of Eden, was suddenly transformed into face-off between the returning Prince and the men who orchestrated the coup that abolished the reign of the three princes. The sight of blood stained Prince Asa arriving without Elam or Abaddon rattled the small group and at first no one seemed to know what to do. It wasn't until one of the men, by the name of Blaine, spoke up over the roar of the waterfall, that things began to escalate.

"Where's Elam and Abaddon?"

Travis eyed the assembly, "They're not coming."

A murmur resonated through the men.

Blaine spoke again; taking the opportunity to advance himself among the inner circle.

"You arrive without an army and expect to take over what we have built for the pass six hundred years." His voice thundered over the rushing water, "A new regime is in place, you have no authority here. Your days of reigning were over some time ago. "

Motioning to the small militia, he barked out his orders. "Escort Asa and the women to prison."

The armed men moved into position, surrounding the rocky plateau situated behind the falling water.

Bronwyn's heart hammered against her chest as she looked out over Abaddon's personal mercenaries. They were men fighting only for individual gain and the approval of their malicious leader. Their kind had no conscious and would do unspeakable acts just to advance themselves to a place of significance.

Travis surveyed the men, only fourteen of them were armed, the other six stood to the side; devious politicians and not warriors ready to engage in combat.

"Get down and stay down," he directed Bronwyn pushing her deeper into the cut out cavern "Keep hidden behind the rocks as best you can. Let me fight them off. They won't kill me, but they will you."

Grabbing Bethany by the hand, Bronwyn pulled her down behind a row of large boulders. She wore no expression and appeared numb, as if she was in a hypnotic trance waiting for the snap of fingers to wake again. There was no time for Bronwyn to console her or try and explain any of the craziness that was transpiring and for the first time ever, she asked no questions.

Once safely behind the rocks, Travis drew the pistols from his belt, simultaneously pulling back on the guns. His gaze lingered on Bronwyn, stealing her breath much more than the panic squeezing in.

The men froze at the sight, not sure of what to do. Should they fire, they might kill him, thus sealing their doom, yet if they advanced, they would surely be shot. So the stand–off ensued. No orders were voiced audibly, only transmitted through the mind so not to give away the tactic. Two men covertly, backed away from the rest, and began advancing around the back side of the falls. Another two, took to the opposite side while two others darted around the back, preparing to scale the rocks and then descend down into the cavern shielding them. The remaining eight faced off, aiming directly at them. Their directives were to maim Travis enough to disarm him and take him prisoner. But by no means were anyone to kill him. Blaine along with his five cohorts waited in great anticipation but seemed somewhat at a disadvantage without Elam or Abaddon. Neither one of them aware that their greatest defeat would transpire among themselves, each one trying to usurp authority over the other, taking command of the throne until Abaddon returned.

Travis fired the first shot; the victim fell from the one of the higher boulders on the left side of the falls; his body crashing into the jagged rocks below. The men in front began firing at will, bullets zipped through the falling water buzzing into the hollowed out cave like bees swarming their hive. More than anything Bronwyn desired to see how Travis was faring, yet she dare not lift her head into the line of fire. As long as he continued moving and discharging his pistols she knew he was okay.

Bing…a bullet hit the rock, barely missing her hand. Another exploded on top of the boulder gouging out a small hole, detonating a dust cloud into the air. Another hit the rock wall sending loose stones cascading down upon them. Covering her head with the book, Bronwyn hunched down further, her heart accelerating with every fire of the weapons.

Travis continued shooting. Each deafening blast echoed in the small cavern. That, combined with the roar of the falls, was earsplitting and left no way of knowing if anyone were stealing around the sides ready to ambush.

The gunfire began to lessen; Bronwyn could only hope the reason was that Travis had taken out most of the mercenaries. Then a sinking sound… the click of an empty gun. Raising her head just enough to get a peek, she saw Travis toss his weapons aside. Out of ammo, he pulled a dagger from his belt just in time to engage in a knife fight with an assailant slinking around the sides. Then to her horror she saw another aggressor coming up behind him. Thinking fast she snatched one of the rocks that recently plummeted down on top of her, hurling it at the guy with all the strength she could muster. She'd never been that great at sports and spent most her childhood in the theater or piano recitals, yet she landed the rock to the back of his skull with such accuracy that he doubled over, grabbing his head in pain. Recovering fast, he whirled around to face her. With fury blazing in his eyes, he charged her way, and as he did she threw another stone. Dodging it, he pulled his knife and yanked her from behind the rock. Trying to fight him off, she grabbed another rock hitting him hard at close range, and then gave a swift kick to his groin. Growling like an animal, he spun her around and pressed the blade against her neck. Bethany's scream drew Travis' attention to the skirmish. Just as he was making his way over, two mercenaries crashed in from above. Surprisingly, one jumped the man holding Bronwyn, while the other fired a round into Travis shoulder.

Rising to a crawling position, Bronwyn scooted back against the wall and for the first time noticed Travis' wound. Her spirit faded at the sight. Yet in spite of the agony etched in his face, he continued to fight. The mercenary, who took down her assailant, fired a shot into his comrade, killing him.

Grimacing in pain, Travis lunged toward the man, jerked the gun from the man's hand and pressed it into the man's forehead.

"Who are you?"

"My name's Cenric, I've come to help you."

Travis pulled back on the gun. "Why?"

"Because I have been praying for the return of you reign, vowing if I ever have chance to put you back in power I would take it."

"I don't trust you!" Travis grunted through the pain.

"I tell you the truth." Cenric spoke up over the roar. "Two men will be charging across the waters any minute now to divert your attention from the person poised on the rocks to your left. He has a direct line of fire to your lady."

Keeping his gun aimed at the man, Travis glanced at the rocky ledge to his left. Cenric was right; there was movement along the stalagmite catwalk. Travis fired sending the stalking culprit toppling over the ledge to his death. Tossing his wet hair from his eyes, he aimed at the rocky bank shooting point blank the two revolutionaries charging the falls. With the shooting of these final three, Travis had incapacitated the small army leaving only the six unarmed representatives of Abaddon's inner circle. Still not sure whether or not he trusted Cenric, he pulled him to his feet, and with one hand clutching his collar, he pulled him close to his face.

"You're coming with me." Biting through the piercing pain he ordered Bronwyn and Bethany to stay put. Then with a running leap, he soared through the falling water, taking Cenric right along with him. Storming across the shallow pool, he grabbed Blaine and pushed him up against the rock wall. Wrapping his fingers around his neck, he knocked his head hard against the stone. With his other hand he pulled back on the gun, and at the same time shoved the barrel directly beneath Blaine's chin.

"Since you seem to be calling the shots among your contemporaries, you can send the order to release Haytham."

Gasping for air, Blaine choked out his objections, "I have no authority to order that release. Haytham is being held for high treason, Abaddon…"

"Do it now!" Travis growled, shoving the gun deeper under Blaine's chin. "Have Haytham brought to the Ferry landing at the east shore. Secure us a boat. Once Haytham is in my care and I and the ladies have safe passage, I will set you free; otherwise you can join your fallen men in death."

Although Travis had the upper hand, Blaine audaciously challenged the once reining Prince, "You're the giver of life, you won't take mine."

"That's where you're mistaken," Travis clenched his teeth to mask his pain. "Sometimes you have to take one life to preserve others. Just so you know; I find no joy in this." Having said what he did, Travis pulled the trigger spraying parts of Blaine's head across the granite wall. Then like a mad man he grabbed the next cabinet member of the inner circle, shoving him up against the place where Blaine once stood.

"I'll execute every one of you if I have to," He didn't have to say another word.

The rough barbaric actions of Travis surprised Bronwyn. She'd never seen this ferocious side of him and could only attribute it to the possibility that since Kenalycia was not among them that something dire happened to her. That would no doubt explain his wild possessed behavior. Her heart ached at the thought, especially after remembering Falcon's accounting of the anguish he'd already suffered. Now after remaining true to his love and waiting for six hundred years could she be gone? As much as Bronwyn desired him for herself, she regretted this turn of events, feeling her impulsive decision to reunite the two may have caused the tragedy. She hoped he would not distance himself from her because of it.

She and Bethany walked in silence, following Travis, Cenric and the hostage. Bethany hadn't uttered a word since they came through the portal and this concerned Bronwyn. Travis was quiet too; focused on the task at hand. The blood from his wound soaked through his tee-shirt but she couldn't tell if his behavior stemmed from pain or controlled fury; and for the first time since she met him, she felt somewhat frightened. He hadn't informed her as to what they were doing or why Cenric was accompanying them. He didn't give a reason for shooting Blaine in the head or why he took one of the unarmed men as prisoner. But in all reality, he never gave reasons for any of his actions back in Moonshine either. His life was a total enigma; she consoled herself with this reasoning.

About an hour later they arrived at the banks of an enormous lake. Several large fishing boats floated in the water along with sailboats and a few other smaller vessels anchored near the docks. Old-world buildings seemed to grow from the ground and sat nestled near the shoreline; creating a picturesque little fishing village. Fishermen milled around, tending to their boats, making last minute preparations before setting sail for a long night of fishing. At the arrival of the battle weary party, the quaint village came alive with curiosity. Shopkeepers left their stores, fishermen stopped mending their nets, everyone gathered in the cobblestone streets eager to see what history turning event was transpiring.

Cenric ran ahead and in no time was back pointing out the boat they would be traveling on. Not letting his guard down for a minute, and keeping his gun buried in the back of his prisoners head, Travis climbed aboard the vessel and checked every compartment making sure it was unoccupied so there wouldn't be any surprise attacks. Once he deemed it safe he told Cenric to bring Bronwyn and Bethany aboard.

Bronwyn felt the stares of everyone as she climbed the ladder into the boat. She could only imagine what they were thinking. What a sight she must be in her torn, dirty evening gown, and sporting a busted bloody lip. Would there ever come a day when she would be clean and dry and well-dressed again? A day where she wouldn't get hurt and bleed and have to make a mad dash for her life?

Cenric offered his hand when she topped the ladder, helping her board. Once on deck she glanced at Travis who motioned for her to come over to where he was. Bethany joined them leaving Cenric waiting by the ladder as if he were expecting someone else. Bronwyn wondered who they were waiting on but decided not ask. Travis still had a strong hold on his hostage and remained quiet like he did when he was communicating mentally with someone. That was it, possibly the reason for his extended silence. He was back in Eden now; maybe he was in contact with old friends trying to elicit some help.

A ruckus from the crowd drew her attention to a small group on the street headed toward their boat. Stumbling along, surrounded by four guards and two of Abaddon's men, was Falcon. Her heart rocketed at the sight. Travis must have taken the man hostage to bargain the release of Falcon. Her heart warmed at the thought, increasing her admiration for him. In the midst of losing Kenalycia he still had the fortitude to save Falcon.

"Remove his chains," He ordered from the deck.

Without an argument the guards unlocked the collar and shackles binding Falcons, wrist and ankles. Despite his weakened battered state, his eyes danced in mischief as he lifted his head and tossed the hair from his face.

Bethany gasped at the sight of him, not knowing there were two. Noticing her confusion, Bronwyn touched her on the arm promising to explain later.

With much effort, Falcon made his way to the boat. The crowd grew quiet as he staggered along. Bronwyn pitied him for the unwarranted brutality he suffered at his own brother's command; and as she watched him teeter along, making every effort to climb up the ladder, her heart burned with an all-consuming hatred for Abaddon.

Running to his aid, Bronwyn reached him just as he topped the ladder and collapsed onto the deck knocking her down with him. Rolling off her and staring up into the blue autumn sky he flashed an impish grin.

"Looks like you and I were invited to the same party Scribe. Glad to see you've survived. I taught you well."

Smiling through her tears, she reveled at the sound of his voice; even in weakness, he stayed true to form, choking out his sarcasm.

"Get the boat underway," Travis ordered Cenric, who immediately obeyed by pulling in the ladder and scurrying about the deck, pulling in the lines, preparing the boat for their departure.

Travis bound his hostage and pushed him to the ground. The man protested vehemently reminding Travis of his deal to set him free once Haytham was released and safe in his company.

“I’ll set you free once we’re underway, Travis snarled, “You can swim back.”

Bronwyn remained by Falcon, as the boat left the shore, watching Travis haul in the lines and chart their course. She was able to relax some, feeling confident now that she was with Travis, and Falcon was safe. She wasn’t sure about the Cenric fellow but figured if Travis trusted him enough to have him along then she would too. After all, he did save her life.

Bethany still leaned against the railing disoriented and staring into nothingness as if she were under hypnosis. Bronwyn’s heart went out to her. As soon as things calmed down she would console her and try and help her mind grasp what was happening.

Leaning against the deck wall she stared up into the pure autumn sky. White fluffy clouds drifted along with the boat, as birds raced with the wind, gracefully gliding along the deep blue expanse. The late afternoon sun warmed her skin bringing with it a gentle breeze, wafting onto the boat, stirring her hair, and drying her damp dress. She inhaled enjoying its fragrance. It smelled like freedom.

CHAPTER THIRTY-NINE

Madison carried in the vegetables from the garden, and placed them in the basket on her kitchen counter. She was up earlier than usual; sleep wasn't coming easy these days. She spent the better part of every night, waking suddenly and checking her cell just to see if Bronwyn had called. Lying in bed, staring at the ceiling, only brought dire thoughts. So she got out of bed, even though she was still tired, and busied herself to try and give her mind something else to think about.

"It's going to be another hot one today," She said taking her frying pan out of the cupboard.

Martin joined her in the kitchen after having retrieved the morning paper from the front lawn. Placing his reading glasses on the tip of his nose, he removed the daily from the narrow plastic bag.

"Oh No!" he groaned after seeing the headline.

Leaving the bacon sizzling on the stove, Madison joined him at the table, reading over his shoulder.

"Agent Betancourt is dead! But how? And Bethany was with him, does it say anything about Bethany?"

"Call her." Martin said, skimming the front page.

Grabbing the remote, Madison turned on her small kitchen TV before dialing the phone.

"Put it on CNN," Martin told her, still scanning the front page.

Holding the receiver with her neck she changed the channel.

Sure enough the correspondents were discussing the latest development out of New Mexico while aerial footage of a burning house and emergency personal tending to slain and wounded victims covered the screen.

"What you're seeing here is footage from yesterday's carnage at the old Elwell property right outside of Cedar Crest New Mexico. At approximately 7:36 yesterday morning a call was placed to 911 operators alerting authorities of an attack taking place on the property. The caller identified herself as Bethany Baker of Los Angeles California. Miss Baker is a longtime friend of Bronwyn Sterling. Miss. Baker told the operator that she was in the company of special agent Betancourt and was requesting police back up. Here is a recording of the call."

Martin laid aside the paper, "Turn it up dear."

The printed version of the call appeared on the screen as Madison and Martin listened in to Bethany's frantic call.

Operator: "911 Emergency."

Caller: "My name is Bethany Baker and I'm with Agent Betancourt of the FBI. We are three miles off of Penny Lane at the old Elwell property. He needs back up." (Woman screaming) "Oh my God! He just killed someone! Oh my God, Oh my God! He just stabbed him."

Operator: "Calm down ma'am, I need you to calm down. Who got stabbed?"

Caller: "I-I-I don't know, some man. Travis killed him...."

“And that’s where we lost the call,” The anchor took back over the story.

Madison hung up the phone, a look of despondency etched on her face. “It went straight to her voice mail.”

Before introducing her special guest, the newscaster recapped the events of yesterday’s mysterious bloodbath. “Yesterday’s massacre left five dead, including agent Betancourt, and two wounded, one critically. The dead men carried no identification which is consistent with all the deceased in this baffling case. An unidentified man survived the attack and was taken to Baptist Memorial Hospital with a knife wound to the throat. The fugitive by the name of Dakota was taken into custody. The caller, Ms. Bethany Baker was not located, neither was Ms. Sterling found at the scene. Her whereabouts are still a mystery.”

Madison clicked the remote, turning off the TV.

“Call the police, Martin and tell them we want to talk to Dakota. I want to know what he’s done to my daughter.”

Abaddon stared at the TV hanging high in the corner of his hospital room. Having half of his face bandaged made it difficult to focus in on the broadcast. He didn’t care to see it, but he did want to hear it. Something the starchy reporter’s guest said sparked his attention. Fumbling around for the remote, he yanked at the white cord, untangling it from the railing of his hospital bed.

She was interviewing Taylor Elwell, a family member of Agent Betancourt’s, who was unknowingly equipping the man who caused his cousins death with valuable information.

"Jacob was obsessed with the family mystery and had been since he was nineteen. At first we all humored him, everyone adding their own bizarre stories into the mix. But then it seemed to consume him. We all thought his obsession had driven him insane but it was when he uncovered the mysterious book buried in the spring house that we all thought he might be on to something. I was intrigued so I sort of joined him on his investigation; doing research for him when time permitted."

"What sort of book?"

Abaddon sat up at the question.

"It was an old book, written sometime around the fourteenth century. There was a letter hidden inside the back cover written in a dialect we were never able to place. The author is unknown. The funny thing about it was my great grandfather's name was mentioned in the book. How can that happen? How can someone write about a person who hadn't been born until six hundred years later?"

The reporter appeared stoic, going through the motions of the interview, asking the appropriate questions.

"There was also an old book recovered at the crime scene in Ryan Reese's condo in California. Do you know if there are any similarities?"

"I don't. The last I heard from Jacob was Sunday. He called and said there was a huge break in the case and was flying to New Mexico. He said he'd call and catch me up." Taylor sighed, "He never got the chance."

"So it seems he died without the answers he'd been searching for, or do you think that possibly it was the knowledge of those answers that took his life?"

Taylor shrugged. “I guess we’ll never know.”

“So what about you, Mr. Elwell? Will you continue your cousin’s investigation?”

“Well right now the family is grieving and we have funeral arrangements to make. I think I’ll let the FBI handle this for now.”

Abaddon switched off the set just as a very pretty nurse smiled at the police guarding the door and slipped inside his room.

CHAPTER FORTY

The cabin creaked as the boat rocked in the peaceful waters. The rhythm of it relaxed Bronwyn, to the point where she could barely keep her eyes open. She'd gone below after Travis equipped his hostage with a life preserver and tossed him overboard telling him to swim toward the horizon and eventually he'd see land. She's always heard of men having to walk the plank but had never actually seen it in action until now. The man was hostile, cursing and making threats the entire time while speaking disparagingly against Travis and his deceased brothers. She thought it kind of Travis to volunteer the life preserver considering his belligerent behavior; and had Falcon not been incapacitated, she was sure he'd have done the man in himself.

They'd been traveling for several hours now, all was calm. Travis gave Bethany a concoction of something to drink, soothing her troubled mind and putting her to sleep. Cenric took over on deck, steering the boat while Travis helped Falcon below to administer healing to his wounds. After steaming various parts of plants he collected on the walk to the village, he cooked them to a thick oily paste, and set them aside to cool. It was when he drew his dagger from his belt and offered it to Bronwyn that her drowsiness subsided.

Pulling off his shirt, he motioned to his wound, "I'm going to need you to remove the bullet."

"Me?" she was wide awake now. "I'm not sure I can, I might hurt you more."

"It's not very deep, you will feel it if you probe a little. Once you get it out I can heal the wound. Once I'm whole, I can heal Falcon."

Her stomach constricted at the suggestion of probing the wound. She'd always had a strong aversion to blood, nearly fainting at the sight of it, however she'd seen enough of it in the past week to make her immune to such a phobia. Besides, this was Travis, how bad could it be? It was his blood, his wound and nothing about the man repulsed her. This was an opportunity to be near him, to touch him and maybe have some kind of conversation so she could find out what happened to Kenalycia back at the ram shacked house. With those thoughts tumbling around in her head, she took the dagger from his hand.

"I'll do my best."

Swallowing back her fear, she dug the knife into the small hole only to pull it back out when she noticed pain take residence in his eyes.

"Don't look at me," He said, "Or you won't be able to do it. Just concentrate on the wound."

Nodding, she chewed on her bottom lip and following his direction, tried again. She stirred the knife around, and when she did, blood oozed from the puncture. Her mouth began to water and her stomach squeezed; just when she was about to tell him she couldn't do it, the blade hit a hard object.

"That's it," He said quietly but still she heard the discomfort in his voice. "Try to get behind it and scoop it out. Biting down harder on her lip, she cut around the object digging it from the hole and catching it in her trembling hand.

"Good job, now if you don't mind, will you apply the paste to Falcons wounds while I take care of mine."

Again she nodded, saying nothing. Grabbing the pot of cooling balm, she stole a glance at Travis, who was sweating profusely while mopping up the blood from his chest. Picking up a thin piece of gauze she dipped the fabric in the mixture and dabbed it on each slash in Falcon's back. He sat slumped until the balm touched his wounds, then he arched his back wincing at the touch.

"I'm sorry," she whispered keeping her voice low.

"It's okay," he groaned through the pain, "You owed me one anyway."

She smiled, lifting her eyebrows, "Only one?"

He grinned, "What I'd give for a damn cigarette."

"It's a fishing boat, I'm sure I can rummage some up, somewhere on here."

"You do that Scribe and I take back ever thing I ever said about you."

She laughed softly this time. "I'm glad you're okay Falcon. I missed you."

"I missed you too Scribe. I was proud of the way you handled Elam at dinner. You showed a lot of courage. You did good…real good."

"Not so good," she lowered her voice and glanced over at Travis. She doubted he'd hear her anyway. He seemed to be engaged in some sort of healing ritual. His eyes were closed. One hand was pressed against his wound while the other was placed against his heart. His body trembled and perspiration dotted his forehead, rolling down his face.

"I messed up really bad. In my hurry to right a wrong, I may have caused Kenalycia's death."

Falcon cut his eyes up to hers, "How so?"

"She asked me to take her to Travis. She had it all planned out, the guards helped us escape to the portal, but somehow we were followed. I think they might have killed her."

Falcon didn't show any signs of surprise let alone remorse, his only reaction to her dismal news was a reprimand. "What's the one thing I kept telling you Scribe?"

"Not to trust anyone but you."

"Uh huh," he gritted his teeth in pain. "I also told you you'd come face to face with the enemy and it wouldn't be what you expected."

Bronwyn dabbed the moist goo, stirring it up; the aroma somehow soothing her own aching muscles.

"I'm not quite sure I'm following you."

Falcon propped his leg on the table allowing Bronwyn easy access to his wound?

"I think you should talk to Travis about it."

"Maybe," She said and then began applying the ointment to his leg.

"Looks like your friend managed to stick her nose in a little too far."

Bronwyn glanced over at Bethany who was curled up on one of the bunks asleep.

"That's for sure. I don't know how she managed it, but she shows up with a man claiming Abaddon is his great grandfather."

"That was my great grandson Jacob." Falcon said pointing to an abrasion on his pectorals. Rolling her eyes, Bronwyn applied the mixture. "I'm sorry, I guess you know..."

Falcon sighed, "Yes."

Travis joined them, taking over for Bronwyn. She was fascinated to see his wound had all but disappeared. He moved along silently, and although his injury was gone, hurt still showed on his face. Too ashamed to look him in the eye, she stepped aside allowing him to do his work on Falcon. With a heavy heart she excused herself, leaving the confines of the cabin for the deck.

Cenric had dropped anchor, but remained on watch for safety measures. She smiled at him and he returned the silent greeting.

The night was cool and peaceful. The moon reflected off the waters creating a silver path all the way to where she was standing. The breeze wafted over the water touching her face and tousling her hair. The night was serene, the water tranquil, and the weather pretty much perfect; a stark contrast to the past several days. She fought back the tears pooling in her eyes at the thought of what her parents might be going through. They probably thought she was dead by now. How could life take such a drastic turn in such a short amount of time? Just a month ago her major source of anxiety was getting over Ryan and trying to salvage a poorly written script. She shook her head thinking about Bethany. In a way she was glad she was down below in the cabin. Having her along brought some sense of normalcy to this bizarre experience. She's never seen Bethany in such a traumatized state. As soon as she woke she'd console her and try and explain some things. She sighed; Falcon suggested she talk to Travis about Kenalycia. The conversation was inevitable, she knew that; but how to go about it was what unnerved her. She thought back to the craziness of it all. She'd come through the portal with Kenalycia, Hamza and Conall. She'd left them by the car when she went to retrieve Falcon's journals. That's when she ran into Travis. The thought of that moment caused her heart to ache. He had been happy to see her, she could tell. He had walked towards her but she had stopped him sending him outside. That's when she bolted from the house only to run into Elam. Could he have already killed Kenalycia? No there wasn't time. Something wasn't right. Perhaps Hamza and Conall betrayed her, killing Kenalycia to get to Travis. Whatever the reason she felt she was partially to blame and hoped somehow Travis would forgive her for her part in the whole tragedy.

The feel of a soft blanket being draped over her shoulders interrupted her thoughts. Turning around she faced Travis. Her heart hammered against her chest at the sight of him. Would this ever stop?

"Thank you," she said pulling the blanket tight around her shoulders. "How's Falcon?"

"He's doing much better, should be back to his rascally self within a few hours."

"Bethany still sleeping?"

"Yes."

She smiled, "And what about you? You doing okay?

He nodded and looked out over the railing, watching the water."

She continued on with the questions, trying to dispel the awkwardness she was feeling. “So what’s next? Where do we go from here?”

“It just so happens Cenric has been forming a small army, over the years, in hoping of starting an uprising. When Falcon was in prison he was able to communicate with some old friends; all of which knew about Cenric and his plans. Some of his men are on a boat headed our way. We will join them and sail to their secret location where we can hide and plot out our next course of action.”

Bronwyn nodded and everything became quiet because she couldn’t think of another question other than asking what happened to Kenalycia. And as much as she wanted to know, she didn’t have the courage to ask. In spite of the awkwardness of the moment, she refused to turn in but continued to stand alongside the man of her dreams, starring out over the water. The rhythmic waves splashing against the side of the boat only accentuated the silence.

“Bronwyn,” Travis spoke her name. “That wasn’t Kenalycia. You were set up. They tricked you.”

The boat swayed; that, with the shock of his statement, nearly caused her to topple backwards. Had he not grabbed hold of her she’d of fallen.

“Oh God, oh God… I’m so sorry…”

“Can I ask you a question?”

Still speechless, she nodded.

“Why did you run off? After you sent me outside, to who you thought was Kenalycia, why did you run away?”

Color flooded her cheeks and despite the darkness of the night she knew he saw. Turning her back to him she looked out over the railing, focusing on the shimmering path that led to the moon, and wishing she could follow it to some sort of Neverland and avoid his question.

"Please don't ask me to answer that," she whispered.

He surprised her by turning her back around to face him. "Please, I need to know. Did Abaddon…"

"No," she interrupted, not allowing him to finish. "He didn't."

"Then what?"

She held her breath trying to prevent tears but it didn't help. They came one by one trickling from her eye and rolling down her soft cheeks. She dropped her head.

"I'm ashamed…"

"Please," he lifted her face, "There is no shame in the truth."

If she were to tell him, she needed to look away but he held her chin in his fingers so she lowered her eyes to the ground.

"It was hard…I couldn't watch… As much as I wanted to make you happy, I couldn't bear to watch you and Kenalycia because…" Taking in a deep breath, she released the information. "…because I feel such a strong affection for you myself."

He dropped his hand from her chin and she figured she'd upset him. She didn't have the courage to look at him so she kept her head bowed and kicked at the dirty nets on the deck.

"It's shameful I know and I am sorry." And then, somewhat like she rehearsed, it all spilled out whether she wanted it to or not.

"I can't explain why my heart is so drawn to you. I barely know you, yet my soul has not rested since the moment I met you. I long to be near you and my heart aches at the thought of you as if it's trying to remind me of something I have misplaced and need to find. To be honest, I feel adrift without you and I never realized how lost I was until I stood before you that night. And for a brief fleeting second, I felt as if I'd come home after having been gone for years."

Her heart thundered in the silence that followed her admission. Her face burned hot and a part of her wished she hadn't confessed, but she had, and it was too late to take any of it back. She wanted to sneak a peek at his face but dared not lift her head, not until the color left her cheeks anyway. Not knowing what else to do, she rambled on.

"I'm sorry Travis; I didn't mean to upset you anymore than you already are. I wish I had brought you the real Kenalycia. In my rush to make you happy, I didn't think and I never meant for…."

He stroked the side of her face, and when he did she lost all train of thought and her long-winded discourse stopped abruptly. Running his fingers along her lips, he stopped at the swollen split.

"Is it painful?"

She shook her head, "Its numb…I can barely feel it."

"Good." He said, and then leaning forward, he kissed her lips.

The rush of heat detonated inside of her and the tears poured out, the saltiness mixing with the sweet taste of his lips. He pulled away gently and smiled searching her eyes. Raising her hand she stroked his unshaven face, running her fingers across the stubble. She laughed softly through her tears and when she did, he leaned in and kissed her again. This time she returned the affection. Holding nothing back, she kissed him with more passion than she ever thought capable. He lingered before pulling away.

"Bronwyn, I've kept a secret from you..."

EPILOGUE

Taylor thanked the UPS driver and carried the small box to his kitchen table. Laying his cigarette in the ash tray he grabbed a knife and cut into the taped box. It was an eerie feeling to receive a package from his cousin, five days after his death.

Pulling back the cardboard flaps he lifted out an envelope addressed to him and an airtight Plexiglas case and set both objects on the table. Inside the container was an antique book titled Moonshine. On the far end of the casing were two holes, with gloves made of a thin nylon fabric. Slipping his hands through the openings and into the gloves he carefully opened the cover of the book and thumbed through the pages.

After a few minutes he removed his hands, took a draw off his smoldering cigarette and opened the envelope. Pulling out a letter he read,

Dear Taylor,

I'm sending you the book. Put it in safe keeping. I believe it to be very important; especially the letter hidden in the cover. I'm heading up to Moonshine to do some investigating. There is a chance I may disappear for a while if not for good. There are some things we are not meant to know and once one possesses the knowledge then the universe must deal with them because of it. There is a reason God told us not to eat of the tree of knowledge. I have nibbled and fear I will pay the price eventually.

One day people will come for this book. Protect yourself and protect it. Another world's survival depends

on it. Only release it to Bronwyn Sterling, she is the author, and the cryptic letter is for her.

Sincerely,

Jacob Betancourt

ABOUT THE AUTHOR

Denise Daisy is described as one of the purest storytellers of all time; pulling of romance, suspense and a touch of the supernatural, all in the same piece. Born and raised in Tennessee, Denise Daisy sets her stories in the Deep South and her natural southern style charms all her work.

In addition to writing, Denise enjoys directing for the theater, and has brought to the stage many wonderful stories, from The Legend of Pocahontas to Great American Tall Tales. To Denise, there is nothing more thrilling than bringing characters to life, whether on stage, behind the camera or in the pages of her books.

In her free time, she enjoys spending time with her four daughters, watching fireflies in the evenings, dreaming up her next story and inspiring others.

Denise Daisy's books include, *The Secrets of Moonshine, The Secret in the Rubble*, and *The Storyteller's Secret* all a part of her Moonshine series.

Once Last Time, a historical time travel romance coming soon by Kensington/Lyrical and *The Haret*, the first book in The Haret series.

You can follow her at, Author Denise Daisy on facebook.